A Predatory Mission

by

Judith Campbell

Mainly Murder Press, LLC
PO Box 290586
Wethersfield, CT 06129-0586
www.mainlymurderpress.com

Mainly Murder Press

Editor: Judith K. Ivie
Cover Designer: Karen A. Phillips
Cover Photo by Judith Campbell

All rights reserved

Copyright © 2013 by Judith Campbell
Paperback ISBN 978-0-9887816-5-8
E-book ISBN 978-0-9887816-6-5

Published in the United States of America

Mainly Murder Press
PO Box 290586
Wethersfield, CT 06129-0586
www.MainlyMurderPress.com

Dedication

This book was written for all those dedicated and worthy people in the world who are healers. You know who you are, and you know what you do. Thank you.

~

Acknowledgments

Thank you to Frederick/Chris, my beloved best friend, first reader and editor. Thank you to the Oak Bluffs Library writing group, the "3 on 3" writers in Kingston, MA, and my "same-time-next-year" writing group in the UK. You folks keep me honest. Thank you to my experts in religion, the law and human nature who have helped me get it right. Thank you to the friends and colleagues who have added your words of endorsement for all to see on the back cover. And finally, profound gratitude to the Creative Source of Being which calls and challenges me daily.

Praise for the Olympia Brown Mysteries

"In *A Predatory Mission,* author and minister, the Reverend Dr. Judith Campbell takes on the highly charged subject of clergy sex abuse. She writes honestly and clearly about this much talked about but poorly understood subject. She does not back away from the truth or the untoward and illustrates plainly how a predator sexually assaults those whom he was called to pastor. I have added Campbell's book as required reading, next to those of Nathaniel Hawthorne, John Updike and Sinclair Lewis, in the courses and programs I offer on clergy sexual misconduct. Like Hawthorne in *The Scarlet Letter,* Campbell writes about the real and serious damage done to people by clergy hypocrisy and abuse of power. But unlike Hawthorne, her novel is accessible and entertaining. You will not be able to put it down."

The Reverend Dr. Deborah J. Pope-Lance, minister, psychotherapist and consultant on clergy malpractice and creating safe congregations

"*An Unspeakable Mission* is an engaging and thought-provoking story of two dedicated and impassioned clerics struggling to find the truth when secrets and silence are the expected norms. And when 21st century religion gets involved with religious and cultural expectations of the past, the story doesn't always turn out as expected. I kept turning the pages to see what would happen next."

Rev. Keith Kron, Director of the Transitions Office for the Unitarian Universalist Association

Preface

This was not an easy book to write, but to quote Olympia's beloved Frederick Watkins, "Knowing you as I do ... I understand that you don't see any alternative but to go ahead with this."

--Judith Campbell

One

Search for Doctor's wife and children continue as concerns for their safety grow. The whereabouts of Yolanda Emerson Nikitas and her two children remains a mystery since they vanished on Thursday of last week. Concern for her whereabouts began when Mrs. Nikitas, the estranged wife of Doctor Nicholas Nikitas, a family practitioner in the community, failed to show up at the home of her mother. Mrs. Nikitas was planning to leave the children with her mother for the afternoon on the day of her disappearance, but the three never arrived. Her abandoned car was discovered the next day in a commuter rail parking lot. Police are exploring all possibilities as the investigation continues, but for now they are treating it as a missing persons situation and not a kidnapping. Anyone having information regarding this incident is asked to call Millbridge Police Department or the anonymous information hotline listed in the town directory.

Detective Inspector Steve Vages handed the folded newspaper across the desk to Officer Ginny Simon.

"It's not even been a week, and they've already demoted the story to page three."

"It's a disappearance, Steve. Unless there's a dead body or a suicide note or a paper trail to some romantic hideaway on a tropical island, it's hard to know exactly where to start looking or to know what we're looking for. We've followed protocol to the letter, and we've come up with a big fat nothing.

Vages opened a manila folder marked *Nikitas*.

"This is the narrative of the interview I did with the husband. I want to go over it one more time and see if anything jumps out that we might have missed." He cleared his throat and began to read.

"Dr. Nikitas states he first learned that his estranged wife and their two preschool-aged children were missing when his mother-in-law called on Thursday to ask if he knew where they were. They were expected two hours earlier, and she was getting concerned because Yolanda wasn't answering her phone. Nikitas cancelled the rest of his appointments and drove to the family home, where she lived with the children. Upon arrival he noted that her car was not parked in its usual spot in the driveway, nor was it in the garage. Using his own key he entered the house to find no one there. He said that this was totally out of character, that his wife is highly organized and very punctual. Later, when questioned, he would say there was no sign of any kind of struggle in the home, and nothing seemed to be missing other than maybe some articles of clothing, but he couldn't be sure.

"Dr. Nikitas said his wife had been despondent of late, but he didn't think she was suicidal. He also noted that despite their marital difficulties, she was a devoted mother, and taking off with the children without some sort of explanation was something she simply wouldn't do."

Vages closed the folder and set it on his desk. "That's it as far as the actual interview goes. The rest of the stuff in here is pictures and personal information."

Ginny shook her head. "I went to school with Yoli. We were in the glee club together. She sings in the local church choir, or at least she did up until she started going to that church across the street. This whole thing is unreal. I know we're in the crime business, but when it involves someone you grew up with, it really does change your perspective on things."

Steve sucked in his lower lip. "No kidding, and the first place we always look is the next of kin."

Ginny nodded. "Don't think I didn't start there, but the good doctor is a total Mr. Clean. He doesn't even have speeding tickets. Medical stuff is all in order, highly respected in the community and a regular church go-er. No skeletons in that closet unless they're left over from an anatomy class." She made a face and shook her head again before saying, "They were living apart, so we know there were problems, but lots of people have problems. Sometimes all you need is a little time off to clear the air."

"Yeah, but what isn't being made public is that there was absolutely no sign of foul play in either the car or the house. Her cell phone was switched off and locked in the glove compartment."

Steve tapped the folded newspaper with the tips of his fingers. "Somebody somewhere knows something, and that somebody isn't talking."

"Or there's something big and nasty that we totally missed."

"It's strange that after a whole week we've come up with absolutely nothing. On the other hand, the fact that there was no explanatory note, no sign of a struggle and nothing of value missing from the house doesn't give us much to go on, but it's not as worrisome as a trail of blood."

"Are you sure about that? If she's still alive, and she's got the kids with her, which appears to be the case, she might be holed up somewhere cooling off and thinking things over. I've seen that happen before. But if it's one of those cases of hideous domestic abuse that no one ever suspected, she may have taken off for good. It's not easy these days with so much of our private lives on display for all to see, but with planning it can still be done."

"You just said it, Steve: if she's still alive. The picture gets worse every day that goes by. I have to tell you, I don't have a very good feeling about this."

"You're not telling me anything I don't know."

Vages closed the file and slipped it back into the top drawer of his desk. "I'm calling the husband back in. If he does know something, he's eventually going to crack and let it slip."

"If not, then it's back to square one. I was there for the first go-round, remember? I think he's telling the truth. I don't think he has any idea what happened or where she is."

The police inspector stood up, laced his fingers together, stretched them back over his head and grunted. "I'm not so sure about that, Ginny. There are some really sick puppies out there, and they can look just like you and me. I'm going across the street. You want a coffee?"

Two

May 13, 1862

A woman alone has to make her own way. I do not know who will find and read these words when I am gone, but whoever you are; do not castigate me for my transgressions but rejoice with me in the ways I was able to transcend their consequences. In these pages I invite you to read these very private words written in times of joy and anguish by a woman who believed she could create a better world for herself and her child — and a woman who worked day and night to make it happen.

More anon, LFW

Reverend Olympia Brown closed the worn leather diary and hugged it to her chest. She'd found it hidden away in a cupboard shortly after she'd purchased the antique New England farm house she was slowly restoring. It was a window on the life and times of a previous occupant, Miss Leanna Faith Winslow, parallel descendent of Otis Winslow, who came to Massachusetts on the Mayflower. Olympia had become friends with the indomitable Miss Winslow through the carefully formed words that recorded the fleeting images of her daily life and the deeper secrets of her heart. When Olympia needed advice or guidance, she often read and re-read these words, written long ago by a woman who had hopes and fears and dreams not unlike her own. This new assignment was surely going to be one of those times.

The day was as lovely a one as May in New England could produce. There was a clear blue sky overhead and mild, shirt-sleeve temperatures that promised to climb into the seventies. Weather-wise Yankees knew the chill of March still lurked in the shadows and prudently kept an extra sweater in the car just in case. Spring flowers were coming up in the gardens and along the sidewalks of Millbridge, a picturesque town in southeastern Massachusetts where Olympia Brown and her significant other, Frederick Watkins, were looking for All Souls Church. He was at the wheel, and she was calling out directions she'd printed off her computer.

"Are you sure you want to do this, Olympia? I thought we agreed that if you were going to take a parish position, it would not be one fraught with dissension. You've seen enough unpleasantness in the last year to make anyone a little wary. "

"Who could have predicted that summer ministry on Martha's Vineyard would turn nasty? That was a surprise to both of us."

"You have a point, my darling, but why is it that wherever you go, within days of your arrival something nasty bubbles up that needs fixing, and you get sucked into the middle of it? After the Vineyard incident, a hospital chaplain and religious fanatic actually tried to kill you. The difference this time is that we already know there's a problem, so at least you won't be blindsided. But I have to tell you, I have my doubts about the wisdom of your taking this on."

She began tapping her fingers on her handbag.

"That's just it, what is the problem? I suppose that's what Zak Bilecki, the District Coordinator, wants me to find out. Right now all I know is the settled minister resigned abruptly, and these folks are in a total tizzy. I never got to know her, and that may be a good thing, because it means I come without preconceptions. " Olympia threw up her hands. "There were some rumblings about misconduct, but what kind and on whose part? That's the real question. Misconduct is a generic word that could describe anything from the pilfering of church funds to sexual abuse. Hell, I've seen churches fire a minister because he or she used the word God too often … or not often enough."

"One of the many things I've learned from you, reverend lady, is that churches can be hotbeds of turmoil and trouble carefully concealed under flowery hats, white gloves and pot luck suppers."

"Whatever it is or may be, the higher-ups want me to go in there as kind of an interim-consultant and hold the place together until some of the feathers settle and then see if I can restore some peace and harmony."

"And while you're there, do a little sleuthing and see if you can find out what really happened."

Olympia rolled her eyes. "There are always two sides to everything."

"That's on a good day, Olympia. I don't know whether your reputation precedes or follows you, dear girl, but you do have a nose for trouble."

"And your point is?"

"That they don't pay you overtime for risking your life."

She made a face that was half exasperation, half resignation and aimed it in the direction of the man beside her.

"At most it's a four-month appointment. The church is less than a half-hour from home. I'm coming back to you and the cats every night. It's a perfect situation. I didn't teach in a college for almost thirty years and not learn how to put out fires and circumvent land mines. Besides, I'd much rather have a challenge than a sinecure. You know that."

"Only too well, my dear and I think we're here. Is this it?"

Olympia leaned forward and squinted out the window.

"White steepled church in need of a paint job with a Church Parking Only sign in front, directly across the town green from another white church that looks almost exactly like it?"

"Spot on."

Frederick rolled the canary yellow Ford pick-up past the sign post and came to a sputtering stop next to the curb.

"You're sure you don't want me to come in with you."

Olympia smiled and shook her head. "No thanks, sweetheart. They said it would be a short meeting, just formalities. Go have a cup of coffee and dig into one of your crosswords. I should be through in less than an hour. I've got my cell phone. I'll call you when we're finished, and you can come back and get me." Olympia looked off to the side and toyed with the collar of her blouse. "Maybe we can go for a little walk around the town before we head back. It's really pretty."

"You mean do a little snooping."

Olympia slipped down from the front seat to the sidewalk and then turned to respond through the passenger window. "I prefer to think of it as acquainting myself with the local flora and fauna."

"A rose by any other name, my darling, is still ..."

"A worrywart," said Olympia, "and speaking of roses, will you look at the display on either side of the church steps? They're incredible, and the ones on the right are totally different in color and shape than the ones on the left. I wonder why that is? Usually people want more formal landscaping surrounding a church building, especially in the front."

Frederick harrumphed. "Of course, they are not as lovely as our English roses, mind you, but I suppose it's a noble attempt for the colonies."

Olympia harrumphed right back and followed the brick path around to the side of the church as instructed and spotted the door marked Office. Before opening it she did a quick check of her reflection in the glass panel above the door handle.

She was attired in what was now called *business casual*. She'd chosen a beige and coral flowered linen jacket, coral blouse and beige linen slacks. Linen was supposed to look slightly wrinkled, and Olympia was forever pushing its limits. She was not a grey flannel pinstripe suit kind of minister. After smoothing her hair into place with her fingertips, she pushed open the door and stepped into a carpeted entryway where she found clearly marked doors indicating the church office, the ladies parlor, the minister's study and the social hall. She paused and checked out the pamphlet table, moved on to the church activities bulletin board and finally the church school activities notice board before calling out a cautious "Hello" in the direction of the office.

"Is that you, Reverend Brown? I'll be right out. Everyone's waiting for you in the parlor. The ladies room is through here if you need it."

Within seconds a woman of middling age and height, with an open and engaging smile, came out of the office, extended her hand and thanked her for coming so soon. She introduced herself as Franna Buckland, the office administrator, and immediately offered Olympia any assistance she might need to help her settle in and get acquainted.

"Well, I'm not exactly hired yet," said Olympia, returning the smile and falling in step beside her. "It's a board decision, is it not?"

Franna stopped walking and lowered her voice. "You come highly recommended, Reverend. After what we've just been through, unless you have a warrant outstanding for your arrest, they're going to ask you to join us."

Olympia leaned closer to the woman. "I don't know exactly what happened here. All I know is that your previous minister, Julia Grafton, resigned abruptly. This never happens without serious cause."

"Oh, it was serious, all right, and everyone here has a different understanding of what happened, including me. Now, there's coffee and snacks on the table by the window, but I'll get you tea or water if you'd prefer."

"Coffee is my drink of choice for the moment, but thank you for offering."

Franna stopped in the doorway and allowed Olympia to pass in front of her before announcing her and introducing her to Stephen Cook, the president of the board.

Olympia held out her hand. "I'm pleased to meet you, Mr. Cook."

"Call me Stephen. We really appreciate your coming. Would you like a cup of coffee or a glass of water before we get started?"

"Coffee, thanks, and I can get it."

The ladies parlor was a pastiche of faded elegance from an earlier generation and several local attics. It was comfortably furnished with an oversized, slightly worn, oriental carpet, a clawfoot, marble-topped buffet and side table. There were several Victorian wood frame, upholstered arm chairs and a big, ugly, practical plastic folding table set up in the middle where everyone was sitting and waiting for her. It was all so very familiar. "This is lovely," she said, trying to make eye contact with each of them. "Where would you like me to sit?"

Cook pointed to an empty chair and then asked the five other people in the room to introduce themselves and say what responsibilities they held as part of the running and management of the church. In turn, Olympia was greeted by the board secretary, the treasurer and two of the three trustees. It all sounded very proper and formal. Olympia knew that she would have to get underneath all of this if she were ever to learn the real reason for her being there, but day one was not the time to start. She did, however, unintentionally crack open the veneer by asking if they could give her some history and background about the events leading up to the resignation of their previous minister.

This was greeted with eye shifting, leg crossing and general discomfiture. Finally Peter Boak, a tall, slender man, said, "How long have you got?"

"To be honest I have about another hour, and I'm already thinking that's probably not going to be enough. When Stephen called me, he said this would be a short meeting, dealing with the formalities of deciding whether you would like me to work with you for the next few months and whether I think I can be of help."

"Please say you'll come," said Cook.

"This has been really stressful for all of us," added Joanna Zee, the board secretary. One of the trustees then spoke up. "Nothing like this has ever happened before, and, well, we don't know where to begin. At least I don't. And then there's the whole thing about Yoli."

Olympia looked confused.

Joanna offered to explain. "Yoli Nikitas. She's the third trustee, or at least she used to be. She's been missing for over a week now, just disappeared into thin air. The police are investigating it, but so far they've come up with nothing. I'm surprised you haven't read about it in the newspapers. None of us knows what to think. I'm beginning to think this place is cursed."

This was seconded by several unhappy nods.

Olympia put down her coffee cup and looked at the troubled faces around the table.

"Providing we can come to an agreement, when would you like me to start?"

When the cautious applause died down, Stephen Cook stood and said, "I think I speak for all of us when I say you can begin whenever you'd like — or maybe I should say as soon as possible."

"Why don't I come and preach this Sunday? That way you can get a sense of my style and how I conduct worship. In the meanwhile, would you please e-mail me a letter outlining your needs? After I preach, if you still want me to come, we can go over everything. If we can reach an agreement with regard to expectations for both sides, I'll start officially on the first of next month."

"That's ten days' time," said Stephen.

"Is that too soon?" said Olympia.

"Not soon enough," said Joanna with a warm and inviting smile.

At the conclusion of the meeting, which ran a little more than an hour, Olympia called Frederick, and the two went back to the local coffee shop, where Frederick was greeted like an old friend and asked if he'd like "the usual."

"Actually, I think something a bit more substantial might be in order," said Frederick, pulling out a chair for Olympia. "I don't suppose you've got kippers and eggs, so perhaps a tuna sandwich for me. The lady is a vegetarian, so …"

"We make a terrific mozzarella, tomato and fresh basil Panino. How about that?"

"I think two of those might be in order and another cup of tea for me." He looked at Olympia.

"A Diet Coke, no ice, please" she supplied.

Once they were settled at the table, Frederick made a great show of polishing his glasses and then asked, "So how did it go, and when do you start?"

"If all goes well, in ten days. By the look of them, there's been one heck of a lot that's gone very badly of late."

"So I gather."

"Frederick, what in the world are you talking about?"

"This little restaurant appears to be gossip central for the town of Millbridge. The minute they heard my accent, they all wanted to know where I was from and what I was doing here. I told them I was waiting for a reverend lady who was thinking about coming to the church on the green that had just lost its minister."

"You didn't!"

"I did, and why shouldn't I? After all, they just love my accent, and because I'm a foreigner, they'll tell me anything I ask."

"So what did they say?"

Frederick looked around at the unobtrusively attentive diners and whispered, "They told me it was in confidence, so hang on until we get in the car."

Once they were buckled into Frederick's truck and on the way back to Brookfield, Olympia once again asked Frederick what he had learned in the restaurant about the church and the town where she would be spending the next four months. He told her that All Souls had a contentious history. Back in the 1800s there was a huge argument over child baptism and whether sprinkling or dunking the baby was most pleasing to The Lord. "The church actually split over it, and the dunkers built their own church across the green. The two have been more or less at odds ever since."

"So much for so-called Christian charity," said Olympia.

"There's more. Over time the church across the street from yours, The Church of the Sanctified Believers, has become progressively more conservative and fundamentalist. Since they got their new pastor, I forget his name, they've been growing like crazy, and your little church seems to be really hurting because of it."

"That's a heck of a lot of information for one cup of tea, Frederick."

"I'll admit to having a second cup, but more interesting than the quantity of tea I quaffed was how much they wanted to talk. It was as if I opened a veritable floodgate when I asked about the church."

"Hmm, sounds more like a tsunami to me."

"You're going to take the job?"

"I haven't signed anything yet, but the more I hear, the more I want to find out what's going on and see if I can do anything to help."

Frederick was looking both pained and resigned. "Olympia, must you always …"

"Yes!" came the answer to his rhetorical question.

The two drove in silence for a while, each picking through their own thoughts and concerns about what might lie ahead. As Frederick signaled for their exit, Olympia introduced an entirely new subject.

"Did I tell you Jim Sawicki called yesterday while you were working at the bookstore?"

"No, you didn't. We haven't seen much of the good Father Jim since he got back from Kentucky. How is he doing?"

"I think that's what he wants to talk to us about."

"Is there a problem?"

"Not so much a problem, Frederick, as a sea change."

"Well, we were talking about tsunamis just a few moments ago, were we not?"

"Jim is not one to rush into anything. You must know that by now. That's why he wants to talk it over with us."

"When's he coming?"

"Tonight."

"Shall I stop for a proper bottle of wine?"

"Don't worry, he'll bring it. You know what a wine snob he is."

"I still like him," said Frederick.

Three

After Olympia Brown left the church the members of the board remained seated around the table.

"Well, she seems likeable enough," said Stephen.

Joanna was folding and refolding a paper napkin. "Likeable is one thing, but can she do the job? That's what I want to know. The truth is we are inviting her into a mess and asking her to perform a miracle. I'm not sure that's fair."

"It can't get any worse than it already is. Four weeks ago Rev. Julia handed me her letter of resignation saying that for personal reasons she could no longer continue. Then bang, she was gone. She refused to say what those personal reasons were other than she cared too much about the church to involve us or let us down. Well, what the hell does that mean? Even Zak Bilecki, the District Coordinator, was stunned. He didn't know anything about it. What he did say was that this Olympia Brown person is really good in conflict situations."

"We're conflicted, all right. Our minister just up and walks away, and three weeks after that one of the trustees disappears off the face of the planet. What the hell is going on here?"

"Maybe there's something in the water."

"Look, Peter, this isn't funny. We've got two big problems. One is the previous minister, and the other is Yoli. Her husband is a member, and the two kids used to be in the Sunday school. We all feel it, and it feels worse every day that she remains missing."

"And you expect the new minister to sort this out in, what, four months? That's not fair."

"Look, the police are handling the Nikitas situation. I spoke to Officer Steve Vages this morning. I think they may want to question people who knew Yoli."

"Could you please say *know* her, as in the present tense? I need to believe she's still alive somewhere."

Joanna started sniffling. "This is just terrible. I just don't know what to think."

"I'm just as concerned as the next person, but it's in the hands of the police. Our job is pulling the church back together. You know that there are a few people who are totally elated over all of this. They couldn't stand Rev. Julia. Some of them even went so far as to imply that maybe she and the guy across the street had something going."

"That's just vicious gossip," snorted a man named Tamreh Herlihy. "I'm surprised you'd even say something like that."

"I think the rest of the congregation wanted to shield her from small town politics," said Peter Boak.

"I always say where there's smoke, there's fire," said Herlihy, "and from what I hear somebody was really smokin' up a storm over there."

Peter Boak stood up and made the time out sign. "Hold on everybody. Let's get back to Rev. Olympia. That is what we're here for, isn't it? Her references are good, and the District Coordinator gives her high marks for conflict resolution. I say we get to work on the terms of our agreement."

"Second that," said Joanna.

That evening Olympia, Frederick and Jim Sawicki were in agreement about the excellence of the first bottle of wine Jim had brought with him. Now they were seated at the table in Olympia's oversized kitchen, preparing to open a second and enjoy the eclectic meal before them. Frederick was homesick for something English, so Olympia decided to try her hand at bangers and mash, a skillet combination of smashed leftover potatoes and sausages. To this she added a bowl of Brussels sprouts, boiled to extinction. Jim was happy with that, but it left vegetarian Olympia to come up with something for herself which her men, as she thought of them, could share. She decided on one of her own favorites, fresh mushroom and asparagus risotto with cracked pepper and grated parmesan cheese.

The two cats, Thunderfoot and Cadeau, now a rough and tumble teenager of six months, were in ready attendance, awaiting their share. It was a contented scene: three people who cared about one another, who enjoyed good food, and who had nowhere else to go that evening so they could fully savor a second bottle of wine and the promise of an equally elegant vintage brandy later on.

Olympia carried most of the conversation during the meal, telling Jim about the church she was almost certainly going to be working with and some of the apparent and not-so-apparent issues connected with it. She described the abrupt resignation of the previous minister and the troubling disappearance of one of the members and went on to say that it was actually her District Coordinator who had suggested that she might be able help.

"So it's not only Frederick and I who recognize your sacred sleuthing abilities," said Jim, holding up and then draining his wine glass.

"Famed in song and story," responded Frederick. "Regular little Sherlock, she is now."

"Well, then, which one of us is Watson? That's what I want to know." Jim held up the remains of the bottle and poured it into their glasses.

"You both are, depending on who's talking." She paused, putting down her glass and looking back and forth between the two of them. "Actually, I don't mind admitting I'm a little out of my comfort zone on this one, and it may well be that I'll be asking you both for your advice and wisdom."

"Now there's a change. Usually you go charging off, damning the torpedoes, and only when the fertilizer hits the fan do you call in the reinforcements. Why do you think this one might be different, Olympia?" Jim broke off a piece of bread and began to butter it methodically.

Olympia put down her fork and leaned back in her chair. "Don't think I haven't thought about it, Jim. There's a twofold issue going on here, and the police are already involved in one part of it. We have a minister who just up and walks out of a church. Clergy don't do that unless there is one hell of a good, or bad, reason behind it. Then within weeks of that happening, one of the former pillars of the church, a trustee and member of the choir, takes off with her kids and doesn't leave a note."

"How did you learn all that?" asked Frederick.

"I picked up a copy of the local newspaper on the way out of the restaurant. It was open to the article describing the disappearance."

"You just took it without asking?"

Olympia made face. "Research, Darling. Reading the local paper is the best way to learn about the ins and outs of a town, especially the letters to the editor. And to your raised eyebrow, I asked for it when you were in the loo."

"Ohhh, she's ever so English," said Frederick.

"Wiseass," said Olympia.

"Now, children," laughed Jim.

Olympia folded her napkin and set it beside her plate. "I think I need coffee and some of that brandy."

"Shall we go for a walk before we have it?" It's a lovely evening. That way we'll have a bit more room for that incredible dessert I slipped into the fridge when you weren't looking."

"Wha …?"

Jim pointed a loving finger at his friend. "Gotcha! I'm not just the wine merchant, you know, and although I don't have much of a sweet tooth, I haven't known you this long without knowing you do."

It was on the walk around a neighborhood that had houses dating to the mid-1700s, when Olympia's house had been built, that Jim began to outline his plan for the future.

"Starting in June I will be on what is called personal administrative leave. What that means is, while I'll still be considered a priest, I'm not going to be actively working as one. So I'm not going to be saying mass or hearing confessions or otherwise offering the sacraments. I'll move out of the rectory at Saint Bart's and get an apartment on my own. For now, anyway, I'll continue teaching part-time at Allston. I should be able to get by on what I earn there while I sort things out. I think I'd like to continue in higher education, maybe teaching at a secular college, but I'm not completely sure. There's so much to think about."

Both Frederick and Olympia were listening intently to their friend. He was at a turning point in his life, and they knew it. They also knew that they were committed to supporting him however they could, wherever the next chapter in his personal journey would take him.

"What about your physical health, Jim?"

"The doctors tell me I'm doing very well. Those three months at the monastery in Kentucky did me a world of good both physically and spiritually. I'm still HIV positive, that's not going to change, but I've got a very different, and I'd say very healthy, personal prognosis for myself. I'm not ready to leave the priesthood yet, but I've come to understand that I do need to step back from it for a while and decide where to go from here and what shape a future priesthood might take for me."

"That's a huge decision, Jim," said Olympia.

"Not as huge as it felt six months ago. I'm much more comfortable with where I am since I got back. I'm also convinced that when the time is right for me to take the next step, I'll know what it is and when to take it. I guess faith will do that for you."

"I wish I felt as comfortable with taking on that church I went to today," said Olympia. "I'm pretty sure I can help them restore some peace and harmony. That's plain old-fashioned organizational management skills, and I have those. It's what caused all the disharmony in the first place that troubles me."

"That's why they want you to go there. If anyone can sort it out, you can."

"I need to sleep on it, Jim, but before I do, I need to examine firsthand whatever you snuck into my fridge."

"How does tiramisu sound?"

"Sounds like a cross between the holy grail and the meaning of life!"

The three friends had just settled down, intent on making serious inroads on the tiramisu, when they heard the simultaneous jangles of the telephone and the antique clock on the mantel. Olympia put down her plate and started toward the phone in the kitchen.

"Oh, dear," said Frederick, looking in the direction of the clock and then towards his lady love. "This sounds important. Perhaps I should say, it would appear that Miss Winslow may have some thoughts on the matter."

"So your resident house-ghost is as nosy and garrulous as ever?" asked Jim.

"Actually, she's been a bit reticent of late. Not like her. I think she might have an opinion about Olympia's latest venture. That's probably what she was chiming the clock about."

When Olympia returned to the sitting room, she was clearly troubled.

"Church?" asked Jim.

Olympia shook her head. "It was my daughter Laura. She's been offered a really good job and wants to come and discuss it with me."

"Jolly good," said Frederick, smiling through a tiramisu enhanced ecstasy.

Olympia shook her head. "Not exactly. The job is in California."

"Uh oh," said Jim.

"Damn," said Olympia.

The clock said nothing.

May 29, 1862

I have neglected this diary for too long a time. It would seem that my short stories, two published now and a third sent off for review just yesterday, consume what little extra time I am able to prise from my very full days. I do not complain. I have so much to be grateful for. I am now a published author and have seen my words printed for all to read on the pages of Godey's Ladies Book. But those stories are for anyone to read. This precious book is mine alone, and perhaps one day my son's.

It is late May and with the longer evening light upon us I am able to walk, yes walk, about the garden with Aunt Louisa and with Jonathan between us. What a curious little boy he is. Every leaf, every flower and tiny pebble are all to be examined, and if I don't take care, to be tasted.

I often wonder if I did such things when I was a child. I have no mother to ask, and when I was a babe, Aunt Louisa lived so far away she did not see me every day. Thus, I take great care in noting every triumph, every new discovery, and more recently, every word in his expanding world. He has three words to date, Mama, see, and Weeza, his best effort at his great aunt's name.

On some days Mr. Fuller, the gentleman from across the way, will come and walk with us, and truth to tell, my Jonathan has taken quite a fancy to this man. He has no wife, therefore no children of his own, and is quite content, he says, to be a bachelor. He has a most personable dog and two aging cats to keep him company and asks for nothing more. He is a good neighbor, helpful when needed, and does not ask questions. I repay his kindness with gifts from my garden and my kitchen. I don't ask questions either.

More anon, LFW

Four

On the following Sunday, Olympia met with the Parish Board, and together they worked to define and articulate the terms of her employment. In reality the contract looked like any other letter of agreement between a church and a minister, but they all knew that the document on the table could in no way accurately outline the task that lay before them. Preaching, pastoral care and spiritual guidance were the expected duties of ministers serving a church. What was not written down, but was evident in the anxious faces around the table, was that something bad had happened within the tastefully painted walls of this historic New England church. Olympia Brown was being tacitly encouraged to try and find out what it was. When they finished, she shook hands with all present and told them she would give them a schedule within the week. Then she added that she would hold office hours by appointment on Mondays, Wednesdays and Thursdays from ten until noon, starting tomorrow.

The treasurer, Peter Boak, who was the obvious t-crosser and i-dotter of the group, asked why not Fridays so she could balance the week. Olympia replied, "Friday is usually my work-from-home sermon day, and it really does take that long. Twenty minutes in the preaching is ten to fifteen hours in the preparation."

"But Friday gives you only eight hours," said Boak.

"The rest is thinking about it, and I won't charge you for that."

The bean counter nodded his assent, but it was clear from the angle of his peaked eyebrows that he wasn't too sure.

I'll keep an eye on that one, thought Olympia.

The next morning she turned up at the church at nine-thirty, plastic travel mug in hand, to begin her day. Franna, the church administrator, was already at her desk and waved her in. "There's hot coffee in the kitchen if you're empty and a vintage microwave if it needs warming up."

When Olympia returned with fresh coffee, Franna was holding out a sheet of paper.

"Nothing like jumping in with all four feet. Three people have already called to make an appointment to see you this morning, and the gay couple that Rev. Julia was supposed to marry next month asked you to call them. The wedding is already marked in the church calendar, but they told me with everything that's happened, they want to meet with you in person."

Franna paused and cocked her head to one side. "You don't have a problem with that, do you? The same sex marriage stuff?"

Olympia chuckled and held out her free hand for the paper. "Oh, gosh no. My best friend in the world is a gay man. I've been doing same sex weddings since way before they were legal. I believe it's *that* you love, not how or whom you love. Love is the operant word here, and it's a gift that does not need explanations, qualifications or man-made barriers."

"Go, Reverend! That's nailing your colors to the mast."

"For better or worse, it's what I do," said Olympia, then added, "and it has sometimes been a very mixed blessing."

"Say no more," said Franna with a knowing wink.

Olympia returned the wink and touched the side of her nose with her index finger. With the unspoken acknowledgment established between them, she took the sheet of paper listing her appointments and messages and went through the door labeled Minister's Study.

Her first meeting was scheduled for 10:00 a.m. She looked at the name, Letitia Blume. It was not a name she remembered from the people she'd met on Sunday and wondered who Letitia might be and what she wanted to talk about. She barely had time to take a second sip of her coffee before she heard sounds in the outer office, followed by the commanding entrance of Mrs. Blume.

"Oh, don't get up, Reverend. I'll just sit in the chair I usually do when I come to visit the minister. I know right where to go and exactly how long to stay. Twenty minutes, right?"

"Well, I …"

The cheery, rosy-cheeked woman sailed across the room and dropped into an arm chair next to the window. She was wearing a pink flowered dress and a rose bedecked hat, and she was trailing a cloud of rose perfume.

She looks and smells like a walking flower garden, thought Olympia.

"Everybody calls me Letty, dear, and I'd like you to, as well. I've just dropped in to make your acquaintance. I didn't get to introduce myself to you yesterday because I was in the kitchen tending to the refreshments. That's what I do. I'm the lady who makes the coffee."

"And you like flowers," said Olympia.

Letty smiled and twisted her fingers in her lap.

"Why, however did you know that?" she said.

"Maybe it was your perfume. Roses are among my favorite flowers."

"Well, then, I'll have to have you over to tea sometime soon. Mine are all out. Perhaps you noticed some of them on the right side of the front door of the church. I have several varieties." She dropped her eyes. "I don't mean to brag, but I've taken a few prizes with them, and the other minister always let me put them on the altar."

Olympia smiled at the flowery lady. "I certainly hope we can continue with that. May and June are the months for roses."

"They'll bloom again in October and sometimes even into November, if we don't have an early freeze."

"I think we'll be having lots of roses, and I can't think of anything nicer."

Letty drew herself up in the chair. "I'm glad you said that, because for some reason Rosemary Madder thinks her roses are better than mine. But now that we have this all sorted out, I'll just let her know that I'll be doing the roses for the next four months." She paused and looked over her glasses. "That is how long you'll be staying here with us, isn't it?"

"That was the agreement with the board, Letitia."

"That's wonderful, and do call me, Letty. Now tell me what kind of cookies you like so I'll be sure to have some for you on Sundays."

Olympia took a deep breath. "Letty, that's so very kind and thoughtful. I really don't want you to go to any extra trouble. It's enough to say that I never met a cookie I didn't like, so whatever you do I'm sure will be just wonderful."

Olympia wondered how it was possible for the woman to draw herself up any taller or to puff out her flowered bosom any farther, but she managed. "I take care of the minister, dear. Letty Blume, committee of one, dedicated to the care and feeding of ministers. Only ..." she paused, glancing toward the door and lowering her voice.

"Only what, Letty?"

"I should have taken better care of Rev. Julie."

"Can you say more about that?"

Letty was twisting her fingers. "I've probably said too much already. Rev. Julie was just too good and too kindhearted. She wanted to think the best of everybody. I tried to warn her, but she wouldn't hear it."

Olympia didn't like prying information out of people, nor did she like being manipulated. On the other hand, one of the reasons she was here was to get information, and to that end Letty might be helpful. It was clear she enjoyed the game of I-know-something-you-don't-know, and Olympia wondered just how far she should play along with this woman. She'd met her kind before. They were a mixed and manipulative blessing.

"Tried to tell her what, Letty?"

Letty's voiced dropped to a barely audible whisper. "About that man across the street."

Olympia felt like she was trying to unwind the Gordian Knot, one twisted thread at time. She tried to keep the exasperation out of her voice. "What about the man across the street?"

"Just be careful," she hissed.

They were interrupted by a gentle tap at the door. Franna apologized for interrupting and announced that Olympia's next appointment was outside.

"My goodness, time sure does fly when you're having fun," said Letty and made rather a grand production of getting up and fussing with her extravagant hat.

I don't think goodness has anything to do with it, thought Olympia, mentally crediting Mae West with the sentiment as she walked Mrs. Blume to the door.

"Thank you for welcoming me, Letty, and I look forward to seeing those roses of yours."

Olympia stepped into the outer office to find Peter Boak seated on one of the chairs with an open magazine on his lap. She was momentarily flustered because she hadn't recognized the treasurer's name on the list that the administrator had given her.

"Oh, hi, Peter, I'm getting a glass of water. Can I bring you one?"

"No thanks, Olympia. I'm driving."

They both chuckled, and Olympia went off to the kitchen where she took advantage of the time alone to refocus. Dear little Letitia, with her roses and her cookies and her whispered warning, had left her a bit unsettled. None of this is making sense, she thought, but this is the first morning of the first day on the job. It's not supposed to make sense yet.

When she returned Boak was seated inside her office, and as soon as she sat down, he got right to his point.

"I don't know how much you know about what happened here, Olympia, but I think it's imperative that I tell you what I experienced and observed. We are speaking in confidence, are we not?"

Olympia inclined her head. "It goes without saying."

"I just like to be sure." He glanced toward the door.

"Would you like to close it?

He nodded. When he was back in his chair, he began to speak. "Things got really messy here with the minister, and most people don't know the half of it. Then to have Yoli Nikitas and the kids disappear on top of everything else ... well, I guess I don't have to tell you. Everybody's spooked, and nobody knows what to do next. These kinds of things happen somewhere else, not in nice little white picket fence towns like this." He shook his head and then looked down and picked at his watch.

Olympia waited for a few moments before responding. "Bad things happen anywhere, Peter. It would help if you tell me all that you know, but before you start, it is okay with you if I take notes? I'll even let you look them over, if you want. It just helps me if I write things down."

"I'm prepared to trust you, Olympia. Trouble is, I trusted Rev. Julie, too, and even I don't know the whole of it. She stopped talking to any of us." A look of pain creased his face. "I feel like I let her down. Maybe I could have done more."

Olympia said nothing. She was thinking that in the space of less than an hour, two members of the church had come to her in confidence to tell her they felt they had personally failed to help or protect the previous minister.

"Start at the beginning," she said.

"The beginning is a little over two years ago when Rev. Julie arrived. Everything seemed to be going well. More people coming on Sundays, a few more families with kids, you know, definite signs of progress. Anyway, maybe it was about six months ago, give or take a couple of weeks, I began to notice a change. I didn't say anything at first, but she seemed distracted.

She was forgetting things, like skipping the offering, or giving out the wrong hymn number. That can happen to anyone, right?"

"It's certainly happens to me," said Olympia.

"But then she started staying away from the parsonage overnight from time to time. Not that it's any of our business where she goes or who she goes wit.'She's a grown woman, and she isn't married or partnered. But this is a small town, Reverend, and people notice things. Then they start talking."

"What else did they see?"

"That's just it, not much, really. Some nights her car was not parked in her driveway until late. That could be anything. Lots of meetings are held at night. No tall dark strangers meeting her in the coffee shop, no letters from faraway places."

"How would you know about that?"

"My brother's the postmaster. Believe me, if you want to know anything about anyone in a small town, ask the mailman."

Olympia shivered involuntarily as he continued.

"Where was I? Oh, yeah, distracted." He chuckled and pointed to himself. "Anyway, because I'm on the board, I called her up one day and asked if we could get together sometime, that I had something I needed to ask her. When we did, I told her I had noted that she'd seemed a little preoccupied of late and asked if something was bothering her. If you're asking yourself why me and not the board president, the answer is I don't know. I just seemed to have more of a connection with her."

Olympia nodded. "What did she say?"

He shook his head. "She looked really sad and said she was sorry she'd let a personal problem become apparent, and she'd make sure it didn't happen again."

"Was that all?"

"Basically, yes. I asked if there was anything I or anyone could do to help, but she closed up like a little clam and thanked me for my concern. Three weeks later she called and asked the president and me to meet her at the church. When we came in, she handed us her letter, turned around and walked out the door. Just like that, bang!"

"What did the letter say?"

"Classic letter of resignation. She could have taken it off the internet, for all I know. She just stated that starting immediately she was leaving the position. Said she regretted she couldn't give us more notice, but the circumstances were beyond her control. The one thing she added was that her reasons for the sudden departure were personal and had nothing to do with anyone in the church. She ended by saying she deeply regretted leaving in such haste but felt that it was in the best interests of all concerned."

"Wow," said Olympia, shaking her head. "Something went very wrong. What did the District Coordinator say?"

"What could he say? He said he'd find us another minister as soon as he could. We know where she is. She went to stay with a brother in Indiana, but for all practical purposes she's incommunicado. It's not like she broke a law or anything, so there's nothing we can do. I'll tell you, it's a real mystery, and we all feel guilty. It's terrible."

"Do you have the letter, Peter?"

"I do, but what difference would that make?"

"I don't know, but I'd still like to see it. It's part of the bigger picture."

"I'll bring it on Sunday unless you need it sooner?"

"Sunday is fine. Oh, and one more thing. Not that it matters, but was Julie gay or straight?"

"I'm sure she was straight. She's divorced. No kids. Said her ex was a minister, and he had a church somewhere in North Carolina. That came out in a casual conversation and didn't seem to be a big thing. Maybe I missed something?"

"I don't think you missed anything. I'm just fact-checking. Whatever happened has left this church in pieces. From what I gather people are feeling bad and wishing they could have done more to help her or prevent whatever happened that caused her to leave. Add to that, nobody knows what that might have been — or somebody isn't talking."

"Bingo, Reverend."

Olympia shifted in her chair. "One of the reasons I was asked to come here was to try and sort things out here at All Souls. If I can find out what happened to Julie, so much the better, but if you don't mind I'd just as soon keep that part of my assignment between us just now."

Peter held out his hand. "My grandfather helped start this church, and I and my father before me grew up running around the pews and eating ham and beans at the pot-lucks on Saturday nights. My commitment to this place goes way beyond religious dogma, Reverend Olympia, it's in my bones. It feels broken right now, and I want it fixed."

Olympia took his hand. "I believe you. I'll do everything in my power to help, but before you go I have to ask you one more question."

Peter crossed his arms and cocked his head to one side, "And that is?"

"This is a bit of a stretch, but do you think the disappearance of Mrs. Nikitas and the children is in any way related to this business with Reverend Julie?"

"Does make you wonder, doesn't it, having two unexplained disappearances within a month. My answer to that is, I'm not sure." He frowned in thought. "I do know that Yoli, uh, that's Mrs. Nikitas, started going to the church across the street. She said it was because she wanted the kids to have more exposure to the Bible than they were getting here."

"The church across the street is more scripture based?"

Peter made a sour face and shook his head. "Rather more than somewhat. I swear we can hear the Bibles thumping over there even with the doors and windows shut." He paused and self-corrected. "Look, I know we're supposed to be accepting of all traditions, but that guy over there is virtually pulling them in off the streets. I hear he's one hell of a speaker – oops, sorry about that."

Olympia waved away the apology. "What else can you tell me about him?"

He looked down at his watch. "Plenty, but I've got a meeting five minutes ago. I'll just say this, and we can finish another time. Word is that despite all the pious words and the charitable deeds, he's a real hit with the ladies."

With that rather cryptic remark he turned and almost collided with a potato shaped lady who was also wearing a lilac and pink floral-print dress. She was carrying a bouquet of deep purple-red roses.

"Oh good, Reverend, I was afraid I'd missed you. I'm Rosemary Madder. I've brought some roses to welcome you to All Souls.

Expletive, thought Olympia as she plastered her most engaging smile onto her lightly freckled face. *If I didn't know better, I'd think we might have a latter-day war of the roses being waged right here in my office.*

"Why, hello, Mrs. Madder. Are these from your own garden? I've heard tell you grow some of the most beautiful roses in this town." *And I'm not lying.*

"Why no, dear, I grew these right in front of the church to the left of the front door. The light is better on that side, bright but not too sunny. That way they don't get parched."

Five

Olympia's daughter, Laura Wiltstrom, was sitting by the window in her second floor apartment in Somerville. She was making a list of yays and nays and weighing a decision that had life altering professional and familial consequences. Laura had been born out of wedlock and given up for adoption when Olympia was only seventeen. She and her mother had reconnected only recently, and their relationship was still new and fragile as they worked to know and understand one another.

Now Laura, a single mother with a seven-month-old daughter of her own, was struggling with a major career decision. She could accept the fantastic job offer on the west coast, along with its concomitant risk, or stay nearer to home where things were familiar, safe and without challenge. Here in Massachusetts she had family nearby to help if she needed it, which, as the single mother of a healthy and active infant daughter, she often did. In California she had the opportunity of a lifetime, a significant position in a cutting-edge company where she would be her own boss doing what she loved, project management and market research. The biggest challenge was not the known *vs.* the unfamiliar, but rather moving away from her brother, the adoptive parents who had raised her, and Olympia Brown, her birth mother.

Laura had three parents here who loved and supported her and wanted to see her succeed, people who would encourage her and never stand in her way. These same three parents would be heartbroken to have their beloved daughter and granddaughter three thousand miles away, but not one of them would ever try and stop her.

Laura continued to ponder her options. The company in California offered on-site day care, flexible hours, the opportunity to work from home several days a month and a total resettlement package. It did not provide homemade chicken soup, the voice of maternal experience, a shoulder to cry on and a grandfather who could fix anything except a broken heart.

Laura put down the pencil and looked at the list in her lap and then at the telephone beside her. What she really needed was a summit meeting with her dad and both mothers at the table. She already knew what they would say and knew it would be she who would come to the final decision. She just wanted them all there with her when she did.

While Olympia was fending off the rose ladies in Millbridge, Frederick Watkins was wandering around their antique farmhouse in Brookfield. It was a wonderful, rambling old house with a quirky personality all of its own. Along with its historically documented colonial New England lineage dating back to 1739, it provided him with an unending list of renovations and repairs and fix-it jobs that kept him out of mischief on the days he wasn't working at the bookstore. Added to that, he had the occasional company of Miss Leanna Faith Winslow, Mayflower descendent and nosy, opinionated house ghost. Olympia's English gentleman had more than enough to occupy his time. Today he was contemplating replacing the outside door and frame, which was completely rotted and about to fall off on its own. The day was warm, and there was no problem being without a door for a day or maybe two. Frederick was neither fast nor particularly efficient when he undertook a repair job, but when it did finally get done, it would be done right.

Because of the history of the building, Frederick wanted to be faithful to the age and provenance of the structure. So rather than going to a lumber company for his wood, he knew of a building salvage yard where a man could spend hours looking for just the right bit of oak for a proper post and lintel. He loved that old house, and slowly, nail by splinter by mitered corner, he was making it his own. He enjoyed these days by himself. Much as he loved her, his darling Olympia was a force of nature, and a quiet day alone with the ghost and the cats was balm to his gentle soul. But before getting started, he extracted and checked his pocket watch. It was time for a cup of tea. Frederick had learned long ago that it was never good to rush into things.

After bidding Mrs. Madder a fond farewell Olympia sat at her desk and shook her head. It was the same the whole world over, whether it was prize winning roses in Millbridge or skillet-tossing on Martha's Vineyard or growing giant leeks in the North of England. People took pride in and enjoyed recognition for their accomplishments. Part of the unspoken job of ministry was to look for and commend those human accomplishments, and woe betide the thoughtless callow cleric who did not. Olympia knew the rules. She would find a way to have both ladies' roses praised and displayed, come hell or high water.

She looked at the digital clock on her desk. It was almost noon, and there was one last thing to do. That was to call the two women who were planning a mid-June wedding. She would need to meet with them and see what kind of a service they wanted and just how grand or modest the event would be. Olympia smiled at the thought of it. She was glad she could do this. She liked weddings — well, most weddings — and the fact that two people in love, whatever their gender preference, could legally marry was something she felt had been long overdue.

Just as Olympia was hanging up the phone, the administrator stuck her head around the door to ask if there was anything else Olympia needed done before she left.

"I don't think so. I just spoke with Maggie and Danny about their wedding. They were worried that they wouldn't have a minister, but we had a good talk, and they'll be coming in next week. I'll let you know when I have the exact day and time."

Franna cupped her two hands together. "You've had a full morning for a first day on the job, but I didn't hear any screaming and yelling, so I would venture to say that you survived the rose ladies."

Olympia rolled her eyes. "They'll be fine, at least I think so. I'll find a way to use all the roses. I'll bet they would be great for that wedding. Maybe they would like to work together on it?"

Now it was the administrator's turn to roll her eyes. "Only if you want to start world war three right here at All Souls. Those two have been thorns in each other's sides for years. Good luck, Reverend. In this case I would not even think of the phrase, 'Everything's coming up roses.' If I were you, I'd soft *petal* it on this one."

Olympia groaned theatrically and clapped her hand to her chest.

Franna laughed at her own joke and ducked out of the door as Olympia fired a scrunched up church bulletin at her retreating back.

I like her, thought Olympia. I like people who can laugh at themselves and with others. I think I got lucky with this one.

She was congratulating herself on a successful first day and collecting her papers and folders when she heard the outside door open. This was followed by the sound of approaching footsteps and then the appearance of a tall, dark eyed, rugged and very good-looking man of indeterminate middle age. He was wearing dark slacks and a nondescript grey sport coat over a lighter grey clerical shirt.

"Rev. Olympia Brown?"

Olympia stood up but stayed behind her desk.

"I am, and you are?"

He held out his hand. "I'm Pastor Jerrold Markham. I'm the minister of the church across the street. I waited until now to come over because I thought by midday you might be hungry. I'd like to invite you to lunch and, if we have time, show you around the neighborhood."

Olympia came out from behind her desk and took his hand.

"How very kind of you. I am ready for something to eat, and I'm delighted at the opportunity to get to know one of my colleagues. Is there a clergy group here in Millbridge?"

"There is indeed. We meet on the second Monday of the month. I'll tell you more at lunch. You will do me the honor, won't you?"

"Just something quick and local, if you please."

"Got plans for the afternoon?"

"Only the ever-present sermon to think about and a wedding to look over."

"A wedding so soon?"

He opened the door and allowed Olympia to pass in front of him.

"It was already on the calendar, but I need to meet with them."

"Do you need to lock up?" He stood with his hand on the doorknob.

"I suppose I'd better," said Olympia, digging for her keys.

"There's a little Greek place I'm fond of. They have a nice lunch menu."

"How far a walk is it? I'm wondering if I should change my shoes."

"Keep your shoes on. It's in the next town. My car's in the lot behind the church. I don't know about you, but when I have a meal, I want to have it in peace. If we have our lunch in town, half the locals will be talking about it, and the other half will sit down at the table with us."

Olympia laughed as they made their way around to the back of his church to where he parked his car. It was a late model black and silver BMW. Very impressive.

"I know what you mean," she said. "It's hard to be a public face and find private time when you need it."

Pastor Markham leaned over, pulled open the passenger door and said in a low voice, "I manage."

The restaurant, Taverna Athena, was indeed small, quiet, friendly and a very scenic twenty minutes west of Millbridge. When they were settled into a booth by one of the windows, Jerrold took it upon himself to extol several of the luncheon offerings before Olympia could finally say she was a vegetarian and would likely have a Greek salad or a piece of Spanakopita, or maybe both.

He looked mildly surprised. "Oh. Well, what about chicken and fish?"

She shook her head. "They're animals. I've been doing this for years. I'd like to say that it keeps me trim, but the fact is I love to eat, and moderation is not my middle name."

Jerrold laughed before saying, "Women worry too much about weight and waistlines. If God wanted us all to be thin, he wouldn't have made food taste so good. What is that old line about temptation? 'I never worry about resisting temptation, I just give right in. No worries!'"

Now it was Olympia's turn to laugh.

When they both had placed their orders and declined the wine list, Olympia asked her new colleague about the town, the other clergy and his church, in that order."

"I've been here for about five years, Olympia. It's a really nice little town. Not much excitement, that is until poor Yolanda Nikitas disappeared. It's a real mystery. From what I hear there's no sign of foul play and so far, anyway, no word from her. She just vanished. You haven't heard anything, have you?"

He leaned closer and lowered his voice. "I only bring it up because she was a member of your church, but she started coming to mine a couple of months before it happened. I don't know if anyone has said anything, but I just thought you should hear it from me first."

Before she could respond the table server arrived with their meals, Spanakopita and a Greek salad for Olympia, lamb with string beans for Jerrold Markham and two diet sodas. It looked wonderful and smelled, appropriately enough, heavenly.

Olympia decided to share nothing of what she'd heard so far, which in fact was little more than nothing. The only things she did know were that Mrs. Nikitas had started attending the church across the street and that Pastor Markham was said to be an attractive fellow. Well, that much was right.

"I just started at the church this morning, so we both know I'll be settling in for a while. People take time to warm up to a new person ..."

" ... especially when the previous minister left under shadowy circumstances," finished Jerrold. "Did you know her at all?"

"No, I didn't. She didn't come to district meetings. What was she like? You must have known her at least a little?"

Jerrold laid down his knife and fork and appeared to be collecting his thoughts before answering Olympia's question.

"Well, of course we had very different theologies. I believe that the Bible is the inerrant work of God, and men and women can only find salvation through accepting Jesus Christ as their personal Savior. She, and I suspect you, are on the other side of that theological coin."

Olympia peered over her glasses and nodded. "The phrase *polar opposites* does come to mind, Jerrold, but that's what makes the study and the ministry of religion so endlessly fascinating."

He looked interested. "What do you mean?"

"I mean there is always something new to learn, another mystery to be explored and a new truth to be revealed. I see religion as a living thing, growing and evolving as we do. I probably differ from you because I prefer questions to answers. I think searching for something is every bit as wonderful as finding it, perhaps even more so." Olympia had set down her own utensils and was emphasizing her points with her hands.

Jerrold cocked his head to one side and smiled at her. "I love your passion, Olympia. I may not agree with you on matters of faith, but no one can resist that kind of enthusiasm. I certainly can't. We need to have another lunch and another conversation sooner rather than later. But meanwhile, I'm on a tight schedule today, so finish up, Reverend. If you're very good and clean your plate, I'll order some Baklava."

"What was that you said about temptation? Give me five minutes, I love that stuff."

Jerrold smiled and signaled the waiter.

When they were totally stuffed and driving back to Millbridge, they talked more about the social and political nature of their two churches, the challenges of ministry in a small town and the importance of maintaining a healthy balance between one's personal and professional lives. As they were turning into the church driveway, Jerrold stopped the car, opened the window and waved at a woman walking across the lawn towards them.

"Hi, Jenny, come meet the new minister at All Souls. "

The grandmotherly woman smiled and extended her hand to Olympia.

"Welcome to the neighborhood, Reverend…"

"Olympia Brown," said Jerrold Markham. "She's done me the honor of having a get-acquainted clergy-to-clergy lunch with me."

Jenny shook Olympia's hand enthusiastically and said, "Well you may be from across the street, but I think we're all doing the Lord's work. Isn't that right, Pastor Markham?"

"If you say so, then it must be true; but I believe if you give Reverend Olympia a piece of your ginger-apple pie, she just might see the light and change her ways. What do you think, Jenny? That pie could make a blind man see."

"Why, Pastor, you'll turn my head."

"I always speak the truth."

Jenny was blushing and grinning like a seven-year-old as he eased up on the brake and slipped past her. When he came to a stop Olympia started to open the door, but Jerrold reached over her and held on to the handle, preventing her exit.

"Before you go, let me say I hope we can do this again sometime. Having good colleagues is really important in this business. You know that by now. There are things ministers need to talk about that only another member of the clergy would understand."

Olympia nodded slowly.

"You know as well as I do, ministry can be very lonely. We are surrounded by people we really care about, but we can't take a one of them into our confidence."

He pushed open the door and then added, "Oh, yes, and before I forget, there's a clergy meeting next Monday at the Methodist Church across town. It's at ten in the morning, and I suggest you bring your own coffee unless you're fond of beige dishwater."

Olympia made a face. "Thanks for the warning, my friend. Forewarned is forearmed. I'll bring a thermos of my own special high-test."

"Say, I've got an idea. Why don't you go with me? I know where it is, and that way I can introduce you."

"Sounds like a plan," said Olympia. She stood beside the car, turned her face up into the warm May sunshine and took a deep breath. "Thank you for lunch, Jerrold; it will be my treat next time."

A few minutes later, when she was getting into her van, Olympia asked herself what had just happened. As she began to drive off she realized she didn't have an answer, but she was prevented from thinking any more about it by the sound of her cell phone. She wondered who might be calling her but knew better than to hunt for the damned thing while driving. She would return the call when she got home.

It wasn't until after dinner that Olympia remembered she needed to make a phone call. Frederick was out in the back yard, turning over the soil in the raised beds he'd been working on all spring. This was the year he would have a proper garden. Olympia watched him out of the kitchen window and admitted to herself that she was quite pleased with the way things were progressing. Their life together was beginning to have a rhythm, and it was good. *I can get used to this.* She fished out her cell phone so she could return the call she'd gotten earlier, but when she checked, the number wasn't one she recognized.

She tapped the redial button, and after two rings a woman's voice said, "Reverend Olympia Brown?"

"This is Reverend Brown."

There was a slight hesitation before the voice continued, "This is Yolanda Nikitas speaking. I'm a member of All Souls. My children are with me, and we're all safe. I'm using a friend's phone so you can't trace this call. I have to have your promise of complete confidence before I say anything else."

Olympia remembered another time she'd been sworn to secrecy. She hadn't wanted to do it then either, but like that other time, she felt she had no choice. "I promise," she said.

"Thank you, Reverend."

Olympia took a deep breath and reached for a pencil and the notepad she kept in her purse. "Start at the beginning. Tell me what's happened and then how you think I can help."

"That's why I called you," said Yolanda Nikitas.

Six

June 2, 1862

The bright shining sun and chattering birds are a cruel mockery to my grieving heart. Jonathan's father is dead. The awful news came to me in a brief letter from a lawyer in Boston saying only that in the event of Rev. Jared Mather's demise he had been instructed to send notice of same to me. There was no mention of the cause and it is likely I will never know, nor will I ever know where he was laid to rest. I can no longer grieve for what was and might have been. Now I can only grieve. Perhaps it is for the best. I may never know that either.

More anon, LFW

Frederick didn't come in from his gardening until it was almost dark, but one look at how she was collapsed in her chair told him that Olympia was deeply troubled.

"Good heavens, my love, what's happened? Is it one of the children?"

Olympia looked up at him and shook her head. "No, thank God, it's not them, but it's every bit as serious. Go get yourself a cup of tea, and I'll tell you what I can."

"Shall I make one for you as well?"

"Oh, please. The herby stuff, otherwise I'll never sleep."

When he returned and they were seated, each with a cup of tea in hand and a cat in lap, she began.

"First of all I'll start by saying I'm not supposed to be talking about this to anyone, but we both know that clergy partners are often taken into to clerical confidence."

Frederick stroked the purring cat with his free hand and nodded. If he was pleased at being referred to as her partner, he knew better than to make an overt display of it.

"I got a call this afternoon on my way home from church that I didn't take because I was driving. I returned it while you were outside in the garden. It was from Yolanda Nikitas, the woman from church who disappeared last week."

"The minister?"

"No, the young mother and her two children."

"Crikey, what did she say?"

"To be honest it was rather hard to decipher, and she didn't tell me everything. What she did tell me is that she and the children are in a safe place, and she wanted to get word of that to her estranged husband."

"Did she say why she'd left or where she was?"

"I asked her, but all she would say is she had to protect herself and the children, and it had nothing to do with her husband. That's why she wanted me to tell him, but she had to make sure he wouldn't say anything to anyone yet."

"I don't understand."

"I'm not sure I do either, Frederick. I'm giving you the condensed version. She wouldn't say anything more."

"Meanwhile, according to what I picked up in the coffee shop, he's one of the prime suspects in the disappearance."

"That's where it gets sticky. She understands that and feels terrible about it but made a huge point of making sure I would make him promise not go to the police. She told me that once he knows they are all alive and safe, she'll call me again and tell me more about what happened. It's understandable, I suppose. She doesn't know who I am. She's taking a huge chance, and I suppose she's testing me."

"How will you tell her?"

"She told me she's opened a free e-mail account under another name. I'm to contact her on that."

"What about you, Reverend Doctor? How do you know she is who she says she is and not some cruel sadist who's going to make it worse? People do that, you know — give false hope, or even more heinous, demand ransoms for missing people."

"Now that you mention it, I don't really know, but she did tell me enough about herself and the situation that I've chosen to trust her. She told me something only her husband would recognize, the inscription inside her wedding band. It's the date plus the words *te amo*. That means I love you in Latin."

"I knew that, but what if you're wrong, and this really is a hoax?"

"I don't have an answer for that, Frederick. I can only hope she's telling the truth, and I've chosen to believe her."

Their conversation was interrupted by a double chime of the antique clock sitting on the shelf over the woodstove, the vehicle by which the resident house ghost, Miss Winslow, could make her opinions known to them.

"Well, it seems Miss Winslow has an opinion."

"Yes, but what is it?" asked Frederick.

"I don't know, but I'm convinced I need to call on Dr. Nikitas."

As if on cue, the clock sounded a second double chime.

"Did you hear that? I think she's saying she agrees with me."

"Frederick clasped his two hands to his chest, rolled his eyes in the direction of the clock and said, "I plead no contest, and I hope to God you're both right."

Even though it was almost nine-thirty, Olympia decided she really had to speak with Dr. Nikitas in person. No matter what the hour, she'd never forgive someone who withheld that kind of information from her for as much as ten minutes, but what to say and how to say it? She had a church directory in her home office. With a quick silent prayer for courage, she pulled out her cell phone, walked into the next room and closed the door.

He picked up on the fourth ring. "Dr. Nikitas."

"Dr. Nikitas, this is Reverend Olympia Brown speaking ..."

"Oh God, don't say it."

"No, it's good news. I've just spoken to Yolanda, and she and the children are safe."

"Wh ... where are they? How do you know? Are you sure it was her? Have you called the police?"

"Hold on. I know I should be saying this to you in person, but as a parent myself, there's no way I could wait until morning. She told me that the inscription inside her wedding ring is 8-14-02 along with the words *te amo.*"

She heard the ragged, guttural sounds of the man sobbing.

"I'm still here," she said gently, "take your time."

"What else did she say?"

"That above all else she loves you, and we are not to go to the police, at least not yet."

"But they think ..."

"I know and she knows the police suspect you, but she implied that her safety and the children's might depend on not saying anything to them, at least not right away. Anyway, I agreed."

"When can I see them?"

"I don't know. She wouldn't tell me where they are. She used a friend's cell phone. She also opened a Yahoo account and told me to e-mail her after I'd talked to you, and then she would call me back. She has my cell phone number."

"What do I do now?"

"Would you like me to come over there and just sit with you and have a cup of tea? I know it's late, but if you feel you need to talk to someone, I'm very willing to do that."

"Thank you, Reverend, it's very kind of you, but no thanks. Just knowing they're okay is more than I ever dared hope for. I can't begin to tell you. This has been a nightmare."

"I can only imagine, Doctor. Do you think we could sit down together some time tomorrow? It may be that if I have a little more understanding of the situation from your perspective, I might be more able to help when she does come back."

"That's probably a good idea. I haven't been able to talk about this to anyone. First it was humiliating, then it was terrifying."

"Ministers listen. That's probably the biggest part of what we do."

Olympia heard the catch and then the change in the man's voice.

"If you ask me, some ministers don't know the difference between listening and interfering."

"I not sure I understand, Doctor."

"Ask that sonovabitch across the street, Reverend. I'll give you an earful about him tomorrow, too. That's when this all started."

Olympia said only, "What time would be good for you?"

Once they'd agreed on a time, he thanked her again for calling and rang off. Olympia went back to the sitting room, where Frederick was stroking a comatose cat and waiting to hear about the latest development.

When she finished Frederick said, "This is more like a made-for-television mystery than a real-life-steeple-on-top-of-the-church ministry. How do you manage to get yourself into these situations? I'm simply not going to let this one slide through as a mere coincidence, no matter how you try and explain it away."

Olympia smiled. "Frederick, I was asked to go to Millbridge because of a difficult situation that my District Coordinator thought I might be able to help with. Like it or not, I seem to have earned myself a bit of a reputation as a problem solver. The original task was to try and find out why the minister left so abruptly. I already knew there were going to be some landmines there when I accepted. What I wasn't expecting was the double whammy of the Nikitas disappearance. It certainly does complicate things, and although there's nothing pointing to it right now, I think it's possible the two things could be connected in some way."

"I suppose anything's possible, but now that you mention it, two women, both members of All Souls, suddenly drop out of sight within a couple of weeks of one another. It is a rather strange and uncomfortable coincidence."

Olympia began drumming her fingertips on the arm of her chair. "The major difference is that the former minister left a forwarding address. We know where to find her. She's just made it clear that she'd rather we didn't try. Yolanda Nikitas simply vanished, and even now that she's been in touch with me, I still have no idea where she is." Olympia frowned and rubbed her chin. "I wonder what she's doing for money. It would be easy enough to trace her through credit cards and phone calls."

"Didn't the police say they found her cell phone in the car?"

"I think so, and that's only one piece of the puzzle. There are a million things I want to ask, but I'm sworn to silence until she says otherwise. Speaking of that, I'm going to e-mail her right now and tell her I've spoken to her husband."

"Are you going to tell her you're meeting with him tomorrow?"

"No."

If he wondered why, Frederick decided not to ask. He said only; "I almost forgot to tell you, I had a call from Jim. He's found an apartment in downtown Boston, and he wants to borrow your van."

"Well, that's fortuitous. I was planning to give him a call and see what sage advice he might offer or what strings he might be able to pull at the BPD for me."

"BPD?"

"Boston Police Department. A good buddy of his is on the force and has access to all kinds of information and criminal records, stuff the average person, like *moi,* could never get hold of. He's been extremely helpful in the past."

Frederick groaned. "Olympia ..."

Olympia rolled her eyes in the direction of the man she loved, and then she winked.

"Later, darling!"

Seven

Before she left for Millbridge the next morning, Olympia, with a second cup of coffee, and Frederick, with his oversized mug of tea, were seated at the kitchen table. They were going over their respective to-do lists, something she felt necessary to organizing her day and something which Frederick dutifully acknowledged and then largely ignored.

She would be at the church until mid-afternoon and would pick up something for supper on the way home. Frederick didn't have to be at the bookstore before one in the afternoon, so he planned to continue sketching out ideas for replacing the outside door and frame leading to the kitchen.

At the mention of it, Olympia turned to the aforementioned and said, "Well, get as far as you can on it, Sweetheart, and let's just pray that we don't have a hurricane in the next week or so."

Frederick looked at his lady love with amazement. "Whatever do you mean? I would have started yesterday except I had trouble locating exactly the type and color of wood I want."

"Yikes! Look at the time. I want to be in my office before Dr. Nikitas arrives. Mrs. Buckland, our administrator, isn't in on Tuesdays, and I'm there by myself, so I have to open up."

Olympia carried her empty coffee mug to the sink and rinsed it out.

"I thought she was there every day," said Frederick.

"Nope, Mondays, Wednesdays and Fridays, mother's hours. It's all the church can afford. When I think about it, it's probably better that she's not there today. I think Dr. Nikitas might like total privacy for this conversation."

"Given all the turbulence over there, I think I'd feel better if she was there when you were. I want you to give that some thought, Olympia."

Olympia turned, smiled reassuringly and put her hands on her hips. "Frederick, whatever has happened at All Souls, it's happened outside the building. That much I'm sure of. It may or may not involve the mystery man across the street, but he's over there, and he doesn't have a key."

"Just be careful, will you?"

"Aren't I always?"

"No."

Olympia stretched out her hands and wiggled her fingers in the man's direction and chanted, "Think doors and door frames and mitered corners, Frederick, doors and corners. Think about them all finished and in place." She kissed Frederick on his bald spot and went off to begin her day.

When the energy she left in her wake stopped swirling, Frederick took a long, languid breath and reached for the book he was almost finished with. Once he got that out of the way, he'd get cracking on that door. So many pages, so little time.

As planned, Olympia was seated at her desk when Dr. Nicholas Nikitas arrived. She stood and held out her hand and then offered him his choice of chairs. He was a striking man of medium height with the dark eyes and smooth olive skin that reflected his Greek ancestry.

"Good morning, Doctor. Can I get you a cup of coffee before we get started? There's some fresh I just made in the kitchen. "

He shook his head. "No, thanks. Have you heard any more from Yolanda?"

"I e-mailed her last night right after I talked with you. I used that Yahoo address she gave me, but I haven't heard anything since." Olympia arranged herself in a wooden armchair opposite the doctor.

"What did you tell her?"

"Only that I had done as she asked, called you and told you that she and the children were safe and under no circumstances were we to go to the police."

"You haven't heard anything back? Well, I suppose we could take matters into our own hands and go to the police anyway."

Olympia gasped and held up her hand. "No! She made that clear. We can't, at least not yet." She paused. "Last night you said you wanted to talk about what might have led up to this. Do you still want to do that?"

He nodded.

She sat, looking in his direction, but carefully avoided fixing him with her eyes.

He shifted in his chair and cleared his throat. "This is going to be harder than I thought." He raised his head and began. "How do you tell someone that your wife's left you for another man? It's even harder for a Greek man to say that. I'm Greek, and she's a Yankee, related to Ralph Waldo Emerson, no less. What a mix. In our culture the man is the head of the household, and the woman is the heart. I'm enlightened, but it's ingrained. Anyway, it all started about four months ago when she started going to a Bible study group at the church across the street from All Souls. First it was just Wednesday nights, and then she started going there occasionally on Sundays. She said it was because she wanted a more traditional Sunday school for the kids, but I think she got suckered in by the minister."

Olympia kept her voice low and even. "Why do you say that? What did she do ... or not do?"

He rubbed at his forehead before responding. "It was gradual. First it was just the Bible study once a week. Then she started attending a mothers' group on a different morning. The next thing I knew, there were church ladies coming over to the house a couple of times a week with their children for Christian play dates. At first I thought it was all rather sweet. The kids were cute, the ladies were nice, and our kids loved it."

"When do you think things started to change?"

"Probably by the end of that first month, but I'm away from the house a lot. It comes with being a doctor. I guess I didn't really notice how bad it was until it was too late."

Olympia nodded. "What made it too late?"

He cleared his throat again and looked down at the floor. "The obvious." In response to her puzzled look he said, "She started sleeping in the guestroom."

Olympia winced. "What then?"

"When I tried to talk to her about anything other than the children, she just clammed up. She started losing weight, too. She's always been a little round – not overweight, mind you, just nice. All of a sudden her bones are sticking out and she's leaving the kids with her mother a couple of times a week, saying it's so she can do volunteer work at the church. Her mother noticed the change, too, but she's so keen on not interfering that she didn't say anything until after the disappearance." He paused. "God, how I wish she had spoken up."

They were interrupted by the bleating of Olympia's cell phone. As she yanked it out of her purse she apologized for taking the call. "I'm sorry about that. I usually turn it off, but in this case I'm hoping it might be Yolanda."

As it turned out, Olympia was right. She nodded vigorously and pointed to the phone. "Can you hold on for a second? I want to take this in another room."

Nikitas jumped out of his chair and reached for the phone, but Olympia waved him back. She pointed to her lips and mouthed the words, "Me first, then you."

Back in Brookfield Frederick and the cats were having a perfectly lovely morning. He'd finished his book and was thinking about how to tackle the door project when the phone rang. When he picked up, a male voice said, "Is Reverend Brown available?"

"Who's calling, please?" said Frederick.

"This is Pastor Jerrold Markham speaking. I'm the minister at the church across the street from All Souls in Millbridge. Is she available?"

Even though he was alone in the kitchen, Frederick drew himself up to his full height. "I'm afraid The good Reverend is not at home just now. Is there a message you might care to leave or a number where she can reach you?"

Frederick was giving him what Olympia referred to as The Full English, meaning he was speaking the Queen's English in the most pompous and forbidding tones he could summon.

"Not really. I was just confirming that she'll be riding with me next week to the clergy meeting. I've invited the Baptist minister to come along with us as well. That way she can get to meet another colleague in town."

"How very thoughtful of you. I'll be sure to tell her. Might there be anything else?"

"Uh, no, not that I can think of."

"Cheerio, then" said Frederick, making a nasty face and dropping the handset back into the cradle. He looked across the room at the cats sprawled in a pool of sunshine flooding in through the kitchen window and smiled. He liked those two cats.

"Now where was I? Oh, yes, the door." He looked around the room. "I need to find a proper doorknob. Mmm, where did I put that catalog?" Cadeau opened one green eye, flicked the tip of his slender black tail and remained silent. "You might at least give me a hint," Frederick said, adding a touch of mock irritation to his voice. Cadeau closed his eye and resumed his nap as the antique clock chimed from the mantel shelf in the other room.

Frederick felt a prickling sensation along the back of his neck. He knew by now that one did not ignore Miss Winslow when she had something to say. He followed the sound into the sitting room where he began looking around for something that might be out of place. After a few moments he saw the catalog on the shelf beside the clock. He didn't remember putting it there, but he also knew there were times when things moved or were moved by an unseen hand in that house. He also knew that on the best of days, he could be a bit scattered. He picked it up and started back toward the kitchen when the clock chimed a second time, followed by the sound of something falling to the floor behind him. It was one of Olympia's several Bibles that she'd left on the table beside her chair.

"Are you trying to tell me something, Miss Winslow?" Frederick wasn't really expecting an answer. Nonetheless, he often found himself treating the house ghost like an old friend and chatting to her as he went about the house, fixing it up and slowly bringing it back to its former grace and functional elegance. He looked at his watch. "Wherever has the time gone?" he said to the clock. It was time to go to the bookstore.

Olympia returned to the office and held out the phone to Nicholas Nikitas. Then she walked out of the office and shut the door to give the man some privacy. She was about to go into the kitchen for a cup of coffee when she heard the outside door opening and a cheery voice calling out, "Oh, Reverend, you are here. Come look at what I've brought you."

She turned to find Letitia Blume standing behind her, holding out a huge bouquet of roses. The rich, heavy scent of them instantly filled every inch of the church foyer.

"These are from my garden. I just picked them this morning. I know they won't last until Sunday, but I wanted you to see how lovely this variety is. See how the edges of the yellow petals are tinged with peach and red. In England these are called Joseph's Coat, as in coat of many colors. Isn't that just the sweetest name?" She took a quick breath before rattling on. "I thought I'd make up two baskets of these for Sunday, and then afterwards you can take one of them home to your house, and I'll take the other to the nursing home down the street.

Sometimes we divide them up and take them to the shut-ins. That's what we usually do with the Sunday flowers. We do have our little traditions here at All Souls."

She was beaming from ear to ear, but underneath the smile Olympia could see her teeth.

Eight

Nicholas Nikitas remained in Olympia's office with the door closed until after Letitia had left the building. Olympia stood and listened for the sound of voices before tapping on the door. She half-smiled at the dark absurdity of the situation. She had a lady with a rose vendetta on one side of her, a man whose wife had fled in fear for her life on the other, and unanswered questions piling up like thunderheads over the church across the street.

Olympia called through the door. "The coast is clear. Is it okay to come in?"

Nikitas pulled open the door himself and stood, holding out Olympia's cell phone. It was clear to her that the man was deeply troubled. He made a good show of trying to appear composed, but his olive skin was deeply flushed, and his hand was shaking.

Olympia took the phone, slipped it into the pocket of her jacket and said, "Let's go get some of that coffee I offered you earlier, and if it's too lethal after sitting on the burner for this long, I'll make us a fresh pot."

One sniff, followed by a sour grimace, told her it was new coffee time. The kitchen bustle of dumping the grounds, rinsing out the pot and locating the coffee stash provided the two of them with a little breathing space before settling down to talk about the conversation between Nikitas and his estranged wife.

Once they were settled back in the office with the In Conference—Do Not Disturb sign hung on the door, he began.

"She's not ready to tell me where she is. She assured me that she and the kids are safe, and in time she will be ready to meet with me in person. She wouldn't let me talk with the kids, because she thought it would upset them. That really bothered me, Olympia. They're my kids, too, and for the past week I've been thinking they might be dead, for God sake. She said …"

Nikitas turned away and pressed a fist against his mouth. Olympia sat in silence, knowing he needed to get this out. She thought about her own boys, Malcolm and Randall, and now Laura, her daughter. She shivered at the thought of how she would feel if even one of them went missing. It was unthinkable. In time Nikitas picked up his coffee mug and took a sip.

"She said she was so upset about what happened that she just can't face anyone yet, least of all me, but she won't tell me what it is. Oh, for God's sake, Olympia, she messed up, so fucking what! She's alive, and I want my wife and my kids home where they belong."

Olympia waited before responding. "She reached out to me first, Nick. Do you think she might be willing to meet with me? In some ways I'm a neutral person in all of this. Even though I seem to be right in the middle, neither of you really knows me. Sometimes it's easier to say difficult things to someone you don't know than to someone you do. Do you know what I mean?"

"I do," said Nick. "We call it the airplane or the bartender syndrome, where you spill your guts to someone you don't know and will likely never see again. You don't care what they think, am I right?"

"Generally speaking, yes. The fact that I'm a minister casts it in a different light. I'm a helping person. I listen, and I'm committed by the vows of my ordination to keep a confidence. People say things to me they might never say to anyone else. Do you want me to ask if she'll meet with me in person?"

He raised his head and looked at her. "I'd give anything if you would. If it involves any travel, I'll pay your expenses."

"Let me talk to her, Nick. It might be a beginning, but I have to be honest. I can't say where this might end. You also have to know that I can't tell you what she says unless she gives me permission. Are you still willing to have me try?"

"I don't know where this may go either, Olympia, but I'll do anything, go anywhere, say anything ..."

Olympia looked at the man sitting across from her. "The hardest part is going to be doing nothing for a while. Later, it may be that we uncover something very ugly, and then it could get really nasty. I just can't say."

His face and his voice hardened. "Olympia, I have money, and I have connections. The Greek community is very tight. Something happens to one of us, it happens to all of us, if you get my drift."

"That could be some of what concerns me. Right now everything depends on keeping Yolanda safe, and that means letting her make the next move."

He nodded reluctantly. "I understand. Oh, and I almost forgot. She does want us to tell the police to call off the search. She suggested you go with me over to the station. If you're there with me, they'll believe it. Are you willing? It may end up involving you more than you might have wanted."

A little too late for that, Doctor, thought Olympia. "Of course," she said.

"Well, then let's go right now. I'll drive."

Olympia hesitated. "It's not much of a walk, ten minutes maybe. The fresh air will do us both good."

"Reverend, with all due respect, I don't care to alert the whole town to the fact that we've been talking. Walking through the center of town together will do exactly that."

Olympia bit her lower lip and nodded, "Of course, Nick, I should have known better."

In a tiny cottage set back off a dirt road in the island town of Oak Bluffs on Martha's Vineyard, Yolanda Emerson Nikitas was finishing up the breakfast dishes. Her two children were playing in the back yard, and her cousin Sia was standing at the kitchen counter, folding laundry. There was a cup of fresh coffee on the table in front of her. The yips and squeals of happy voices coming through the open window were a stark contrast to the gravity of the conversation between the two women.

"So near and yet so far away," said Yolanda as she set the mug she'd just dried onto the shelf beside the others, upside down with the handle turned out.

"For someone who tells me she's been the equivalent of an open book all of her life, I'd say you've managed the logistics of your mysterious disappearance like a CIA professional."

Yolanda shook her head sadly. "If this whole thing weren't so awful, I'd probably wisecrack and say I'm the evil twin you've always heard about, or I read a lot of spy stories, but the truth is I'm scared skinny."

"You're sure they have no idea where you are?" said Sia, flapping out another towel.

"That's probably the one thing I am sure of. At first Nick thought I went out to stay with my sister in Indiana. That would be the logical thing, but he's not pushing her." She grimaced. "Everything I've ever done in my life has been logical and predictable. Now look at me. I'm totally messed up, afraid to go home and completely ashamed of myself. How could I have been so stupid?"

Sia smoothed a little pink jersey over her knees and carefully folded it into thirds one way, then the other way, until it was a neat pink square. She added this to the pile on the counter in front of her and reached for a pair of yellow cotton underpants.

"From what you say that slick-talking minister could charm the birds out of the trees."

"It seems he had a lot of practice." Yolanda lowered her voice. "I wasn't the first, you know."

"So you said."

"That's the worst part. He had me convinced that nothing like this had ever happened before. It was only when I overheard him saying the exact same things he'd said to me to another woman in his own church that the awful reality hit me. I can't believe I was so gullible."

Sia smiled sadly and stopped folding. "Yoli, you aren't the first, nor will you be the last, tired and overwhelmed young woman to be taken in by a fast-talking snake-oil salesman. You were lonely and frazzled, stuck at home with two little kids and not much help from a husband who, because of his profession, is often away in the evening. It's easy to understand from my perspective. Um, how exactly did you find out about the others, that is, if you want to tell me?"

Yolanda shook her head and laid the damp dish towel over the edge of the sink. "I'd been out of town to see my sister in Indiana and came back a day earlier than expected. That night I went out for some milk and noticed a light in his office. I decided to sneak in and surprise him. I surprised him all right, only I didn't say anything right then."

"What happened?"

"He never knew I was there. I slipped in through back door, and it didn't take me two seconds to figure out he wasn't alone. I tiptoed up to the door and listened, and that's when I knew. He must have that script memorized." Yolanda brushed away a tear of anger and frustration. "Same thing, word for word. This was different. She was special. This was God's secret and precious gift to the two of them." Yolanda clenched her fists. "What bullshit, and I fell for it."

"What did you do then?"

"I crept back out of the church, threw up in the parking lot and crawled back to my car. Poor Nick wondered what in the world had happened when I got back. I must have been white as a sheet. I know I was shaking. He thought I was coming down with something and tried to take my temperature. Needless to say, I couldn't tell him. I stewed and steamed all night long, and the next day I marched myself down to the church and confronted him."

"You didn't."

"I damn sure did. By then I was furious."

"What did he do?"

"What could he do? At first he tried to smooth talk his way out of it, but when I told him I knew who it was and was going to go and talk to her, he went crazy. That's the only way I can describe it. He jumped up, grabbed me by the arm and said if I ever mentioned as much as one word, he'd hurt the kids and ruin my husband's practice. Then he said he'd tell everybody I'd been chasing after him ever since I started coming to the church. He told me he had pictures, and he'd publish them. That did it."

Sia shuddered. "That is absolutely vile. You must have been terrified."

"You can't imagine. Nick and I might have grown apart, but there was no way I was going to let my indiscretion ruin him or bring any harm to the children. So I took a deep breath and said I'd never mention it again. He had me, and he knew it."

"And then you started plotting."

"Exactly. I called my sister, told her only that I'd gotten myself into some trouble and needed help with no questions asked. That's when she called you. Now I'm here, and I have time to think. I thank you for this. As long as he doesn't know where I am, he's going to be uneasy."

Sia sipped at her cooling coffee and nodded. "Curiously enough, Martha's Vineyard is a place where people can disappear. Little back streets, a somewhat transient population and a place where people don't ask questions. I often have short-term renters in this place. The neighbors are used to it."

"The neighbors are lovely."

"I know. I used to live in this house. Anyway, we'll talk more about that later. What are you going to do now?"

"I took a chance and contacted the new minister in my old church. Her name is Olympia Brown. I needed to let Nick know that the kids and I are okay and get the police to call off the search. I told her only that I'd gotten myself into a difficult situation involving the church across the street, and getting out of town seemed to be my only option. I told her I'm not ready to talk about it, but when I am, I'll come home. Then I asked if she'd be willing to talk with me sometime. So in addition to telling the police I was safe, I asked her not to do anything other than be there for Nick."

"And she agreed?"

"I can't say that she was enthusiastic, but she said she would. I really don't know her at all, but like I said, I took a chance. Talking about it with you now, it feels as if I did the right thing."

"Her name rings a bell. I think she may have preached here or something. I can find out, if you want me to."

Yolanda took an involuntary step backward. "No, not now. I really don't want anything said or done that might direct any attention toward me. That's why I'm using my maiden name here, Yoli Emerson. I never dropped it when we got married, so the kids are used to hearing it.

Sia shook her head in admiration. "I have to say that leaving your car in a commuter parking lot and taking the train into Boston, then a bus down to the Vineyard, was brilliant. Talk about blending into a crowd and hiding out in the open."

"Like I said, I may have done something really stupid, but I'm not naïve. Besides, I really do read a lot of mysteries."

"You're not stupid, Yolanda, just human. I may be a second cousin three times removed, but we're family, and I'm glad I can help."

"You are a godsend, cousin. There are three things I'm sure of right now. Nick is a good man, Jerrold Markham is a snake, and it's up to me to make things right."

"I believe you will, Yolanda."

"You know what? I think I'm going to ask Reverend Olympia if she'd be willing to come down here and talk."

"Do you think that's wise?"

"Don't ask me why, but I feel I can trust her."

"If you say so." Sia paused and looked up at Yolanda. "If she is who I think she is, I'd say you're right. She made quite stir when she was here last summer."

Nick Nikitas held the door for Olympia and then caught up to her so they could approach the main desk together. Detective Inspector, Steve Vages was at the desk and was immediately concerned when he saw Nikitas and Olympia coming toward him. He looked first at the doctor and then at the minister standing beside him.

"Uh oh. Are you here to tell me you have news about Mrs. Nikitas?"

Nick nodded. "It's good news. I've just talked to her, and she and the kids are safe. Is there a room that's a little less public where we can speak privately? This might take a few minutes."

Vages stood and held out his hand. "You can't imagine how glad I am to hear this, Doctor. Is she back home?"

Dr. Nikitas shook his head and briefly touched the other man's outstretched hand. He turned to Olympia. "I've brought the good Reverend along with me because as it turns out, she was the first person my wife called, and I think she might be able to give us a more complete picture of what's going on."

"Of course, Doctor. Come with me. Can I get you a glass of water or something?"

"No, thanks, Steve, just find us a room with a door we can shut."

"Okay if I take notes?"

"Of course."

When the three were seated in a small, closed room at the far end of the building, Olympia was the first to speak. Nick was sitting forward in his chair, twisting his fingers and staring at the floor. She cleared her throat and glanced over at him before speaking.

"I'm the new minister at All Souls. I've been there less than a week so I don't really know everybody yet. Yolanda Nikitas called me at home last night to say she wanted me to contact her husband and tell him that she and the kids were safe. She said she called me because as the minister, I would know how to contact her husband without anyone else knowing."

"Did she say anything else at that point?" asked Vages.

"No. She's determined not to be found right now, and she's gone to considerable effort to make sure of that."

"What do you mean?"

"She told me not to try and call her back or try and track the number, because she was going to destroy the cell phone. She told me that after I had spoken to Nick, I was to e-mail her on a Yahoo account she would access at a local library or on a friend's cell phone. She called me at church this morning, and this time she wanted to talk to her husband."

Nick shifted in his chair, crossed his arms and held them tightly across the front of his body. He looked as if he might fly apart if he let go. He took a deep breath before beginning to speak.

"This is really hard."

"Take your time, Doctor. I'm not going anywhere." For such a large and imposing man, Vages' voice and manner were surprisingly gentle. Olympia watched and listened. She wondered how the poor man was going to say all that needed to be said, but Vages was a true professional. He made the opening and just waited.

Nick continued, "She didn't go into detail, but she said she'd gotten herself mixed up in something involving the minister in that church across the street from ours, I forget the name of it."

"The full name is Amazing Faith Fellowship of Sanctified Believers," supplied Olympia.

"Oh, them," said Vages, rolling his eyes. "I never did much go in for that fundamentalist evangelical stuff. They're a little too sure of themselves for my taste. Um, did your wife say what it was that happened?"

"She wouldn't go into detail over the phone, said she would eventually, but she wasn't ready yet. She said she was afraid of him and afraid to bring the kids back." Nick was punching his right fist into the palm of his left hand. "So help me God, Steve, if that sonovabich hurts Yoli or the kids, I'll kill him."

Steve held up both hands. "Easy, Nick. For the record I didn't hear you say that, and neither did you, Reverend, okay? Right now we don't have enough to go on to say or do anything official, but that doesn't mean we can't do something. I've had my doubts about that guy ever since he set up shop over there a couple of years ago. Oh, he makes all the right noises and shows up at the right things, but there's just something about him that doesn't ring true. Maybe it's a guy thing, but I don't think so. To be honest, I'd love a chance to do a little background check. Might find something interesting."

"What do you mean by a guy thing?" asked Olympia.

Steve folded his hands over his ample stomach and leaned back. "Oily. Smooth talking. Ladies all nodding and making big eyes at him. Ever see one of those televangelists? Whenever I've heard him speak, I think he sounds like one of them. I don't trust those guys either. Ever notice that it's all about sending them money? That fast-talking Pastor Jerrold Markham wears designer suits and drives a very expensive car."

"Well, whatever happened, she's not ready to come back. I want to know why, and it's up to the police to go and find out."

Olympia held up her hands. "Wait a minute. Yolanda made a point of saying three things. First was tell the police she's safe and call off the search, but not to make that news public in any way. In other words, don't alert the press or the media. She's afraid of what Markham might say or do. Second was not to do or say anything at all until she decides what she wants to do next. And finally, she asked if I would call her back after we talked to the police. I said I would.

"As long as people think she's a missing person and therefore safely out of the way, then Markham, if he is responsible for her disappearance, isn't going to be worried. Ergo, we might have a better chance of watching him when he doesn't think he's being observed."

Vages rubbed his hands together. "Well, to be honest, up until now we've been handling this as a domestic difficulty. When a spouse in a rocky marriage needs a little time, sometimes that person just takes off for a breather. Our experience tells us that eventually they come back. Because there was no sign of foul play, no ransom demands, and nothing else leading up to it like 911 calls from the house, we played it down in the media. It's a small town, and when we think it's a domestic, we tend to watch and wait, if we can, rather than charge in. You know, give people their privacy."

"So," said Olympia, tapping her open palm with her forefinger to make her points, "You'll go on like she's still missing and no one has heard anything from her. At the same time one of us takes on a little undercover work and checks out the mysterious minister across the street."

"You aren't suggesting that you take that on yourself, are you, Reverend?" Vages looked distinctly uncomfortable at the thought.

"No, but I have two good friends, one or both of whom could be of some assistance. You see, Jerrold Markham has already taken me to lunch and since then has offered to take me to the interfaith clergy meeting next week. So I have my own opportunity to check him. I haven't exactly sorted it all out in my own head yet, so let me do that first, and then I'll tell you what I think we might do."

Vages looked intrigued. "It sounds like you have done this sort of thing before, Reverend."

"More by default than by design, Detective, but yes, I have sorted out a thing or two in my travels. Let me talk to Yolanda first. Anything I might say or do has to have her okay, or I don't do it. I'm afraid if we move ahead without her permission, we could lose contact with her." She paused and looked at the two men. "So are we agreed, gentlemen?"

Vages started to speak, but Nick interrupted him. "Look, Steve, What Olympia just said makes sense. All I know right now is that something happened that scared my wife so badly, she took the kids and ran. I don't know where she is, and I do want her back, but she's holding all the cards. I say let Olympia talk to her and see what she wants to do next. Meanwhile, we do a little fact-checking on Markham. If you think about it, other than what Yoli said and what you might think about him, we really don't have very much to go on."

"You've got a point," said Vages, nodding with his whole body.

"So we look both ways and proceed with caution," said Olympia.

"What if someone asks what we were doing at the police station?" asked Nick.

"You were asking about the progress of the investigation," said Vages.

Nine

June 10, 1862

Despite blinding summer sun my sorrowing days crawl on. I feel unable to work on my stories. My only joy, and tangible memory, is that I have my son. His simple delight in being alive is most infectious and his daily needs must be met, thus I am kept busy. My grief is such a lonely one for I can tell no one other than Aunt Louisa the truthful cause of my despondence. I don't even have the honor of wearing mourning garb.

Today Mr. Fuller came to my door with an oak seedling and asked if I might like it for outside the kitchen door that it might one day cast a cooling shade upon the house. Jonathan heard his voice and came running, so I asked him in to take some tea with the three of us. His eyes tell me he knows I am heavy hearted, but he is too proper a gentleman ever to speak of it. We all have our secrets. I know nothing of him other than he purchased land that once belonged to my father's estate and he tends it with great care.

For now that is enough.

More anon, LFW

That evening while Frederick was out in garden, Olympia stayed inside and caught up with the writings of Miss Winslow. Curiously enough, her words from a hundred and fifty years ago often offered insights to Olympia's present day life. On the other hand, maybe it wasn't curious at all.

Frederick frequently took advantage of the longer light available in the evening and went out to admire his garden. He was usually accompanied by the cats, who took turns ambushing each other, then freezing mid-charge and chattering at a bird mocking them in the branches overhead.

When it grew too dark to see properly, he came in and joined her in the sitting room.

"How did your meeting with the good doctor go?"

"Not entirely satisfactorily, but better than nothing."

"And what might I deduce from that cryptic utterance?"

"You make us some tea while I capture the cats, and I'll fill in the details."

Later, when she'd related the convoluted events of the day and they finishing the last of their tea, Frederick asked what she or they planned to do next.

"I've e-mailed Yolanda and asked if she's willing to meet with me in person. Of course, I have no idea where she is, but her husband Nick offered to pay my expenses to wherever it might be."

"I don't suppose you've heard back?"

"No, not yet, but I have a few other thoughts on the matter."

"I think I may be afraid to ask, Olympia. Are you getting in over your head again? "

"I don't think so. When I went to lunch with Jerrold Markham, he was exactly what he should be, a local pastor welcoming a new colleague to the community. He was totally professional, and yet there was something about him that made me uneasy. If you asked me what it was, I couldn't tell you. Maybe it's a girl thing."

"What do you mean by a girl thing?"

"The police detective, Steve Vages, said the same thing this afternoon. He said Markham made him uncomfortable, only he thought it might be a guy thing."

Frederick set his empty tea mug on the table beside him and invited Cadeau onto his lap. "What are you getting at?"

"Yolanda said she got into a situation with the minister from the church across the street. Well, I don't have to be a nuclear physicist to figure out that she probably had an affair with him, and he said something that panicked her and sent her running, but I have to say she's orchestrated her vanishing act very well. So I can deduce from this that the woman performs well under fire, meaning she may be down right now, but she's not out. She's likely feeling humiliated and remorseful as hell, but she may well be planning her return as methodically as she planned her departure."

"If that's the case, what now?"

"I think I'm going to try calling Julia Grafton, the minister who resigned from All Souls so suddenly. I'd like to ask her what she knows about Mr. and Mrs. Nikitas, as well as the nasty-pastor across the street."

"Innocent until proven guilty, Olympia. You don't know anything about him."

"Yet," she supplied. "Let's just say I'm getting some really uncomfortable vibrations around this whole thing. She doesn't have to talk with me if she doesn't want to. On the other hand, if something happened to her that made her take off, it may be there's a connection."

Frederick stopped stroking the cat and looked up at her. "Don't you think that's stretching it a bit? I agree two women disappearing from the same church without apparent cause or explanation is rather a strong coincidence. But let's say the nasty-pastor did have a thing with Yolanda. Surely the man is not so driven by his passions that he'd approach two women in the same congregation. I mean, there's foolhardy, and then there's downright suicidal."

"Power is a curious thing, Frederick. Just look at some of our elected politicians."

"I'd rather not, thank you."

She chuckled sadly. "Think about it. Power means different things to different people. For some it's money, and for others it's social or political position and recognition. For some it's fast cars or physical strength and endurance, and for some it's sexual domination—you know, as in notches on the bedpost."

"Is that the girl thing you're getting at?"

"It just might be. I may be a grandmother, but I'm not dead from the waist down."

Frederick grinned and nodded appreciatively.

"I'm serious. Jerrold Markham is a very sexy man."

"Should I be worried?"

"Hardly. Being able to recognize something doesn't mean I'm interested in it. In fact, that kind of person has the exact opposite effect on me. It's kind of like being in a room with a live snake. Even if you're not afraid of it, you know it's in there somewhere, and when it finally does come out, which it will, it's going to startle you and make you uncomfortable. So the best thing to do is to take the initiative and scare it out of hiding. Then you can catch it. That puts you in control and not the snake. See what I mean?"

Frederick cocked his head and looked at Olympia. "When did you learn so much about herpetology?"

"It's one of those things you pick up along the way."

"Olympia?"

"The father of my sons was interested in snakes and lizards and such. I picked up a few things. It was another life, Frederick."

"You rarely talk about him. I'd like to hear more, if you ever want to tell me."

Olympia had a curious half smile on her face. "Maybe someday. That was then, and this is now, Frederick. Times and people change, and considering where I am now and who I have here with me, I'd say that it all worked out for the best."

Ten

Olympia did not sleep well that night because she kept replaying differing versions of what-if and who-but and maybe-I-should-have in her mind. As a result she was up with the sun and sitting at her desk in what passed for a home office, waiting for her laptop to power up.

That's the next project for Frederick, she thought. I need a proper office, one with a door I can shut and a window I can open. The cold room off the kitchen is the perfect one to convert. In days gone by it had been both a walk-in pantry and a storage room. All it needed was a little cleaning out, insulation and some sort of heating. It was certainly large enough to accommodate a desk, two chairs, two cats and a book case or three.

With that decided she put the thought on the Good Ideas list and began to consider her options regarding the issues, actions and principal cast of characters, past, present and across the street, that were of more immediate concern.

First on that list was contacting Julia Grafton, the former minister of All Souls. Olympia checked the time and realized that it was far too early because, according to Franna, she was living at least two time zones west of there. Next on the call list was Jim Sawicki. She needed to connect with him for several reasons. One was to see how he was doing in general, and the other was to find out when he was moving. She also planned to ask if he'd be willing to do a bit of internet sleuthing for her.

She knew Yolanda would be contacting her at some point, but there was no point in scheduling that on her list. Somewhere in all of this she needed to find a title and topic for her sermon. The childhood game of Truth or Consequences popped into her mind, but given the present circumstances at All Souls, it might be too direct an approach.

Finally, in opposite corners of the ring, were the rose ladies. Olympia giggled as she imagined the two of them, swinging their secateurs and brandishing their flower baskets in a do-or-die battle for control of the altar table. Further imaginings were interrupted by the comforting sound and smell of coffee happening in the kitchen. Frederick, bless him, had slipped out of bed and was making breakfast. With at least part of her day organized in her head, Olympia left her computer to its own devices, smoothed out her bed-hair the best she could with her fingers and made her way around the ever-hopeful cats to the kitchen. She smiled, remembering the first time Frederick had made her coffee and thinking that she could get used to this. *Well, I am used to it now, and I think I like it.*

Olympia stayed home and waited until after ten to call Julia Grafton's number. She was comfortably ensconced at her desk in the corner of their bedroom with the door closed. Frederick was out in the garden, and the cats had been banished to the sitting room. If she did manage to get through to Julia, the last thing she wanted was an untimely interruption. She'd gotten the number from the Denominational Directory, now available on line to all members with an authorized password.

There was no point in advertising her plan of action at this point because it wasn't fully formed. Her mother always used to say, the less said, the less mended. Well, in this case the fewer people who knew what she had in mind, the better. That way, if it didn't work, no one would be the wiser, and if it did, she wouldn't have people standing at her elbow micro-managing. This was a very tangled knot she was looking at, and she needed to approach it in her own way and time. If she could slowly extract one thread at a time and see where it connected to the others, she might eventually find out what was at the core of it all, and that is exactly what she planned to do. She had her suspicions, but now she needed facts.

Julia Grafton picked up in middle of the message Olympia was in the process of leaving on her answering machine.

"This is Julia."

"Hello, Julia. I'm Reverend Olympia Brown, and I'm the minister who's been appointed to All Souls."

"If you don't mind, I'd rather not have any contact with anyone from All Souls."

"Wait, please don't hang up. I promise I'm not going to ask you about anything personal. I called you because I need information and maybe some insight about something that's troubling me, and you might be the only person who can help."

There was a long pause before Julia responded. "How do I know you are who you say you are and not some malcontent busybody trying to make more trouble?"

Olympia gulped. She wasn't prepared for such a defensive response, but as the logical side of her brain flashed through what she'd just heard, it was perfectly understandable.

"I agree, you don't have any proof at all that I am who I say I am. I got your number through the Denominational Directory, and I had to use my member password and identification number to get it. You can do the same thing to check me out." She began to restate her name when Julia interrupted her.

"Never mind. I heard through the grapevine that you were going there. What's your question? That will confirm who you are as much as anything, and I can Google you for more information."

"Then you will have heard that Yolanda Nikitas and her two children disappeared in the middle of last week."

"I did know that. Has anyone heard from her?"

"I actually talked with her yesterday and again this morning. That's why I'm calling."

"Then she's all right, meaning she's not in physical danger?"

"Yes and no. That's why I took a chance and called you. Minister to minister, I wanted to ask what you know about her."

Julia hummed for a moment before speaking. "To be honest, I wasn't at my best before I left, but I did notice that Yoli was coming to church less frequently. When I asked her about it one day, she told me she'd been taking the kids to the church across the street because of the Sunday school there. She said she wanted the kids to learn more about the Bible."

"What about her husband Nick? What about them as a couple? If you feel like you can tell me without breaking a confidence, were they having problems that you knew about? I'm trying to get a picture of something I've sort of landed in the middle of. Both of them are talking to me, but Yolanda won't say where she is, only that she's afraid to come back. She says it has something to do with the minister across the street. Something he said or did panicked her so badly that she took off. Can you tell me anything about him?"

There was a long, difficult silence before Julia answered. Olympia could hear the other woman breathing.

"I can tell you about him," she said, taking another breath and letting it out slowly. "I had an affair with him. I broke every ethical code I thought I cherished and lived by. I betrayed the trust of my congregation, and then, when he threatened to go public and say I was the one who came on to him, I just couldn't face myself or my church. In exchange for his silence and the remaining shards of my dignity and self-worth, I left. Only it hasn't worked. I'm absolutely shattered physically, emotionally and spiritually. He's a sexual predator, and I was a willing victim. I know it now, but hindsight is about as effective as a broken condom."

"Oh, God, you're not pregnant, are you?"

"No, that much I'm sure of, and I suppose I should be grateful. That in itself is another story."

"Oh, Julia. You poor thing. I'm so sorry. That's awful."

"It's not awful, Olympia, its vile, and I hadn't planned to tell you all this. It's just that I'm a mess, and I know it, and frankly, it feels so good to finally be able to speak the words." She paused and then asked for a moment to collect herself. When she spoke again, her voice was stronger.

"He's got to be stopped, Olympia. He's going to do it again, if he hasn't already."

"That's what I'm thinking, but I also think he could be dangerous if cornered. If he's so arrogant and sure of himself that he thinks he can approach two women in the same community in broad daylight and get away with it, he's either delusional or else he's very skilled at what he does."

"He could talk the leaves off the trees, Olympia, and I'm Exhibit A. I fell for it, and I was thrilled to be asked. That man could sell air conditioners to polar bears. I know, I bought one, only it doesn't work."

Olympia paused to gather her own thoughts and chose her next words with care. "I need to think on what you've told me, Julia. I don't know all of what happened with Yolanda, but she says she wants to meet with me in person. I'm assuming I'll find out more then."

"You'll love her. She's a real sweetheart. What a total bastard that man is."

"Something else you should know is the congregation misses you and feels bad that you left. They really don't know what happened. There are little murmurings, but I don't think they know the whole thing."

"It's a small town, so I guess I'm surprised to hear that. I'll tell you, the guy has it down to a science. I think part of the thrill for him is doing it, literally, under people's noses and not getting caught."

Olympia shuddered in disgust at the thought of the man using his personal magnetism and power, definite assets in the religious profession, to take advantage of women who came to him in need. If this was true, and it was sounding more and more as if it might well be, then the man was a predator and needed to be taken out of action.

"Julia, you have my promise that I will never repeat anything you've just said to me. Let me have that conversation with Yolanda and see what pieces she can add to the total picture. Pastor Markham has offered to take me to the Interfaith Clergy meeting next week, which could be interesting and informative as well."

"Be careful, Olympia. I think that man is downright evil, and as a minister that's not a word I use lightly."

"I hear you. I think I'm hatching a plot of my own. I just need a little more time. If I'm going to go out on a limb, I'm going to make damn sure the thing is going to hold me up before I do."

Julia chuckled. "I think I like you, Olympia Brown. I hope I get a chance to meet you in person one fine day. Thank you for listening to me and not condemning me."

"All I'll say in response is there, but for the grace of God, go I. There is not one commandment that I haven't either broken or at least thought seriously of breaking. I learned early on that no matter how justified you think you may be, some risks just aren't worth the consequences. I hope I get to meet you, too."

At this Julia actually laughed out loud and then promised to keep in touch.

When she hung up the phone, Olympia took a pen out of her pocket and fished a dog-eared note pad out of her purse. She needed to start writing things down immediately before she forgot. The first thing she wrote was Jim's name. Under that she wrote Frederick's and under that she wrote Yolanda, followed by three question marks. The first two she was confident of, but the third was still very much of an unknown quantity.

Eleven

Out in the back garden Frederick was blissfully up to his knees in peat pots, seedlings and nice, fresh, fragrant compost — his pride and joy. He was particularly proud because he'd found that a lovely colony of worms had taken up residence in the compost bin. They would do a terrific job of aerating the soil for his vegetables over the summer. He had the urge to scoop up a squirming handful of them and take them in to show Olympia, but he remembered she'd asked not to be disturbed. As he stood admiring them a robin flew down and pecked up a wiggly snack. Frederick couldn't tell boy robins from girl robins, but he smiled his approval. It would be nice if a pair set up housekeeping high enough in a tree to be safe from the cats.

He turned at the sound of the back door opening and watched as his lady love, dressed for work, approached him for a goodbye kiss before climbing into her van.

"Were you successful? Was she willing to talk to you?"

"Yes to both questions, but that doesn't mean I have much to report as of right now. I just need to watch and wait and dodge the rose ladies."

"Rose ladies?"

"Much needed comic relief, Frederick. I'll catch you up on everything tonight."

Olympia planted an emphatic kiss on Frederick's dusty, smiling face and headed for her beloved VW. It was time to go to work. Everything from now on depended on her looking and acting like nothing in the world was amiss. Olympia didn't like deception, and she didn't like playing games, but sometimes you had to fight fire with fire. As a result of her conversation with Julia, she had become the predator tracking a predator.

Frederick stood leaning on his spade in the sunshine and watched and listened as Olympia's van sputtered off down the street. There was nothing quite as distinctive as the metallic clatter of a vintage VW engine. He made a mental note to himself to have her check the compression in the not-too-distant future. It sounded as if something was misfiring, not that it would be surprising, considering the age of the thing, but it wouldn't do to have it give out on her and leave her inconveniently stranded.

He was enjoying an imaginary side trip into auto mechanics and engineering when he was interrupted by the unwelcome jangle of the phone ringing inside the house. He truly wanted to let the answering machine get it and stay out in the sunshine. Then conscience and duty prevailed. Thinking the call might have something to do with missing persons or a frantic husband, he dropped his shovel and galloped inside. He caught it before the message began and gasped a breathy greeting into the handset.

"Hi, Frederick, it's Laura Wiltstrom. Is, uh, my mother there?"

He could hear the squeaks and babbles of a cheerful baby in the background and smiled at the mental image of the child he considered his granddaughter.

"She's just this minute gone off to work, Laura. Do you have her cell phone number? She should be there in about a half hour."

"I'll call her at the church, but I'll tell you, as well. I want to talk to you both sometime in the next couple of weeks about that job offer I got. It's really tempting, but I'm still not sure whether I can manage it all on my own."

Frederick knew this was not the time to offer his personal thoughts on the matter. This was still too fragile a situation, and he felt too much of a newcomer on the scene. He was, however, profoundly grateful to be included in her thinking.

"I think that's a really good idea, Laura. From what little I know of you, I think you could take on anything you wanted singlehandedly. However, it's not mine for the telling."

"Funny you should say that, Frederick. I'm only just getting to know my birth mother, and you kind of arrived with her, so I think of you as a pair and therefore, I want to include you."

There was so much he wanted to say about future permanency, the meaning of life and other English and non-English profundities and personal insights, but he said only, "Thank you for saying that, Laura. You can't begin to know what it means to me."

"I hope one day you'll tell me, Frederick, but right now I need to arrange a date and feed a little girl who has just sprouted her first tooth."

"Really!" crowed Frederick.

"Yup, I found it this morning when I was giving her breakfast. I heard it clink on the spoon. Then I stuck my finger in her mouth, and there it was." He could hear the swell of maternal pride in her voice.

"Sure sign of intelligence, you know, early teething."

Laura was laughing. "Who told you that?"

"That's what my red-haired mother always said, and we all knew better than to disagree with her."

"Then it's well documented, isn't it, Frederick?"

When they'd said their goodbyes, Frederick carried the warm glow of this greater and more explicit familial inclusion back to his garden. It outshone the pride in his beloved compost and even went beyond the glistening colony of worms. Frederick Watkins was a happy man.

On her way to the church Olympia stopped for a cappuccino. She loved a good cup of coffee every bit as much as she enjoyed a full glass of good wine. With cup in hand she pulled up and parked in front of the church. There she sat, relishing the taste and rich blended scents of coffee and cinnamon before taking on the day. Inside, waiting for her, were questions about a missing person, a broken family, a wounded minister, and, of course, the challenge of the rose ladies. She'd never expected that life as a religious professional would be so complicated — spell that hair raising — but it sure beat the hell out of boring.

"Well, look who's here!" It wasn't a question.

Surprised out of her reverie, Olympia looked out the open window to find Jerrold Markham standing beside her van.

"You were a million miles away, Olympia, but I wanted to say hello. I hope I didn't startle you.

"You did, but that's okay. I needed to come back to earth and get to work at some point this morning. Hello back. How's it going over there?"

Olympia had been caught off guard and was making nervous small talk. Her opinion of Pastor Markham had undergone a sea-change in the last twenty four hours, but it was vital to everything that would happen from now on that she not let it show. She flashed him a cheery smile over her coffee container.

He gestured toward his church across the village green. "You know what a day in the life of a pastor is like. It takes time and energy, so it's especially nice for me to have a colleague who understands."

He stepped back from the car and pulled open her door with a flourish and a little half-bow.

"Why, thank you, Jerrold. You are a pastor, a chivalrous gentleman and a colleague all in one."

"I hope I'm more than that, Olympia, more than just a colleague, that is." He edged a fraction closer to where she was now standing.

Olympia smiled and dropped a mock-curtsey, to all appearances extending the play-acting. "Good Sir Jerrold, what could anyone want more than a friend and a colleague in this curious business?" She put her free hand to her chest and lowered her eyes in theatrical false modesty. "I am honored to make your acquaintance, and a good morrow to you, kind sir. I needs must not tarry with such mirthful merrymaking when there are countless souls to be comforted and saved."

"And miles to go before I sleep," countered Jerrold Markham. "I'll see you next Monday for the clergy meeting, if not before."

Olympia waved a breezy goodbye and went around to the side of the church to the door that led to her office. Once inside, she called out greetings to Franna, but when there was no response, she relocked the outside door and listened to her own footsteps in the big, empty building.

Once inside her office she pulled out her cell phone and dialed Jim's number. She was worried about him. Her priest friend was in a precarious place mentally and spiritually. Despite being HIV positive, his physical health was stable, but he was having a personal crisis of faith. As a result of this he'd been showing signs of depression. As she listened to the ringing sound, she asked herself whether she should be approaching him at all but decided that in this particular instance, there was no one else she could go to.

"Jim, its Olympia."

"Thanks for getting back so soon. I've found an apartment. There's a professor at Allston going on sabbatical for a year. He's delighted to have me stay in his place if I'll just pay the utilities and water the plants. It's on the back side of Beacon Hill."

"That's a terrific location, Jim but the parking is going to be god-awful, especially in the winter."

"He has an off-street spot. I'm splitting that with him so he can have it when he comes back."

"Well, I guess that's you set for a while, and say the word if you need any help getting your things over there. I'm assuming it's furnished."

"Oh, it's furnished, all right. The guy collects antiques. The place is like a Victorian museum."

"Really," said Olympia, arching a curious eyebrow in the privacy of her office but saying nothing more.

"The only things I have are my clothes, my music system, my books and CDs. The one thing of any size is my grandmother's rocking chair, which I can't get into my car. So I guess if you have a little time, I could use some help with that. It'll go into your van with no trouble at all."

"If you're free this weekend, we could make a Saturday afternoon of it. I have something I'm going to need a little help with as well," said Olympia.

"Uh oh, not so soon. You just started there. You can't have stepped in something already."

"How delicately you put it, Jim, but I'm afraid you might be right. Look, I'll tell you everything on Saturday. In fact let's make a day of it. I'll come in and help you move your stuff, and then you come back home with me and have supper and stay the night. You can check out that room we've reserved for you."

"How's Frederick?"

"He's working at the bookstore. We're not joined at the hip, you know."

"I know that, Olympia, but it's still courteous to ask. Besides, I like the guy. He's funny."

"I like him, too, Jim."

In the church across the street Jerrold Markham double-checked his datebook. His first appointment wasn't for an hour. Thus assured of not being interrupted, he locked the door to his office and powered up his personal lap-top.

Twelve

Friday was often her stay-at-home sermon writing day, and with Frederick off in his bright yellow truck to the bookstore, she was free to concentrate. It was also her day to check in with her three children.

By mid-morning she'd learned that Randall, her youngest, might be coming home for the summer if he didn't find work on the Cape. Malcolm, the elder son, a musician and sometime college student, was thinking about changing direction (again) and finishing up with a double major in business and psychology, and oh, by the way, he and Liz had finally decided to get married sometime in September, and they wanted her to perform the wedding. Her last call was to her firstborn, Laura, who asked if there was a time she could come and talk about her job on the west coast.

"So you've accepted it?" said Olympia.

"I have, and then I start thinking about it, and I panic. It really is everything I ever wanted, and if not now, when? Something like this may not ever happen again. The timing could have been better, I mean, with the baby and everything, but my mother said once I got there she'd come and help me set up the apartment. I thought I'd ask you, when you finish up this assignment, if maybe you and Frederick might come out later in the fall? Maybe even for Thanksgiving?"

Olympia loved Laura's youthful enthusiasm but winced at her use of the word mother. She couldn't help it and was glad she could not be seen.

"It all sounds wonderful, Honey. I'll need to check my calendar, but consider it a yes."

"Oh, thank you." And then, as if Laura had read her mind, she added, "You know, Mom-Olympia, I really do need a name for you."

"I have a name."

"No, a mother name. I call my adoptive mother Mum. So what do I call you? Olympia is too formal. I need to give you a mama name. Olympia, you there? I mean, is that all right?"

Olympia nodded, speechless with eye-drippy happiness, and tried to pull herself together.

"It had to be when the time was right, Laura. Now that it is, something will emerge, I'm sure of it. "

"I'll think of something."

Olympia changed the subject. "So now that you've accepted the job, when are you leaving?"

"I start work on September fifteenth."

Olympia swallowed hard. "That's less than three months away."

"I know. I guess I'll need some help sorting and packing. You up for that?"

"Of course, Honey. I'm a positive whiz with duct tape and cardboard. Just give me a bit of lead time, okay? Things are a little intense here at the church."

"I thought churches were supposed to be oases of peace and tranquility, sanctuaries for the spiritually weary, happy homes for the hopelessly heavy hearted."

Olympia could not help grinning at her daughter's wordy wit.

"That, my darling daughter, is yet another urban, or in this case suburban, myth. Churches are organizations and as such are subject to all the trials, tribulations and human dramas that plague any other polyglot human subgrouping. Maybe the difference is that in churches most of the nasty stuff happens behind the scenes rather than in the office or the boardroom."

"Sounds like you have an agenda, Reverend-mother."

"And you, my dear girl, are as perceptive as you are brilliant. I may not have raised you, and you may not as yet have noticed, but we do share some rather distinctive characteristics."

"I've noticed."

Olympia hung up the phone, smiling, and turned to the sermon that still needed writing.

June 27, 1862

Today I received a letter from Sarah Josepha Hale, the editor of Godey's Lady's Book, asking if I would consider writing a novel they could publish in monthly installments. It seems my stories have been well received and there is great interest in such an undertaking. I am to send them my answer, yea or nay, within ten days. Oh Lord, what shall I do? Were I not so sick at heart I would rejoice, say yes, and carry the letter to New York myself. Indeed, it is a great honor. Perhaps I shall ask Aunt Louisa's advice. I know I can trust her to advise me well.

More anon, LFW

On Saturday after Frederick left for work, Olympia drove into Dorchester to St. Bartholomew's, where she collected Jim and what meager possessions of his that wouldn't fit into his old Toyota Corolla. These were his music system, a small crate of CDs and audio tapes he'd collected over the years, a hand crocheted afghan and a carved oak Victorian rocking chair. These last two personal treasures had been gifts from his *bubcia*, his Polish grandmother, who gave them to him before she died.

The whole operation of moving the accumulated possessions of Jim's life took less than an hour. As they were making the final trip to the car, the housekeeper for the rectory wished him well and handed him a still warm loaf of Irish soda bread for good luck. Other than that, there was no farewell fanfare, no gathering of parishioners waving and calling out their good wishes. There was nothing other than the sounds of a door clicking shut and their feet on the pavement. Jim walked ahead down the brick walkway and got into his car. It was done. Olympia wondered what was going through his mind. There was no doubt that her best friend was at a huge turning point in his life, and all she could do right now was be there for him.

She did her best to follow him through the city, but eventually she lost him and was glad she'd had the good sense to put her cell phone and his new address on the passenger seat. There had been a time when she might have boasted that she knew the ins and outs of Boston like the back of her hand. But after several wrong turns, three frantic phone calls and one shouting match with an irate Charles Street police officer, Olympia managed to find a legal parking space only two streets away from Jim's apartment. This was not the time to worry about how to get the rocking chair to its final destination. She needed a glass of wine and a major rant. Then she'd worry about getting the rest of Jim's possessions, and after that she'd tell him about the unpleasantness in and around All Souls.

As it turned out Jim hadn't had time to go shopping, and the wine closet in the apartment was empty as a tomb and dry as dust.

"Crap!" said Olympia with a despairing look. "Now what do we do?"

"We walk down Pinckney Street to one of the coffee shops on Charles Street where I'll get you a double cappuccino with triple whipped cream, and you'll tell me all about your latest ecclesiastical misadventure. After that we'll get your car, and you'll drive me back to the apartment and double-park while I extract the rocking chair and the tapes and CDs."

"Sounds like a plan, Father."

"I'm not just a pretty face, Reverend."

Over their upscale and pricey coffees, Olympia told Jim about the Nikitas situation and her conversation with Julia Grafton, the former minister. When he finished shaking his head in disbelief, she asked what he thought about attending a Sunday service at the church across the street as an observer.

"You know, Jim, act like you're church shopping, look around, ask questions and maybe even ask to meet with the minister. Lots of people do that."

"Protestants do. Catholics don't ask questions, at least not out loud, and we go to the local parish church. We do not church shop, as you put it." He paused. "However, I know what you're talking about, and I can certainly play the part of the curious visitor. Without my collar, no one will ever suspect."

"I'm not so sure about that, my friend. You're pretty articulate when it comes to theology, but then, it's not his theology I'm worried about. I want you to watch him in action."

"Let me think about it. What exactly are you trying to do, Olympia?"

"To be honest, I'm not sure yet. If Yolanda and Julia are telling the truth, and I have every reason to believe they are, then the man is a sexual predator. He needs to stopped and his treachery exposed."

"Sounds like he's exposing himself pretty well as it is."

Olympia rolled her eyes. "I'm serious, Jim. This guy is bad news."

"Sorry, Olympia, you left yourself wide open for that one. I couldn't resist."

"Sexual predators are evil people."

"Tell me about it. We've got a pretty good record on that one ourselves."

"I'll be doing some observing on my own this Monday. He's going to take me to the interfaith clergy meeting."

"Are you going to be alone with him? What will you do if he comes on to you?"

"The chances of that are minimal, Jim. I'm in my mid-fifties, I'm hardly a glamour queen, and I'm in a committed relationship. On the other hand, men like him will come on to anyone they can. I don't know whether it's an obsession or a compulsion or both."

"Be careful, Olympia, obsessional people can be dangerous if cornered."

"I hear you, Jim. I'll be careful, but I don't think I'm his cup of tea. I've seen pictures of Yolanda. She's beautiful. Anyone would find her attractive."

"So when should I come down? My Sundays are going to be free from now on."

"How about next weekend? This week's a little unsettled. Oh, and Laura called and asked if Frederick and I could go help her pack for California sometime over the summer."

"She's taken the job then?'

Olympia bit her lip and nodded.

"Just when you were beginning to really get to know her. That's too bad."

"I'll be getting to know her for the rest of my life, Jim. Now I know why God made airplanes."

Jim smiled and nodded his agreement and then looked at his watch.

Olympia got the hint. She up-ended the cup, licked the foamed milk off her upper lip and scooped the rest out of the cup with her index finger. Now she was ready to go.

Olympia finished out the weekend by preaching a rather abstract sermon on faith versus belief, then carefully sampling and praising each and every brownie, cookie and lemon square that had been set out after the service.

To anyone who asked if there were any new developments in the Yolanda Nikitas disappearance, she said only that since there were children involved, the police were being very close-mouthed about the whole business. This was not a lie; it simply was not the whole truth and offered just enough to satisfy a curious parishioner but not so much as to encourage further inquiry. The real truth was that neither Nick nor the police knew that Olympia had spoken with Julia Grafton and that later the following week she had a date on Martha's Vineyard with Yolanda. But neither of these would take place until after the interfaith clergy meeting on Monday when she would have the opportunity to observe Jerrold Markham at close range. Until then it was the conscientious and deliberate appearance of business as usual.

Thirteen

On Monday morning Olympia looked up from her desk to see Jerrold Markham standing in the doorway. It was the second time he'd walked in on her unannounced, and she liked it even less than she had the first time.

"Are you early, or did I lose track of time?" She hoped she sounded breezy and conversational rather than irritated and discomforted by his silent arrival.

"Likely a little of both, Olympia, I hope you don't mind. You know what this business is like. One minute you're over your head, then someone calls and cancels, and you find yourself with unexpected free time on your hands. I decided to come over and see if you might want to leave work a little early and go for a ride. I thought we might take the so-called scenic route. It's a total of three or four minutes longer, but it goes through a really pretty woodsy area, and if there's time I could show you the famous Millbridge waterfall."

"I didn't know there was a waterfall nearby, but wait a minute. I thought the Baptist minister was coming, too." Olympia was collecting and stacking the papers on her desk.

"He called and cancelled this morning, hence, even more extra time. I was hoping you'd be agreeable. That waterfall is one of my favorite places. I go there with my camera sometimes. It's really lovely after a snowfall."

"Then you're a photographer, too?"

"Not really. I like to take pictures, and I confess to a lust for fancy cameras, but that's as far as it goes. No, I take it back. I did enter one of my photos in a competition once."

"Did you win anything?"

"No, I was happy just to be accepted. It was a juried show."

Olympia picked up her sweater and her purse, locked the outside door of the church and followed Jerrold to his BMW.

Once they were buckled in, Jerrold moved onto the main street and began to act as a tour guide. He pointed out historical buildings, told her names and denominations of the neighboring churches they passed and where she could get the best coffee in town. Olympia didn't bother to tell him she already knew about the coffee shop. She was busy taking mental notes on how he was treating their time together. So far, it was purely touristy and collegial and, in truth, quite pleasant.

"Oops, I missed the turn to the waterfall," said Jerrold. "No matter, we'll just go to the clergy meeting a few minutes early. That way I can introduce you around, and we'll go there on the way back. Is that okay with you?"

"Sounds like a plan. I have a three o'clock back at the church. I need to be back for that."

"Loads of time, Olympia, these meetings rarely go more than an hour and a half. That means we have a bit more time than I thought afterwards. That's good."

If Olympia wondered what might be good about it, she chose not to ask.

The Methodist Church, where the meeting was to be held, was unremarkable in its churchliness. A large social hall, a bulletin board festooned with Sunday school pictures and announcements of past and upcoming events, and a blessing of parsons clustered around a coffee maker and a plate of assorted bakery muffins cut into pieces. She'd seen it all before and was comforted by the familiarity. Some things never change.

When they all had a cup and a plate in their hands, Rev. Darlene Lodge, the pastor of the church, invited the eight of them into her study for the meeting. It was a tight squeeze around the oval table, but with a little wiggling and friendly jostling, it was accomplished. As host and convener of that month's meeting, Darlene offered a few opening words and then invited them to begin the meeting with personal and congregational updates and items of note or concern.

Jerrold was the first to speak. "Sisters and brothers, I want to introduce you to our new colleague sitting here beside me, The Rev. Olympia Brown. She's come to help out at All Souls until they can find a full-time minister." He turned in his chair and gestured to Olympia, who was seated next to him.

Olympia smiled at the friendly faces around the table and half-turned back toward the man beside her. "Thank you, Jerrold, but I need to clarify one point. I am the full-time minister. I have a four-month contract. This may or may not be extended, depending on what develops at the church. I'll just have to wait and see. Meanwhile, thank you for inviting me to be part of this, and I look forward to getting to know you all better."

There was a moment of eye shifting and uncomfortable silence. Again she looked around the table and wondered if it were she or her church that was the elephant on the table, the thing everybody knew about and no one wanted to talk about. She decided to be the aggressor.

"As you know the former minister resigned without notice, which is why I'm here, and then, in the week before I arrived, a member of All Souls and her two children vanished. I can tell you only that in the case of Mrs. Nikitas, the police are still trying to locate her and her children, but they do not suspect foul play."

The Episcopal priest, Father Robbie Bensley, raised his hand. "Has anyone heard anything from or about Julia Grafton? I'd just like to know if she's okay. She left so suddenly. I'm worried about her."

Olympia felt, rather than saw, Jerrold shifting his position in the chair beside her.

"As far as I know she's had no contact with any members of the church," said Olympia. This wasn't entirely an untruth, given that Olympia was not actually a member of that church.

The remainder of the meeting consisted of little more than catching up on which church was planning what event, followed by an unenthusiastic conversation about the need for a clergy presence at the Fourth of July festivities. There were a few friendly jibes that are common among congenial colleagues, some second cups of coffee, and finally the closing prayer. Some things never change, she thought once again, or do they? The clergy around the table all knew the minister she had replaced left for a very good reason that no one but she and the man beside her knew. They also knew that a woman who had been a member of that same church and her two children had suddenly disappeared. What they didn't know was when the last coffee cup had been delivered to the kitchen, she would go off to look at a waterfall with the man she alone knew was personally responsible for the disappearance of the two women.

"We're almost there," said Jerrold, turning off the main road at the sign that announced the historic Millbridge Falls. "There used to be a sawmill here, you know, water power for the mill. It was built sometime back in the 1800s. There's a marker beside one of the benches that will tell us."

Olympia nodded. She'd already figured out that building a mill beside a waterfall would have been the location of choice and practicality.

"I like local history," was all she said.

"I'd like to know a little more of your local history, Olympia. You're an interesting woman. It's clear that there's a lot more to you than just being a lady minister. I can only hope one day you'll let me know what it is."

"One of the nice things about ministry is that it has so many facets," said Olympia, carefully avoiding saying what hers might be. She knew by now that within the denomination, at least, she'd earned herself a reputation as a problem solver, and she preferred that the man beside her knew nothing of this.

Jerrold pulled off the road and parked the car along the split rail fence marking the edge of the parking area. Olympia could already hear the sound of rushing water. It was a sound she loved, and she was instantly carried back to a time when she'd done some teaching at a hiking lodge in the White Mountains of New Hampshire. One afternoon she'd joined one of her students and hiked down into a deep ravine where together they had watched and listened to a one-hundred-foot waterfall crashing into a jade green pool at their feet. She could still remember the feeling of the tumbled mist on her face and the rumbling and shuddering vibrations of the falling water that seemed to go right through her whole body.

"Olympia, you home in there?" It was an unwelcome intrusion into her reverie.

"I was long ago and far away, but it was nice trip. I'm back now."

"Will you ever take me there?"

"Not likely."

If there was more to be said, Jerrold was clearly not going to be the one to say it. He looked mildly crestfallen but only for a moment.

"Well, then, let's get out and take a look around. I hope you like it. What's pretty to one person can be a total washout for another."

"Surely you didn't mean that, because if you did, I can match you pun for pun."

They both groaned and laughed and got out of the car. The waterfall was very pretty, nothing like the one in New Hampshire she remembered, but well worth visiting. The utter privacy of the place so close to a town made it a real hidden treasure. The jumble of rocks and change in elevation creating the active fall in the rapidly moving water created a sight and sound that Olympia liked so much. She took it all in but said only, "It's beautiful. Thank you."

Jerrold moved fractionally closer. "I thought you'd like it. Maybe we could come back sometime with our cameras and a thermos of coffee. "He pulled back the cuff of his jacket and looked at his watch. "Oops. Back in the car with you, Reverend, I've got to get you to All Souls for your three o'clock."

As she walked in front of him toward the car, he touched the small of her back in passing. *Is this how he operates? The not-quite-accidental contact that appears to be innocent, even chivalrous; the touch that doesn't offend but is the prelude to another and more insistent one?*

"The water here is faster and deeper than it looks, Olympia." He pointed to the No Swimming sign. "Kids still come here, though, and unfortunately, sometimes one of them drowns. Be careful if you come here alone."

"Young people think they're invincible, don't they?" said Olympia, shaking her head.

"But they aren't, are they?" said Jerrold. "No one is."

Fourteen

Olympia was back with ten minutes to spare before her three o'clock prenuptial meeting. She could see two people sitting in a car as she walked across the town green toward the church and assumed it was the couple. She mentally checked her calendar. The wedding would take place in less than a month's time. *Yikes!* Unlike so many other things that had fallen unceremoniously into her lap, this was one of the less complicated tattered ends surrounding Julia's resignation that Olympia was trying to gather up. She stopped beside the car, leaned down and spoke through the car window.

"Hi, you two, I hope you haven't been waiting long. Danny and Maggie, right?"

Maggie smiled and held out her hand. "You're not late. We got here early because we wanted to give ourselves plenty of time. It's been a while since we were here, and we didn't want to be late."

Olympia smiled and nodded. "I appreciate your making the effort. I make a point of being on time myself, but it seems to have gone out of fashion with a lot of folks. But enough of that, come on in. I have your folder in the office. Reverend Julia left things in good order, but I still want to sit down and get acquainted with the two of you. I simply will not marry people I don't know and who don't know me. A wedding is much too big a step in your lives to have the words rattled off by a stranger."

With that pronouncement Olympia stepped back onto the sidewalk so the couple could get out of the car.

Once they were inside the office Olympia arranged the chairs so they were facing one another and then took out their file and set it, unopened, on the low coffee table between them.

"Let's just sit and talk for a while. I'm in no rush."

For the next several minutes they made pleasant small talk about the classic beauty of the church and the challenges the recent restorations and renovations had created when adding a wheelchair ramp. Then they got more specific about the wedding details, such as how many were going to be in the wedding party, and had they chosen their music?

It was when Olympia reached for the folder that she saw Danny glance at Maggie and reach for her hand. She looked as if she wanted to say something.

"Have I missed something?" said Olympia, turning more fully towards her. "Do you have a question?"

Danny cleared her throat and tucked a stray wisp of hair behind her ear before speaking. "Um, well, there is one thing that's come up since we started planning things."

"What might that be?"

"Well, when we first decided to get married, it was only going to be us and our two best friends, but then it sort of grew."

Olympia smiled knowingly. "Weddings do that. Once the decision is finally made, they seem to develop a life of their own. Is that a problem?"

Danny's voice took on an odd tone. "It would appear so. I have a brother, a straight brother, who's been born again and is threatening to make a scene. He said that when you come to the place in the ceremony where you say, 'If there is anyone here who knows of any reason why these two should not marry,' he's planning to stand up and say he does, that God intends marriage to be between one man and one woman. I don't know what to do."

"Have you spoken to your parents about this?"

Danny nodded miserably. "I did, and they're as upset as I am, but they don't know what to do either. He's always been scrappy and hard to get along with. I don't know what it is, but he's happiest when he's making other people uncomfortable."

Olympia wondered for the umpteenth time why weddings and funerals often seemed to bring out the worst in families rather than the best. And for the umpteenth time she didn't have an answer other than the fact that all families have baggage, and significant life events seem to spill some of it out.

Olympia looked thoughtful for a moment and then brightened. "It might be a bit draconian, but the truth is your brother has threatened you. Therefore, you could get a restraining order preventing him from coming anywhere near you. If you do that, I can have a policeman stationed outside the church to make sure he doesn't try to violate the order and get in."

Danny nodded. Her face was a mask of sadness. "I thought we were getting past this. Who'd have thought something like this could come from inside your own family?"

With an involuntary shudder, Olympia remembered another young woman whose worst living nightmare had been her own father. "I'm always dismayed when people invoke the name of God to be hateful. Give me some time to think about this. I don't want anything to ruin your day."

"We tried talking to him, but he just keeps repeating that everything we are and everything we do is a disgrace to God's holy plan, and he's going to everything he can to stop us from getting married."

"Olympia shook her head. "I'm so very sorry this is happening to you. As far as I'm concerned God has given us many ways of being human, just as in my line of work there are many religions. One is not by nature better than another. We are what we are, and we do what works best for us. We can choose which church to belong to, but I know that homosexuality is not a choice."

The two women nodded in silent affirmation.

"Let me think on it, ladies. We've got a month." Olympia opened the folder and looked at the two women. "So let's do what we can now, and that is to go over your wedding ceremony and see if it's exactly what you want. After that we'll take a walk around the interior of the church proper and block out where people are going to stand."

"Wow," said Maggie, "I never knew there was so much to it."

"That's why I get the big bucks," said Olympia with an exaggerated wink. "Now let's get down to business."

Their tasks completed, Olympia packed the two women off with good wishes and the invitation to call her if they had any questions. She took a quick look around the office and decided that anything further she might do could wait until the next day. She was collecting her things in preparation for going home when the telephone rang. It was Jerrold Markham.

"Do you have a few minutes, Olympia?"

Not really, but on the other hand, if I play the innocent, maybe I can ask a few probing questions about your very questionable past. "I've had a long day, Jerrold, and I'm really ready to go home, but I suppose I can spare a couple of minutes for a colleague. I warn you, though, I'm not at my best at this time of day."

"So you're an early bird are you? I'll remember that. I'm a night owl myself. I never start a sermon until after nine at night. I like to think I do my best work after dark."

"Oh, gosh, not me. I never once pulled an all-nighter, even when I was in college. If I didn't know something by 11:00 p.m., I damn sure wasn't going to know it at 2:00 a.m. "

"Look, why don't I run over there right now? I saw a car parked out front when we got back from the meeting, but it's gone now. That wasn't your wedding couple, was it?"

Olympia smiled sweetly into the receiver. "As a matter of fact, it was. They're lovely."

"Wait a minute, I saw two women get into that car. That couldn't have been them."

"That was them, Jerrold, and I'm going to marry them. Do you have a problem with that?"

"Um, yes and no, but that's not why I wanted to talk to you. It seems I've got a bit of a problem over here, and as a colleague I think you might be able to offer me some advice."

"I really do have one leg out the door, Jerrold, but I try never to say no when a colleague makes a request. Can you give me a hint as to what this is about?"

"I don't want to say it over the phone." He dropped his voice. "I think one of my parishioners has got it into her head that she's in love with me. To be honest, I really don't know what to do. I thought maybe a woman's opinion might be helpful."

Olympia wished she could say, oh, I think you very much do know what to do, Reverend Markham, or else the tables are turned, and you really have been caught off guard. Either way, this could be a golden opportunity.

"Come on over, and we can sit outside in the memorial garden. It's a beautiful day, and I've been cooped up inside for too long."

"But I thought we might ..."

Olympia raised one eyebrow, shook her head and hung up the phone.

Minutes later, Jerrold was looking left and right as he walked toward Olympia. She was seated on one of the stone benches in the circular meditation garden situated to the left of the building. With a beckoning wave, she invited him to join her.

"Do you think this might be a little too public for a confidential conversation?" He was looking doubtful as he carefully lowered himself onto the cool granite seat.

"Actually, it's quite private, and if you think about it, what could be more appropriate than two ministers having a conversation in a church memorial garden?"

He didn't look convinced, but it was clear that Olympia wasn't about to move. She spoke in a low voice.

"Tell me what's going on."

Jerrold shook his head and rubbed his forehead. "I can't believe this is happening. A woman in my church, and I'm not going to name her right now, told me she was having some problems and asked if she could meet with me. Well, of course I said yes and arranged a time for her to come in. She started out by saying that she and her husband were having problems. He's a busy professional, away a lot, and she was lonely and frustrated, trying to care for the children and the house by herself. Then she repeated the word *frustrated* and sighed, leaned back in the chair, crossed her legs and just looked at me."

"Is that all she said? What I mean is, that could be construed as her simply being dejected or unhappy. I don't know quite how to phrase this, but did she get any more specific?"

"Yes and no. That's why I called you. It was all kind of ambiguous, or else I am so totally naïve that I even amaze myself."

"What happened next?" Olympia was the very image of pastoral concern.

"She said she needed something to fill time in the evenings when her husband was out and thought there might be something she could do for me at the church. That's when I began to think she might have something other than the word of God on her mind."

"What did you say at that point?"

"I have to tell you, I didn't know what to say. I didn't want to hurt her feelings or turn her away in case she was telling the truth. On the other hand, if she was making untoward advances, I knew I needed to be really careful."

Olympia made her face look innocently puzzled. "So what did you say to her?"

"By then all I wanted to do was to get her out of there, but I couldn't let her know that. I thanked her for her trust in sharing her problems with me, and I promised to pray on it. Then I told her I would think about something she might be able to do at the church. I told her the greatest need for help was usually during the day when people were there for the food pantry and the clothing closet. I said that if she was lonely, what she needed was people, not an empty dark church."

Olympia nodded. "That all makes sense. Did she leave then?"

"I only wish she had. She thanked me, and we both stood up. I thought she was getting ready to leave, but before I knew what was happening, she put her arms around me and kissed me. I mean, she really kissed me."

"Uh oh."

He nodded. "Uh oh is right. I pulled away and stepped back. Then I told her I was a man of God, and I could not and would not under any circumstances break a commandment and commit adultery."

Olympia could not believe she was hearing this.

"What did she do then?"

"She started to cry. Then she said she was sorry and ran out of the office. That was less than an hour ago. That's when I called you."

"I'm glad you told me, Jerrold. If something like this happens, it's really important that you let someone know immediately. Because she's upset and now possibly embarrassed, she might just turn the tables and accuse you of being inappropriate with her. Was there anyone else in the church at the time?"

"No, and now I think I know why she wanted to talk with me when no one else was there. No witnesses."

"Do you have a District Coordinator or some other higher up you can call on for something like this?"

Jerrold shook his head. "I'm a one-man operation, Olympia. This is my church and mine alone. When God called me to buy this church, it was a falling down derelict. Now I have a growing and thriving congregation, and I don't want to lose it because someone has the wrong idea about me. That's why I called you."

Olympia looked, wide-eyed, at the man sitting beside her, and for one of the very few times in her fifty-something years, she didn't know what to say.

"What do you think I should do?"

"It's a very delicate situation, Jerrold. I know you understand that. There is much at stake. Without a bishop or some other credentialed authority for you to turn to, you need to clear the waters, so to speak, and do it as quickly as possible. Maybe you could ask her to meet with an impartial third party, someone who is not a member of the church. Do you know of any professional mediators in the area?"

Jerrold put his hand on Olympia's arm. "Actually, I thought about doing that very thing. I thought about asking you. That's why I called. You're new, you are not from around here, and being a woman minister and all, she might be willing to listen to you. I'm desperate, Olympia, and I don't know who to turn to."

Olympia bowed her head in thought and then looked up at Jerrold.

"I'm not the person to do this. Let me think if I know someone who can."

Jerrold took out a handkerchief and dabbed at his eyes. "Thank you," he whispered, "I knew you'd be the one to ask. As you can probably imagine, this has been terribly stressful."

"Life is stressful, Jerrold. Being a minister multiplies that by a factor of ten. The clerical life is a gift and a blessing when it works, but when we do run into a snag, we don't always have the answers we need for ourselves. While we are searching for those answers, we are almost always under someone's microscope. I don't mind telling you that I get tired of living in a fishbowl sometimes."

Jerrold's face brightened. He reached over and took her hand. "I've got an idea, let's run away and leave it all behind. Do you think they'd even notice?"

Olympia snatched back her hand and made a great show of looking at her watch-less wrist. "Not tonight, I have to do my nails. Maybe some other time. Let me check my calendar."

"You are joking."

Olympia stood and brushed off the back of her skirt.

"Yes, Jerrold, of course I'm joking."

Fifteen

That evening, when Olympia related all of this to Frederick, she did it the way you might tell the story of *Alice's Adventures in Wonderland*. With each new twist the story becomes more preposterous.

"The worst part is I have no idea what, if any, part of Markham's tale has a shred of truth in it." Olympia paused and corrected herself. "No, it might be something worse than that. He may be a pathological liar. The scene with the church member as he described it may actually have happened, or the whole thing is part of an egotistical and narcissistic construct of his own mind."

"Well, if Yolanda and the other minister, Julia Grafton, are telling the truth, then we know of at least two women he's victimized. And if there are two, then by virtue—no, I correct myself. The word *virtue* has no place in this conversation. I'll start again."

Olympia rolled her eyes at the circuitously loquacious man she loved. "Get to the point, Frederick."

"Ah, yes, point. We know of two women who are victims of his unprincipled charms. Both described the same *modus operandi*. This suggests a pattern. It is highly likely there are more of his victims who have not come forward."

"They don't come forward because they feel humiliated, scared and powerless," said Olympia. She could feel her face flushing with rage at the absolute evil of such an act and the regularity with which she knew such things happened.

Frederick waited a long moment before speaking, and when he did, it was in a low and cautionary tone he rarely used.

"This is a man totally without scruples who has practiced and refined his technique over a long time. This man knows how not to get caught, and he's not about to let it happen now. He has too much to lose."

A grim-faced Olympia responded.

"Why do men like him think they can get away with this, and why *do* they get away with it for so long? Do they think they are gods living above the law or just that that the laws for the rest of us don't apply to them?"

"I have a three-word answer for that, Olympia: consider your politicians."

She nodded. "Then one of the victims finally gets mad enough, and it all comes out."

Frederick nodded. "Exactly. Someone is finally so outraged that the fear of reprisal is not enough to keep him or her silent, and then all hell breaks loose. It happens in the UK, too. You Yanks don't have a corner on political and sexual hypocrisy."

"I'm mad enough," said Olympia.

"I knew that when you came through the door. What are you planning to do about it?"

"Find documented evidence, or create it myself."

"Olympia?"

"Yes, Frederick?"

"Before you take one single step in that direction, let us reason together, think it through and make sure *you* are not the one who gets hurt."

"I've already thought about that."

Frederick's voice and exasperation level were rising. "I'm not so sure, Olympia. I am witness to the fact that you can get carried away on a rising tide of your own enthusiasm, and the rest of us are left to pick up the pieces. I seem to remember standing by your bed in the intensive care unit not so long ago, counting the blips and waiting for you to regain speech and movement—oh, yes, and wondering if, in fact, you were going to live. Or had you forgotten that?"

Olympia knew when she'd been bested. "Okay, Frederick, I'll call Jim. God knows the Catholics have had more than their share of dealing with sexual predators."

"Which means you have to talk with both Yolanda and Julia before you do anything else." Frederick's voice was returning to a more conversational level.

Olympia nodded. "Without their express permission, I may not be able to do anything at all."

"What do you mean?" asked Frederick.

"I mean I probably have two options. I can either catch him in the act myself, or I can try and find other people he's victimized and convince them to come forward and press charges. Whatever happens, it's likely that Julia and Yolanda's stories will become public knowledge. Of course, I'll try and prevent that, but I think the man is sick enough or vicious enough to try and take everybody else with him if he knows he's going down."

"Knowing you as I do, Olympia, I understand that you don't see any alternative but to go ahead with this."

Olympia pursed her lips and nodded.

"I wish I didn't agree with you, my darling, but the fact is I do. Call the two women and see what they think and how they feel. Then call Jim and tell him everything and get his opinion. Then we three sit down and talk it through. We may need an alternative plan if the two women refuse to come forward."

Olympia was tapping her fingers on the table beside her chair and nodding her agreement.

Frederick continued. "There are a few other factors here. At some point you are going to have to involve the police. What he is doing is against the law."

"Frederick, I don't think anyone enforces adultery laws any more. In fact, I'm not sure there are any left on the books."

"Adultery may not be a punishable crime, but sexual harassment, intimidation and blackmail are all abuse of power and are punishable crimes."

"Blackmail?" Olympia looked quizzical.

"Blackmail by intimidation. Do I understand that Markham threatened both Julia and Yolanda if they said anything?"

"According to both women, he did."

"Well, there you are, coercion, intimidation, abuse of power, sexual exploitation. It's not new, Olympia, but it is often goes unreported because of the shame factor, and the abusers know it." He paused. "You are playing a very dangerous game. I really wish you'd go to the police."

"I'm not playing, Frederick, and this is not a game. This is deadly serious. And if I do go to the police, what then? This is still my word against nothing. They don't know exactly what happened to Yolanda, and Julia isn't even on their radar screen. Yolanda is listed as a missing person. Only we know she isn't. She's in hiding, and she doesn't want to say why. They know she cares enough about her husband not to have him worrying himself sick over her, and I think she cares about him a whole lot more than that. I'll go to the police again when I have real evidence and real people to back up my accusations and not before."

"I don't like the sound of that. Just what else are you plotting in that clever little clerical brain of yours?"

"It's not completely formed yet, Frederick. The first thing I do is talk with Julia and Yolanda, and maybe even at some point sit down with both of them together."

"What's that going to accomplish?"

"If they are willing, maybe set up a scenario where they show up and confront him, and hopefully, he'll incriminate himself."

"Have you lost your mind, Olympia? From what you've told me this man has no scruples whatsoever. God knows what he'd do if he was cornered like that. I think it's far too dangerous."

"What if I can set it up with you and Jim in the immediate vicinity? Then we'll not only have witnesses, but if it did get out of hand, we'd have reinforcements."

"You probably can understand that I have grave reservations about what you are about to do, but I also think it might just work. You must promise me on ..." he looked around the room, " ... on Miss Winslow's diary that if you do try this, you will not do it without me and Jim in immediate proximity."

"I promise. I may be in a fury over this, Frederick, but contrary to popular sentiment, I have not taken leave of my senses. I'll tell you something else."

"What might that be, my love?"

"I think this is going to get even uglier than it is now. I think Julia and Yolanda are two of who knows how many, and when those two people pluck up the courage to come forward, I'm dead certain that others will get in line."

"I wish you could be something other than dead certain. It does not inspire confidence."

"If I were a man, I suppose I could say I was cocksure, but I'm not, so I can't."

"This isn't a joking matter, Olympia. I wish you wouldn't do that."

"I'm sorry Frederick. I get wise-crackey when I'm nervous or anxious."

"Which are you now?"

"A little of both."

"Well, then?"

"It's late, Frederick. Why don't we wait until tomorrow? You call Jim first thing in the morning and tell him what's going on, and I'll call the two women and see what they think."

With that, she took a bit of folded paper out of her pocket and held it out.

"Take this. It's Jim's new number in Boston. It's too late to call anybody tonight, and I want to sleep on it. I may have only one shot at gaining Julia's and Yolanda's confidence, and I've got to be clear in my own head exactly what I am going to say and how I want to proceed. "

Frederick tilted his head and arched a very English eyebrow in Olympia's direction. "Do my ears deceive me, or are you actually adopting a cautious attitude?"

"Let's just say if I want to line up my ducks in the order I believe to be necessary, rushing at them with my own arms flapping might just scare them off."

"Will wonders never cease?"

"Piss off, Frederick!"

Sixteen

July 8, 1862

Rain today. It suits my mood, or should I say it did when the day began but since then I have had a most interesting turn of events. It was my intention to ask Aunt Louisa's advice about the request from Godey's Lady's Book after Jonathan was in bed. However, this afternoon, Mr. Fuller came to the door with a fish he'd caught and asked if we would like to have it for our evening meal. I told him yes, but only if he would agree to join us. After dinner, with Aunt Louisa in attendance, I took Mr. Fuller into my confidence about my fledgling career as a writer and introduced him to CK Barrow, my nom-de-plume. He was most congratulatory and even offered to entertain little Jonathan should Louisa be away and I needed time to write. How kind he is, and yet there is a secret sadness I see flicker in his eyes when he thinks I am not looking.

I have decided. First thing tomorrow morning I will send my grateful acceptance to the editor at Godey's, and tomorrow afternoon I shall begin work on my first novel.

More anon, LFW

The next morning Olympia decided to make her phone calls from home, where she would have more privacy. She could hear Frederick moving around in the room over the one in which she was sitting. He had claimed the second bedroom for his study-office-music-listening room, so he had a room of his own, while Olympia was still working out of their bedroom. She had plans for the room or rooms off the kitchen, but they were still in the discussion stage. I need to get him onto that before the snow flies, she thought, then amended it to ... before the snow flies this year!

The first thing she did was call the church and tell Franna Buckland she wouldn't be coming in until noon, but when she did, would she like to go out for lunch? Franna accepted enthusiastically and asked if there was anything that needed doing before Olympia arrived.

"Just keep the rose ladies from dumping weed killer on each other's flowers, and check to make sure we have ushers and someone to do the coffee hour for Sunday," said Olympia. She didn't bother to hide her devilish grin, because there was no one to see her but the cats. They were asleep on the bed, nestled back to back like reverse commas with whiskers.

With step one out of the way, Olympia retrieved the telephone numbers of the two women she needed to call and took a deep breath. She would have preferred to speak to Julia first, but when she didn't answer, Olympia left a message asking her to call back when it was convenient. This left Yolanda, an abused and shamed young mother she didn't know but who had reached out to her. There was a thin thread of trust between them that Olympia prayed she wouldn't destroy.

After another deep breath and a quick prayer for courage, she heard the electronic sound of Yolanda's phone ringing, which was interrupted by a cautious, "Hello?"

When they had gotten the social preliminaries out of the way, and Olympia had assured the woman that her husband was okay and this was not an emergency, she cautiously began to broach the reason for her call.

"Yolanda, how do you feel about my coming over there to see you?"

"Um, what do you mean?"

Olympia sat up and squared her shoulders, unconsciously adopting a straighter posture which somehow might improve her credibility and strengthen her own resolve.

"I've been thinking a lot about this whole situation, and I have an idea. If it works, it might stop Mr. Jerrold Markham in his tracks and put a permanent end to his predatory mission."

"I don't want anything to do with it. I don't ever want to see that man again. If I ever get my life back, it won't be anywhere near where he might be. I'm not interested."

"Please hear me out, Yolanda. I want to sit down with you over a cup of coffee and hear your story, every word. I can't go into specifics, but I have reason to believe that this man has been doing this for a long time. If he isn't stopped, he's going to keep on doing it and ruining other women's lives, not to mention their families."

"I'd like to see him dead. I suppose I shouldn't say that to a minister, but I truly wish somebody would do the world a favor and take him off the planet. I may have committed adultery, Reverend, but I'm not going to commit murder."

"Would you settle for calling him out and sending him to jail?"

"How do you propose to make that happen?"

Olympia sensed a turning of the emotional tide and relaxed against the back of the chair.

"I can only say there is good evidence there are other women he's victimized. If we can get even two of them to come forward and make statements, we'll have a case we can present."

"What do you mean, a case? What do you want me to do? He really put on quite a show with flowers, candy, secret love notes. He promised the moon and the stars, and I finally succumbed. Then, once he'd made his conquest, he wasn't interested any more. Do you think I'm going to humiliate my husband and shame my children and my family by going public with that? I don't think so, Reverend."

"Hold on. I haven't suggested anything of the kind. The only thing I asked was if I could come over to Martha's Vineyard and talk with you in person. Anything I do or say after that will be only with your approval, I promise you." Olympia paused before going on. "Yolanda, you've had a terrible experience. What that man has done to you and other women is shameful and ruthless seduction, followed by emotional blackmail."

Olympia paused for breath. "Not to mention it goes totally against the very conservative teachings of the church and the congregation he makes a pretense of serving. It's all about power and numbers, Yolanda, and you were the target of the month, I'm sorry to say."

Yolanda's voice was suddenly strong and clear. "When can you come?"

Olympia opened her date book. "Today is Tuesday. If I can get a ferry reservation, I can come down later in the week. Will that work for you?"

"Park in the commuter lot on Palmer Avenue and take the shuttle to the ferry. I'll borrow a car and pick you up. Just give me a time, and I can work it out from here."

"Let me clear things on this side, and I'll call you back."

"Would you like to spend the night? A roundtrip in one day could be pretty exhausting. I can bunk in with the kids for the night."

"That's a thought. Can I leave it open for now?"

"Sure," said Yolanda.

When she hung up the phone, Olympia let herself relax. It had gone well.

One down and one to go, and a cup of fresh coffee before I do. She closed her calendar and started out of the room. Now the cats were interested. Their mommy-in-waiting was heading toward the kitchen. This could mean food. With whiskers and tails in the air and a spring in their eight collective paws, they followed.

Once she was settled back in her office, Olympia set the steaming mug on the desk in front of her, picked up her cell phone and redialed Julia's number. This time, she picked up.

"Julia, this is Olympia Brown. Have you got a few minutes? I have an idea I'd like to run by you."

"Does this have anything to do with Jerrold Markham?"

"It does, and I beg you to hear me out."

"Oh, Olympia, there's a part of me that never wanted to hear from you again and another part of me that is desperate to see justice done. Either way is going to be painful. I said too much the last time we talked, and I'm feeling very vulnerable. But go ahead and tell me what's on your mind. The least I can do is to listen."

"Thank you, Julia. I have to begin by saying that my thoughts are still pretty unformed at present, but what I'd like to see happen is that he be confronted by one or more of his previous victims with a witness present who will testify as to what happened, namely me."

"Am I correct in assuming that I'd be one of those previous victims?"

"Only if you agree to it."

"So what are you thinking of doing? Mind you, right now I'm only listening to what you have to say."

Olympia released the death grip she had on the coffee mug and flexed her fingers.

"As I said, the plan is still totally amorphous, but here's my thinking thus far. I'm pretty sure he's trying to add my name to his list of conquests. I recognize the signs. I'm going to behave as though I have no idea what his little innuendoes are leading up to and drag it out for as long as I can before letting him actually say or do something explicit. Meanwhile, I'll be keeping careful notes and saving any e-mails or phone calls, although I don't think he's stupid enough to leave a trail. But who knows. Men like him don't exactly think with their brains."

At this Julia laughed out loud and begged Olympia to continue.

"Actually, that's about it so far. He's definitely on the move, and I've gone so far as to tell Frederick, my significant other, and my best clergy-buddy, Jim Sawicki, about what I'm thinking."

Julia's voice took on a darker and distinctly warning tone.

"He's a bad man, Olympia. Whatever you do, don't do it alone. I think he could be dangerous."

"You aren't the first person to say that, and I am proceeding with extreme caution. I just know the man has to be stopped, and I seem to have landed, or maybe thrust into, the perfect position to do it."

"I repeat," said Julia, "be careful, to which I add I'm willing to help, even if it means going public with what happened. My only hesitation is that I don't want to hurt the church. I care about those people, and I let them down. I'd be so grateful for an opportunity to make amends and tell them the truth about why I left."

Olympia slumped back in her chair.

"You are a victim, Julia. I think your congregation would understand if they knew what happened. They hold you in very high regard, you know, even now not knowing why you left so abruptly. Some of them fear it was something they did."

"I would do anything to make it right, Olympia. Nothing can be any worse than what I'm feeling now. Tell me what you want me to do." She was weeping.

"Thank you, Julia," whispered Olympia. She was surprised that her own voice was becoming husky.

"Would you be willing to come back here on short, maybe very short, notice? If there is a way I can arrange it, I'd like to have you and Yolanda show up and confront him together with me as the recording angel, so to speak. Meanwhile, I'm asking my priest friend Jim to go on an internet prowl to see what he can uncover. Men like Markham can sometimes leave a trail they aren't even aware of. Jim has a friend in the Boston Police Department and can get information that your average minister on the street doesn't have access to."

This last remark evoked a weak snuffle from Julia.

"I haven't given you too much to go on, but will you at least think it over?"

"I don't have to think it over, Olympia, I'll do it. There's no way I can get past this and get on with my life and my ministry if I don't."

Olympia expressed her genuine thanks and promised to keep Julia informed as the plan unfolded. What she didn't tell her was that there was a parallel idea germinating in the back of her deviously creative mind. This one would take a lot more thought, delicacy and careful timing. She could share it with no one, at least not yet; but if she could manage to pull it off, she would accomplish much of what she had been hired to do.

She dropped her cell phone into her pocket and stretched, listening to the creaks and crackles in her neck and shoulders. She'd been sitting for too long, and she needed some fresh air and exercise. Mild exercise. A walk around the back garden before getting into the car and heading off to the church should do it, and then *I'll go have lunch with Franna Buckland.*

Olympia liked Franna. She was a kind soul and good at the job she did. Now Olympia wanted to find out how much the church administrator and other members of the congregation really knew about Julia's departure and what had precipitated it. If anyone would know, it was going to be Franna. She tucked a notebook and pen into her pocket, picked up her keys and wondered where they might stop for lunch. Maybe she'd better take that walk around the garden later or perhaps wait until tomorrow when Frederick was home, and they could go for a walk together. *That makes sense,* she thought. *There's no sense rushing into anything.*

Seventeen

While Olympia was presenting her thoughts to Yolanda and Julia, Frederick was upstairs telling Jim Sawicki what was happening at Olympia's church and, to the best of his ability, outlining her ideas on what to do about it.

Jim's initial response was a low moan of resignation followed by, "She does know she's playing with fire, does she not?" After a suitable pause he added, "And what does she want us to do while she chases after this particular flaming windmill?"

"I know, Jim, here she goes again; but if you think about it, she has a point. She's got two women who have told her almost identical stories of sexual abuse and intimidation at the hands of this man. We both know he'll keep on repeating the pattern until someone catches him and puts an end to it."

"God knows, as a Catholic priest I understand more than most about how sexual predators operate and the shroud of silence and denial that allows them to continue. And now that I am thinking about it, Olympia may just be the right person to see that he's stopped. What exactly does our dear girl have in mind?"

"I don't think she's actually come up with anything specific yet. I know she's downstairs right now, talking to the two women she knows who have been abused. She asked me to ask you to use your police connections to see if you can find out anything more about him. Oh, yes, and I made her promise she wouldn't do any kind of actual confrontation without one or both of us within shouting distance."

His voice was incredulous. "She agreed to that?"

"Wonder of wonders, she did."

"Well, that's something, and if it does get ugly, I can play pretty good defense. When I was a kid, I learned a lot on the streets of the West End. I haven't had to use those particular skills in years, but it's like riding a bicycle. It comes right back."

"I hope we won't need it, Jim, but it's good to know it's there. She's still in the information gathering stage. That's why I called you. But now that I've delivered my message, I want to know how you are doing? How's your sub-let working out? How's your health? When are we going to see you again?"

Jim laughed. It was a good, strong laugh, one Frederick had not heard in far too long.

"One question at a time, brother. The apartment is great. I'm loving being on Beacon Hill. Remember, I grew up less than a mile from here, only it was a working class mile. Who'd ever have thought I'd be living up here with the titled and privileged beans and cod Bostonians?"

Now it was Frederick's turn to chuckle. He was pleased that Jim sounded so positive.

"To continue, my health is holding. I feel good, and my stress level is dropping, and the doctors are encouraged, which means I'm encouraged. To the last point, when I'll come down and see you may depend on Olympia and what she has in mind. I'll give my friend, Jerry O'Brien, a call over at the Dorchester PD and see what his day looks like. Then I could come down there and deliver my information along with a bottle of wine?"

"Jolly good," said Frederick, exaggerating his pound-note Englishness for Jim, who clearly enjoyed it.

"I suppose that would be good for another reason, as well. I've been doing some theological research on my own of late, and I need an intelligent sounding board."

"I don't quite understand."

"I'm not sure I do either as yet. You know I've been trying to come to terms with priesthood in a church that doesn't condone my lifestyle. Let's just say for now I may have found something that might allow me to be who I am and continue to be a priest."

"Good heavens, Jim, is there really such a thing?"

"That's what I want to talk to you both about," said Jim.

"Crikey, times really are changing, aren't they? I'll be interested to hear what you have to say. Meanwhile, I'm hearing noises from below, indicating that Her Ladyship is getting ready to leave. I needs must go and bid my sweet dame farewell."

As he was going down the stairs Frederick heard the chime of the mantel clock in the sitting room. Miss Winslow is either pleased or concerned, he thought. As he reached the bottom step the clock chimed a second time, which usually meant *take note*. He stepped into the sitting room and looked in the direction of the clock. It was not in its usual place but was perilously close to the edge of the shelf on which it traditionally reposed. This was not a good omen. When their resident house ghost was really concerned about something, she signaled it by moving the mantel clock. In extreme cases they might even find it on the floor. Now it was close to the edge, in danger of falling or being pushed. This was either a message or a metaphor, neither of which they should ignore.

"Olympia?" called Frederick.

"I'm on my way out the door. Come give me a kiss, I'm running late."

"Olympia, I suspect that our Miss Winslow just issued a warning chime, and she underscored it by moving the clock. It would appear that something has caught her attention, and I think it might possibly have something to do with your latest adventure. You know what she's like."

Olympia was galloping around the kitchen, hopping over the cats, collecting her keys and filling her travel mug with fresh coffee.

"It's hardly going to be a comfort to say I've got some pretty serious concerns myself, but I don't see that I have a choice other than to go forward with this. I will exercise caution, and I repeat my promise not to do anything directly confrontational without you or Jim nearby."

"I wish I could believe that, Olympia, but some of your best intentions can be discarded in the heat of the chase or when you're presented with a window of opportunity."

Olympia wrinkled her nose and nodded in reluctant agreement. "I'll do my best, Frederick. Meanwhile, I've got a lunch date with the church administrator. If anybody is going to know the story behind the story, it's going to be her."

She ran over, gave him a quick hug, then a longer kiss and left a splat coffee on the floor in her distraction. "Damn!"

"I'll mop it up, love, just take care," said Frederick. Olympia knew he meant it.

After she'd swirled out the back door, Frederick mopped up the spilled coffee and was contemplating a third cup of tea when the phone rang. It was Olympia's daughter Laura, asking to speak with her mother.

By way of response Frederick said, "And how's my charming and precocious granddaughter?"

Laura laughed and told him Erica was growing like a weed and recently had mastered the fine art of crawling backward. Then it was Frederick's turn to laugh. He told her Olympia had left for work, but she could probably catch her on her cell phone.

"I'll wait until tonight. I don't want to call her when she's driving, but I do want to talk to her."

"Not to pry, Laura, but is it anything I can help with?"

"I'm not sure, Frederick. Maybe you can. I'm not used to asking people for things, and I've never asked Olympia for anything because, well, we're really still getting to know each other."

"Laura, your mother would turn herself inside out if she thought it would benefit you. What is it that you need?"

"Let me talk to her about it first. You've already helped me by what you just said. It gives me more confidence. When will she be back?"

"She will likely have returned by supper time."

"I'll call back then."

"If she comes in sooner, I'll have her call you. Will you be at home?"

"I'll be in all afternoon. Thanks, Frederick."

"How are the plans for the new job and the move coming along?"

"Actually, that's part of what I need to talk to her about."

Much as he wanted to, Frederick knew that to press for further information right now could be a mistake. Olympia's relationship with her daughter was still relatively new, and the last thing he would ever want to do would be to jeopardize or compromise it.

"Well, whatever it is I stand in support of you both. I hope you know that, Laura."

"I do, Frederick, and I thank you for that."

Jim Sawicki was standing at the kitchen sink in his apartment, gazing out of the open window, listening to NPR and methodically drying his breakfast dishes. The kitchen was located at the rear of the building, and the window overlooked the back side of the hill. At that moment he was probably happier and more content than he'd been in years, too many to remember. He had a place of his own in the elegant and historic city of Boston, which he loved and where he grew up. He could come and go as he wished, eat and drink what he wished, and entertain who he wished without anyone taking note. More important than all of this was that with the move, Jim had given himself time and space to think. He was on professional leave from St. Bart's in Dorchester and had enough money from his part-time teaching to be frugally comfortable and still enjoy a good bottle of wine when the occasion called for it.

Today, Jim was taking his first step on a new journey. He hadn't even told Olympia but would when next they met. She, of all people, would rejoice and be glad in it.

Laura put down the phone and chased after little Erica, who was scooting backward toward the kitchen. She scooped her up, stood with the baby on her hip and looked down at her little daughter, who squealed and made a grab for her mother's nose. This precious little appendage, this mini-self who possessed a will and a determination which matched and perhaps even exceeded her own, had changed everything. Was she really ready to strap this child into a car seat and drive to California, there to put her in day care while she said yes to a career opportunity which, if refused, might not come along again for years, if ever? Laura shook her head. She had already talked this over with one mother; now she needed to consult the other.

Eighteen

Olympia pulled up against the curb and switched off the engine. From where she sat she could see the broad, flowered bottom of Letitia Blume. The woman was obviously doing something at ground level. Olympia wished she could teleport herself into the church without being seen and having to make pleasant, flowery conversation, but the unmistakable sound of a VW engine brought Letitia to attention. She stood with clippers in hand and a smudge of dirt on her face to greet the new minister. Olympia smiled, passed a few pleasantries which included the beauty and size of her blooms, and made it inside the church building in only five minutes.

At the sound of the door opening, Franna called out from her office. "That you, Olympia? I sure hope it is, because I'm starving."

Olympia stood in the doorway. "It is me, and I'm hungry, too. Where shall we go? You must have a favorite, and this is my treat."

Franna made short work of the papers on her desk and grabbed her purse.

"There's a little Thai place that just opened up. I haven't tried it yet. You want to go there and try it out?"

Olympia grinned broadly. "Does that mean we can Thai one on for lunch?"

Franna winced. "If you think I'm going to honor that with a response, Reverend, think again. You ought to be ashamed of yourself."

"Bad habit," confessed Olympia, "but I have to admit it's one of my favorite bad habits. I can bring grown men to tears with some of my puns."

"Do you mean *gro-o-aan* men?" quipped Franna.

"Truce!" Begged Olympia.

"I will if you will," said Franna.

"Any messages?"

Franna made a face. "Only one. Pastor Markham from across the street called and asked for you."

"Did he leave a message?"

"No, he said he'd call back later." Franna glanced toward the open office door and lowered her voice. "I don't like that man. He used to drop in all the time when Reverend Julia was here. He was always polite enough, but he gave me the creeps."

"How so?"

"He made this little joke about being neighborly. You know, when he came in he'd always say 'It's just me, the guy from across the street come over for a cup of sugar.'"

Olympia put her hand on Franna's arm. "Come on, let's get in the car. You can tell me more when we get there. Letitia is out in the front garden, and she could appear at any moment."

Franna clapped her hand over her mouth, rolled her eyes and followed Olympia out to the van.

Once they were seated in an overly decorated restaurant called Thai Cuisine, Olympia remarked on the incongruity of using the French word cuisine to describe Thai food. Franna didn't have time to respond because the soft-spoken, tan-skinned waiter appeared with oversized menus and a pitcher of ice water garnished with lemons carved into pungent yellow roses.

More roses, thought Olympia, wordlessly accepting her menu. Is there no escape? But she had accepted a declaration of truce, so she set about perusing the menu. After they both had ordered and were sipping tiny cups of spiced tea, Olympia asked Franna what she'd meant earlier when she said Jerrold Markham gave her the creeps.

Franna folder her arms across her middle and seemed to hesitate.

"Maybe I spoke out of turn, but I think you should know. This is a confidential conversation, is it not?"

Olympia assured her that it was, and Franna relaxed and let her hands fall into her lap.

"The best way I can describe him is slimy. You know the type, stands a little too close, always with the flowery compliments that sound like they are fresh out of the can. There's no doubt he had a thing for Reverend Julia. I tried to say something early on, but let's just say my comments were not welcome."

"What do you mean?"

They paused while the waiter returned to take their orders, vegetarian pad Thai for Olympia and a green curry for her guest.

Franna continued. "After I spoke to Julia he stopped coming over, and she started closing the office door when she made phone calls. I wasn't born yesterday, you know."

Olympia knew.

Franna paused looked away. "I've never told anyone this, Olympia, but I walked in on them once. Well, I didn't actually walk in on them, but I didn't need to look to know what was going on, if you know what I mean. It was late. I'd left something on my desk and come back for it. They were in her office. They didn't hear me come in, and they didn't hear me leave either. Julia never knew. The thing is, right around the same time I found out that he was hitting on poor Yolanda, as well. I hear and see a lot in that office of mine, and I keep my mouth shut, at least I did until now. After watching him starting to come on to you, I knew I had to say something."

Franna stopped talking long enough to allow the waiter to serve their meals. When he left, they continued between bites of the absolutely gorgeous food in front of them. Olympia was in heaven and trying not to eat too fast. A loud belch might be good manners in many Asian cultures, but here it would be a distinct distraction. Olympia wanted food *and* information.

She put down her fork and leaned forward. "Thank you for telling me this." She hesitated, "Franna, let me ask you something. Would you ever testify as to what you saw and heard?"

"Are you kidding me? I wouldn't do that to Reverend Julia or to Yolanda either. To tell you the honest truth, I wouldn't do it to myself. I think that man is sick, and I think he's dangerous. Who knows what he'd do to me if he found out I knew? Nope, Reverend, I told you this in confidence for your sake as well as mine."

She punctuated her final sentence by refolding her arms and scowling in Olympia's direction.

Olympia spoke carefully. "I promise never to ask you to say or do anything that would put you in any kind of danger, and I will, of course, keep your confidence."

Franna relaxed again and picked up her fork.

"Now I have to ask for your confidence."

Franna nodded, chewing.

I can only say that I have been in contact with Rev. Julia and Yolanda."

"You know where Yoli is, so she's all right then? What about the kids? What about Reverend Julia?" Franna's voice had risen enough that other diners glanced in their direction.

Olympia lifted a finger to her lips. She was taking a huge risk, and she was trying to do it without breaking another confidence. She responded by nodding only once.

"The police are involved. Her husband knows they are all okay. The only thing I can say right now is I've asked them the same question I just asked you about testifying if it comes to that."

"What did they say?"

"I can't tell you anything other than there is interest in seeing that justice is done."

Olympia looked up to see Franna's eyes brimming with tears.

"I'm in," she said and took a deep breath before going on. "I had an uncle who abused me when I was thirteen. He was my mother's brother. I never ever thought I'd have a chance to put that whole awful thing behind me, but doing this might help."

"Did you ever tell anyone?"

Franna shook her head and whispered. "I was terrified of him, and besides, who'd believe me? He was a priest. I just made sure after the first and only time that I was never alone with him, but it was like he was always waiting around the corner, watching me or touching me if I walked too close to him."

"Where is he now?

"Dead," said Franna.

Olympia knew there was nothing to say anything other than, "I'm so very sorry. I suppose I brought it all back up for you."

Franna shook her head. "No, Olympia, you didn't. Jerrold Markham did when he called today. I could just hear it all in his voice. That's what brought it back. Tell me what you want me to do."

"I don't have a plan yet, but I'm working on it, and you can trust that I'll have a long conversation with you before I do anything. This is not something I can do on a whim or on the spur of the moment. The stakes are too high."

"So is the risk, Reverend. That man is evil."

Nineteen

July 29, 1862

After many futile and unpromising efforts, I believe I have finally commenced to work on my novel! Aunt Louisa has gone off to Cambridge for a few weeks, and I think I may join her in September when the heat will not be so intense. I miss her company and the extra pair of hands. Most of all I miss our conversations. She really has become the mother I lost so long ago.

Mr. Fuller has invited me to go out walking with him in the evening, but without Aunt Louisa in attendance I cannot accept, nor can I ask him in, which is a pity. He is a most companionable gentleman.

This writing is an intense and solitary endeavor and I find I am sometimes very lonely at the end of the day. No matter. We make choices — and I have made mine.

More anon, LFW

After dinner Olympia was in the sitting room, trying to read a few pages of Miss Winslow's diary, when the phone on the table beside her chair pulled her out of the world of Leanna Faith and back into the present. It was Jim.

He began by saying he'd been over to see his friend Jerry O'Brien at the Dorchester PD and had uncovered some very disturbing information about Jerrold Markham. He added he was pretty sure there was more, but he'd run out of time and would go back tomorrow and see what else he could turn up. Then if it was still convenient for them, he'd come down tomorrow evening. Olympia assured him that would be great, and what kind of wine was he going to bring so she could create something wonderful to go with it.

"Haven't you got it backward?" asked Jim. "Don't people usually fit the wine to the meal?"

"Not when you're bringing the wine, Jim. What were you thinking of?"

"I saw a light French red described in one of my wine magazines, and I've been anxious to try it. Why don't I get a couple of bottles of that?"

Olympia smiled at his enthusiasm and was already thinking of what she might conjure up in the kitchen to complement it. "If you get a little wiffled, you can always spend the night. Your bed is still here."

"I'll bring my toothbrush just in case," laughed Jim. On a more serious note he added. "I have to tell you, Olympia, if I've got the right guy here, and I'm almost certain I do, he's got some bad history. The thing is, he seems to be able to slide out from under the law, disappear for a while and then start up somewhere else."

"So you think he did this kind of thing before he got to Millbridge?"

"No doubt about it, Olympia. Just from what I've picked up so far—and as I said, I've just really only gotten into it—the man is a highly intelligent and totally manipulative sexual predator who knows exactly how to get what he wants."

Olympia shuddered at the images that were forming in her mind. "And he operates out of a church."

"Churches, Olympia, plural. I suspect that once people get suspicious, he cuts a deal to leave quietly rather than create a scandal which will reflect badly on the church and the community."

Olympia could feel her stomach knotting at what she was hearing. "That's vile."

"It's criminal, Olympia, and if we can get the goods on him this time, we might be able to put an end to his operation once and for all."

"Actually, I think we might just be able to do it."

"How so?" asked Jim.

"I think I may have at least two victims who will testify."

"You're kidding. Really?"

"I talked to the former minister at the church I'm serving and to a former member of the congregation, both of whom he has abused. Both say they are willing to come forward."

"Don't count on that, Olympia." There was a warning tone in his voice.

"What do you mean?"

"Victims of sexual abuse are very fragile. Sometimes just the sight of the person who abused them is enough to send them flying in the opposite direction. They could back out at the last minute and leave you in a very dangerous position."

"I don't understand."

"Oh, for heaven's sake, Olympia, don't be so naïve. You set something up, the accusers don't show, and there you are with Mr. Predator. You have no back-up and no proof of anything, but he knows you know, and he knows where you live."

"I see what you're saying, Jim, but what can he do? He might be mad as hell that I've uncovered his dirty little secret, but other than that, what could he possibly do?"

"Olympia, I haven't finished my investigation into his past, but it would appear that he's been pretty clever at creating new personae for himself. But the most disturbing information I uncovered concerns at least one woman who simply vanished and never was found. There also seems to be a woman in another church he pastored who is suspected to have committed suicide, but that was never proved one way or the other. In other words, there are lots of unsettling questions, no answers and no hard evidence."

"But ..."

"You can't do this by yourself, Olympia, and you shouldn't try. I think it's time to call in the experts. I'll know more when I come down, but for God's sake, don't say or do anything that will raise the slightest suspicion. Better yet, just stay away from him until we've talked and you've been to the police."

Olympia took a deep breath and promised she would do as he asked. He rarely spoke this emphatically, and when he did, she listened.

"Looks like we'll have more than your wine to talk about when you get here," she said, trying to lighten the mood.

"This isn't a joking matter, Olympia. I agree the man has to be stopped, but it has to be done without putting you or anyone else in the line of fire."

"I hear you, Jim. Let's talk tomorrow night. Three heads will be better than two."

"Does this mean we're going to form an unholy trinity?"

"Good night, Jim!"

As Olympia was hanging up the phone Frederick came in from the kitchen, carrying two cups of tea.

"What in the world was that all about? I only heard bits and pieces of your conversation, but what I did hear sounded pretty ominous."

"That was Jim. He's come up with some potentially damaging information about Jerrold Markham, and he's not done yet. He's going to do some more digging tomorrow and fill us in when he gets here. He thinks we should contact the police before we do anything, and I'm inclined to agree with him."

"Well, that's a first for you, Olympia. Whatever did he say that finally has introduced a note of caution into your otherwise reckless and intrepid approach to life?"

"Sit down, and I'll tell you."

But before she could begin she was interrupted by the simultaneous ring of the telephone and a double chime from the antique clock on the mantel.

Olympia's annoyance at being interrupted quickly turned to delight when she heard the voice of her daughter Laura. Then the joy turned to concern when she heard the tension in Laura's voice asking if it was okay for her and little Erica to come down for a while on that coming Sunday. Laura went on to explain that she was having second thoughts about taking the job in

California and being on her own with the baby so far away from everybody. All of a sudden she felt overwhelmed and panicky, and she just needed to talk to someone who wasn't as personally involved in the situation as her adoptive mother.

Oh, if you only knew, thought Olympia, feeling her eyes prickle at the unintended slight.

"Of course you can come down, we'd love it. If you want privacy, we can undoubtedly prevail upon Frederick to take Erica for a stroll around the neighborhood. I'll be back from church by one, so any time after that. Do you still remember how to get here?"

Laura assured Olympia that she did, and she'd arrive around two. That way Erica could nap in the car and be fit company when she woke up.

After they said their goodbyes and Laura sent her greetings to Frederick, Olympia hung up the phone and turned to the man sitting across from her.

"Good news or bad, Olympia? You look troubled."

"I guess a little of both. Talk about being on the horns of a dilemma. The daughter I've only just gotten to know wants to take a job in California but is having second thoughts and says she wants to talk to me. I'd give anything in the world to keep her nearby, but if this is her big opportunity, how can I discourage it?"

"Why not wait and see what happens on Sunday? She didn't say what those second thoughts were, did she? It might be possible all she wants is a sounding board rather than advice. Either way, you can't know what she's going to say until she's actually here. May I suggest you have more than enough to occupy that fertile little mind of yours with what's going on at the church without taking on something you can't do anything about, at least right now?"

Olympia made a rueful face and nodded in his direction. "I know you're right, Frederick, but it's so hard not to jump in my car and go flying up to her apartment in Somerville right this minute."

"We both know you aren't going to do that. Now, I believe you were going to tell me what Jim has learned so far about The Wrong Reverend Mr. Markham."

Olympia smiled in spite of herself and the gravity of the situation.

"You do have a way with words, Mr. Watkins."

When she finished, Frederick sat rubbing his chin and processing what he'd just heard. Finally, he spoke. "I agree with Jim, It's time to go to the police."

Olympia looked troubled. "I know you're both right, especially in view of the possibility of his being connected to the disappearance of one woman and possibly an unsolved murder involving another. I just don't want them to go storming in there with their guns and bayonets before we have indisputable evidence. Right now there is nothing on record here that would arouse any kind of police interest."

"True," said Frederick, "but you went to talk with them after Yolanda Nikitas gave you permission. So you have established a credible connection with them, so much so that you were able to get them to hold off doing anything further."

"That's because I didn't tell them or anyone else why she took off. All I did was report that she's safe and ask them to call off the search and not say anything to the press. One of the points Jim made was that sexual abuse victims can panic at the last minute and refuse to testify. I might not be able to depend on the two victims I know about. We need to catch him in the act and confront him with firsthand evidence before he has time to weasel his way out."

"I don't like the turn of this conversation, Olympia."

Olympia shook her head. "I already promised you I wouldn't do anything without you or Jim nearby. I may be headstrong, but I'm not stupid. I'm certain the man is coming on to me. Even Franna, the church administrator, noticed it and actually warned me about him."

"What did she say?"

"We had a long and very informative lunch today. She knows everything that's happened, and she's prepared to testify, as well. She actually walked in on Jerrod Markham and Julia one evening when they thought they were alone, but they were so preoccupied they never saw or heard her."

"Having an affair is hardly a punishable offense these days," said Frederick.

"No, nor is having affairs with two women at once, but it is further evidence of the man's disgusting behavior, and it will be useful when we can finally catch and stop him."

"Olympia I think I'm going to ..."

She held up her hand. "Hold on, Frederick. Let's put any further discussion of this on hold until Jim can give us a more complete picture. Then we can go to the police. Believe it or not, I do know when I am out of my league, and this one is not even in the park."

"Well, that's a first, coming from you."

"As I said earlier I'm determined, but I'm not stupid. Last winter I came damn close to getting myself killed, and I wasn't even actively in pursuit of the man who attacked me."

"But you were in his way."

"I suppose I was, given his pathological construct."

"The way I see it is if you are standing in the line of fire, it doesn't matter if you get shot with a bullet or an arrow. You are still going to get shot."

"Not a comforting image," said Olympia.

"It wasn't intended to be. Somebody has to watch over you. It just so happens I support and agree with this particular intention of yours, and so does Jim, and we are the voices of caution and prudence you need to hear."

Olympia nodded and then yawned. "It's late, my love, and I'm tired. Let's take ourselves to bed. My mother always said, 'Everything will look better in the morning.'"

"And on very rare occasions, your mother has been known to be right," said Frederick.

Twenty

Olympia spent most of the following day making pastoral visits to shut-ins in the congregation. She loaded up a basket with flowers and small packets of cookies and set off shortly after breakfast. This was the hands-on part of parish ministry that she loved, sitting and visiting and listening to stories these people had likely told countless times before but were new to her. She'd learned long ago how to get a conversation going by asking questions about where the person grew up or the history of the house they were in or the family pet. Asking and, more importantly, listening to all that was said and sometimes to what wasn't said. Listening to the spaces between the words, they called it.

Early in her own ministry she remembered hearing an older colleague say that ninety percent of ministry is being fully present to another human being, and the other ten percent is putting away the chairs after a pot-luck. She was on the way to her third visit when her cell phone began bleating from somewhere in the depths of her handbag. By the time she'd pulled over and dug it out, it had stopped ringing, so she hit the recall button and waited for Yolanda Nikitas to pick up the phone.

"Is that you, Olympia?"

"Hi, Yolanda, it's me. I'm in a supermarket parking lot in Millbridge. I'm out making some pastoral visits this morning. How are you feeling?"

"I'm ready to do something, Reverend, and I need to talk to you before I change my mind and chicken out. How soon can you come over to Martha's Vineyard?"

This is unreal, she thought. Jim is coming tonight, my daughter is coming this weekend, and now this. Olympia did a quick mental scan of her calendar.

"I can come down tomorrow but just for the day. I'd love to take you up on your offer to spend the night, but it's simply not possible right now. It's been almost a year since I've been there, and I'd love to just have some time to walk around and remind myself how lovely it all is there, but that's going to have to wait."

"Oh, that's okay. I just want to …"

Olympia spoke softly, "To what, Yolanda?"

"I want to go home, Olympia. I don't want to hide anymore." She paused and added in a whisper, "But I'm afraid."

"I'll come down as soon as I can. I think I even still have a ferry schedule somewhere in my bag. Shows you how often I clean it out." Olympia heard a snuffly chuckle. "I seem to remember they run every hour and fifteen minutes, so I'll let you know. Do you think you could pick me up?"

"No problem. I can get my cousin Sia to watch the kids for me. If the weather's nice, maybe we could go over to State Beach."

"If not, we can park ourselves in the back corner of any of several restaurants I remember."

"We'll find something," said Yolanda.

"Do you want me to let your husband know you've called?

Olympia heard a quick gasp. "Not yet, Reverend. Let me talk with you first, and maybe we could both think about what I should say to him."

Olympia hesitated for a fraction of a second before deciding it was best to get it all out then and there. "I need to tell you something else, Yolanda. I'm afraid we are going to have to get the police involved."

"I was hoping we could avoid that."

"As was I, but I've been doing a little investigating, and it would appear that this is not the first time Jerrold Markham has done this kind of thing. We need to put an end to his predation once and for all, and unfortunately, you hold some of the key evidence. You may have to go public with it. So far, he's managed to get away with it because his victims are too afraid or humiliated to speak out. That's what he's counting on now. Do you still want me to come down?

I'm sure of it, Reverend. Just call me when you get on the boat. I'll plan on picking you up."

"Um, you don't know what I look like."

"Yes, I do. I found your picture in an old copy of the *MV Times*. Seems like you had a rather adventurous ministry while you were here. Front page headline and all, Summer Pastor Foils Real Estate Scam."

"Oh, that," said Olympia.

"That's what made me call you. I figured you're not afraid to stick your neck out and speak up. Right now, I am. Thank you, Olympia."

"I'll do the best I can, Yolanda. This is going to be considerably more complicated than a real estate scam, but I think I have the beginnings of a plan. I'll be able to tell you more tomorrow."

"Thank you, Reverend."

"Don't thank me until that man is behind bars, because that's exactly where he belongs."

In his apartment in downtown Boston Father Jim was ensconced in the living room with his laptop on his knees and a glass of Pinot Noir within easy reach. On a hunch he began perusing the Personals pages on Craig's List. It didn't take him long to find a man calling himself Gerry Marks from Southeastern Massachusetts who was looking for a little afternoon delight with a discreet young woman who was a princess in the living room and a tiger in the bedroom. No questions asked. Jim looked at the picture in the advert but realized he had no idea what Jerrold Markham looked like. The man in the slightly blurry photograph was looking off to the side. It could have been anyone. Upon closer examination Jim determined the man had a fairly rugged profile, but that could be real or a Photoshopped embellishment. On an ironic whim, he created an alias identity on Yahoo and typed, "Tell me more." In the reply box he signed it Monica and hit Send. The reply was almost instantaneous.

"Hi, Monica, what would you like me to tell you?"

Jim chuckled at the irony of it all. He was a celibate gay priest, assuming a false feminine identity to hook up with a straight man who, if it turned out to be who he was looking for, was going to be in for a very unpleasant surprise. He typed in the response, "Let me think about it, and I'll get back to you."

"Don't be too long☺!" flashed the reply, followed in a nanosecond by, "You sound really nice — send picture."

Now what do I do? thought Jim. What In God's name am I getting myself into? It wasn't the first time he'd allowed himself to be pulled into some of Olympia's misadventures, but this one certainly had to be the most bizarre yet. He frowned and typed, "Will do — just looking for a good one, XOXOXO."

Jerrold Markham closed his laptop and slipped it into the middle drawer of his desk. He looked up to see one of his parishioners standing in the doorway, watching him. He hadn't heard her approach.

"My goodness, Pastor Markham, I'm impressed. I didn't think we paid you enough to have two computers."

Without missing a beat he pointed to the monitor on the desk and said, "More of a necessity than a luxury, Mrs. Johnson. I find it easier to keep all of my church business on one and my personal correspondence on the other. That way I know which is which and where to find it."

"Well, I suppose that makes sense. I'm afraid I'm just learning to use a computer. My grandson is teaching me, but I can't say I'm enjoying it."

Pastor Markham chuckled. "Lucky you. I'm not blessed with children or grandchildren, so I'm afraid I've had to work all this out on my own. It's a necessity these days, so I don't really have a choice, but you must have something on your mind." He stood and directed her to a chair near the window. "Here, make yourself comfortable."

Frederick was standing in the middle of the kitchen, contemplating his next move — or moves. He had three full hours before he had to leave for his job at the book store and wondered how far he could get on the outside back door project. He and Olympia had both agreed the existing door needed replacing. A previous owner had put up an aluminum storm and screen monstrosity that was an anachronistic eyesore and completely clashed with the sturdy elegance of the rest of the antique home. He briefly thought it might be better to have the replacement door at hand before he actually started the demolition, but he wasn't sure what Olympia wanted to replace it with. So, in Frederick's unique way of thinking, that issue could be dealt with later.

What was of prime importance now was getting the door off its hinges and away to the dump in the time he had remaining, which would result in getting the job half done. He was pleased with himself, and he knew Olympia would be pleased with him for getting started on it without her reminding him. It was only when he had the door twisted off and tied into the back of his truck that he realized he didn't have anything to cover the hole and secure the house against weather or the local fauna.

But once again Frederick's quick and convoluted thinking saved the day. He dragged a nine-by-twelve-foot blue plastic tarpaulin from the barn and nailed it over the opening, holding it with a few decking planks he'd found at the dump. He made sure it was secured in such a way that the cats couldn't get out and curious skunks and raccoons couldn't get in. Tonight they'd have dinner with Jim and discuss what kind of a door they should have.

As he started to pull out of the driveway, he stopped to look back at his work and wondered if he might be able to design a suitable door using some of those planks and some antique looking hinges. On the other hand, maybe he could find some real antique hinges at the salvage shop. As he drove off he thought of one more little detail he hadn't considered earlier. He sincerely hoped Olympia had a front door key with her, because if she didn't, she might think less of his initiative than he might have wished. He promised himself he'd call her the minute he got to the bookstore.

Yolanda Nikitas pulled out her phone and tapped in her husband's number. She knew he'd be alone in the office and wouldn't be seeing patients until after lunch, so if he was willing to talk, they wouldn't be interrupted .

Olympia looked at her watch. She needed food, and she needed coffee. These could be picked up at a deli and consumed in her office. Franna would be there, so maybe she'd pick up some pastry for the two of them, as well. When in doubt, eat, but Olympia wasn't in doubt. She was as determined as she'd ever been. She knew what she was up against, and she also knew she had to see this through no matter what the consequences. Men like Jerrold Markham, who abused the unique power and trust invested in them as clergy, who deceived and seduced people who came to them in need of pastoral care and counsel, were the very worst kind of human scum she could imagine.

Across the street from All Souls, Jerrold Markham kept glancing out of the window to see if Olympia's car was outside the church. When she finally pulled up, his first thought was to go over and say hello, but he decided against it. He noted that the administrator's car was there, as well, and the way that woman had been treating him of late made him uncomfortable. There was no way she could have known about him and Julia. At least he didn't think so, but still, he couldn't be too careful, especially now.

Twenty-One

In the soft light of the warm summer evening, Olympia turned into her driveway and coasted to a stop in her usual spot by the kitchen door, or rather to where the kitchen door once had been. She looked at the evidence of Frederick's latest project, noted the absence of his yellow pickup, and wondered if she would have enough time to do justice to the meal she had planned before he and Jim arrived. Then she wondered how in hell she was going to get into the house. They never used the front door. She wondered if she still had a key, and if she did, it was not going to be found in her handbag.

Damn!

Olympia considered her options: look for an open window she could crawl through, break a window she could crawl through, go find Frederick and strangle him or wait until he came home before she did it. Considering that Frederick's sense of time was as creative as his carpentry, that could be any time at all. She was not happy as she dug around for her cell phone.

"Frederick here."

Olympia dispensed with any courteous preliminaries. "How the hell am I going to get into the house?"

"Oh, that."

"Yes, that. Where are you, and when are you coming home?"

"I, uh, meant to call you and tell you but ..."

"You forgot."

"I got busy at the store"

"You forgot."

"I'm almost to the end of the street. I'll be there in two shakes, and we can figure something out. Maybe I can take the front door off its hinges, and we can get in that way."

"Try that, and I'll be unhinged, as well. Just get home, will you?"

His response was muted by the rattling sound of his arrival in the spot beside her.

By the time he got out of his truck, Olympia was storming back and forth in front of the blue plastic tarp.

"Where's the old door? Could you put it back just for the night?"

"I'm afraid I took it to the dump. It wouldn't have gone back anyway. I sort of twisted it when I removed it. You're not angry, are you? I thought you'd be pleased."

Frederick's troubled face resembled that of a wounded basset hound. Olympia melted and threw her arms around him.

"I will be pleased, my darling, but right now we need to get into the house. We are going to have a dinner guest in less than half an hour."

"I can't possibly get a new door by then."

Olympia bit back her first response and took a long calming breath. Then she spoke very slowly.

"Frederick. Go get a crowbar, and take down enough planks so we can get inside. You can put them back for the night after Jim gets here."

"But how are we going to get back out in the morning?"

"We could use the front door."

"Oh," said Frederick.

Once inside, they banished the cats to the bathroom and left the opening at the back of the house unsecured until Jim arrived. Once he did, Olympia thought it best to busy herself in the kitchen and allow Frederick to explain the details of the once and future back entrance to their guest. She'd decided on beef burgundy for the two men and an expanded salad for her vegetarian self. The beef dish was relatively quick, and she would serve it with herbed rice, a helping of her salad and some crusty bread she'd picked up on the way home.

Olympia enjoyed cooking for an appreciative audience. It occupied the mind, and for the moment the rest of the issues confronting her were far outside her thinking and well beyond what now passed for a back door. She was home and happy, padding around barefoot in her kitchen, making something wonderful for the two men she loved most in the world. The smells of the garlic mixed with the beef and wine were intoxicating. The cats, howling in protest from behind the bathroom door, added a certain fillip that perhaps she alone could appreciate. They hated being left out when food was in evidence, but from the thumps of the hammer and the rustle of the tarp, it sounded like the door-hole was being secured, and the fur-faces could soon be released.

Dinner tasted every bit as delicious in the eating of it as it had smelled in the cooking. They were all making noises of contentment as Jim topped up their glasses with the last of the wine.

"Shall I open another?" asked Jim brandishing a second bottle.

Olympia shook her head. "Not if we are going to have a serious conversation, which is, at least in part, the purpose of your visit. Keep it for now, and maybe we'll open it later."

"Would anyone like tea or coffee?" asked Frederick, pushing back his chair and starting to collect the plates.

"Not right now. Why don't we take what's left of our wine into the sitting room. It's a bit cooler in there. We can deal with the dishes later; they don't mind waiting. There's a lot we need to talk about, and I don't have much of a window left."

"What window are you talking about?" Jim looked quizzical.

"I'm a morning person. A full belly and a couple of glasses of wine at this hour, and I'm ready to curl up and purr myself to sleep."

"Maybe I should make you some coffee."

"Thanks, love, but that would make me too wide awake. I've hit a happy balance just now; let's just keep it that way. Who wants to start?"

"I will," said Jim, who was settling himself into his preferred spot in the corner of the sofa. Frederick sank into his chair and was immediately joined by the kitten Cadeau, now almost a cat, a gift he'd given to Olympia for Christmas.

"So what have you come up with?" asked Olympia.

"Quite a bit, unfortunately, and none of it is very comforting. It seems that Jerrold Markham has a history of this kind of behavior. I couldn't get anything from past church records or personal files, because he's not part of any official denomination. He'd likely be running another storefront operation if he hadn't managed to get his hands on that lovely old building. I found some references to him on the internet, and with Jerry's help I followed up on them."

"That quickly? What did you find?"

"Jerry told me that people who change their names or use aliases often choose something fairly close to their given name so they don't slip up and give themselves away. So between us, we looked up Gerard Marks, Mark Gerard, Jerry Markland and a few other similar sounding combinations and then tried using the title pastor or reverend as the first word in the search box. It worked. I managed to get the names and locations of two actual churches he, or someone very like him, had pastored that are still in operation. I tried calling the contact numbers, and I was actually able to get to talk to people who remembered him."

"You're kidding," said an amazed Olympia.

"Fortunately or unfortunately, I'm not," said a grim-faced Jim.

"And what, dear fellow, or should I henceforth call your Father Sherlock, did you discover?"

"Pretty much what you've described over in Millbridge. He's a one-man band when it comes to church organization. That way he can keep outside of the mainstream so no one is checking up on him. He finds a likely spot, opens the doors, then starts preaching a message of hellfire, damnation and salvation through love and hefty contributions. He's handsome and persuasive, and the women begin showing up in droves. He often gets a soup kitchen going or organizes community suppers, if the area is more affluent. That way he's seen as a positive influence in the community. Then he usually starts a women's Bible study group and goes to work on the most needy and vulnerable." Jim grimaced with distaste.

"It's not unlike pedophile priests quietly grooming altar boys or kids from the youth group," he continued. "He's in a position of power and has the admiration and trust of the people in the congregation. It makes me sick even to think about it. It's completely reprehensible."

"How does he get away with it?" asked Frederick.

"Usually these people tell the victim it's their special secret, and it's just too precious to talk about. If anyone does start asking questions or threatening to speak out, he goes into intimidation mode and threatens them with whatever he thinks will scare them into silence. But this is the really scary part. It seems that in one church he was associated with, a woman died of suicide, and in another a woman just disappeared."

"Like Yolanda Nikitas," said Olympia. "She took off with the kids because she was trying to protect herself and her husband. Thank God she called me. Now she's ready to come forward, but she still doesn't want me to say anything to her husband."

"That's inconvenient," said Frederick.

Olympia nodded. "Exactly right. That's why I'm going over to Martha's Vineyard tomorrow. She wants to sit down and talk with me in person."

"You didn't tell me you were going over there," said Frederick.

"I would have. I guess I got distracted by the back door situation."

Jim snickered and tried to disguise it by clearing his throat.

"I can't imagine why," said Frederick, looking genuinely perplexed.

"We're veering off point," snapped Olympia.

"You're right," said Jim. "Where was I?"

"You were describing Markham's *modus operandi*," said Olympia, "people disappearing." She shuddered. It was too awful even to consider, but she had to. "Was foul play ever suspected?"

"Of course, but there was no evidence. I found what I did by going to the archives of the local newspapers published at the time of the disappearance."

"You really accomplished quite a bit in a very short time," said Frederick.

"Don't forget, I had Jerry O'Brien helping me. He knows the ins and outs of this kind of thing."

"So what did he suggest?"

"He said if we could gather some hard evidence, meaning if we could get the victims to come forward and make an accusation that would stick, we would probably be able to go back and look into some of the other questionable situations. He also said it's highly unlikely we'd find any victims willing to cooperate."

"Well, that's where he's wrong. I've got two women who say they will testify, and I'll be the third if I can get him to incriminate himself by approaching me directly."

"That's where I get nervous, Olympia. I have every reason to believe this man is very dangerous."

"I totally agree with you, but he's clearly coming on to me, and he has no idea I'm aware of what's happening. That's how narcissistic and sure of himself he is. Don't you see that I'm the only person who can set this kind of thing up?"

Jim nodded in grim agreement and added, "The other thing my Dorchester detective friend said was that we do need to go to the police. No matter what your curious track record is in terms of stopping crimes in progress, Olympia, you are way out of your league on this one."

"I will go and talk to the police, I promise, but not before I talk with Yolanda and her husband and with Julia Grafton. I have to have everyone's permission to give the police the facts. Don't you agree?"

Frederick and Jim both agreed.

"Okay. I think we have a plan. I talk to the two women and Dr. Nikitas, and then I go to the police and ask them how they want to proceed. Meanwhile, I let the Nasty Pastor from across the street think he's making progress. I promise I will not allow myself to be alone with him, and I'll keep the door of the church locked when I'm there by myself."

Jim and Frederick turned toward one another in disbelief.

"Am I to understand that for the first time in your fifty-something years you are exercising a modicum of caution?" asked Jim.

"This guy made me uncomfortable before tonight. Now, hearing what Jim has uncovered, he terrifies me. Believe me, gentlemen, I'm taking no chances." She paused. "But I will do my damnedest to see that he's taken out of action."

"There's more," said Jim.

"I'm afraid to ask," said Olympia.

By the time Jim finished telling the two of them about his Craig's List exploration and "Monica," all three of them were laughing, but it was a cautious, hollow laughter.

"I agree it's pretty out of character for me, and it is rather laughable, but it adds one more very ugly dimension to all of this. If Gerry Marks is Jerrold Markham, it means he also has a penchant for stalking and grooming younger women on line — and who knows what else."

"What a thorough-going bastard," snarled Frederick.

"That about says it," said Jim.

"Jim, didn't you say you wanted to talk to us about something else? Not that this isn't pretty momentous, but I know you are examining the nature of your vocation. That's why you are on professional leave, isn't it?"

"Yes, and before I start, I think this calls for some more wine. Any takers?"

Frederick and Olympia both raised their empty glasses in his direction.

"Just a half-glass for me." Olympia held up two fingers. "I don't want to be dancing over the high seas tomorrow with a hangover."

From the kitchen she could hear the familiar *thuck* of a wine bottle being uncorked, then Jim scolding himself as he returned to the sitting room.

"I probably should have let it breathe for a little while. It might not be at its best."

"Your infinite degrees of perfection will be lost on me, Jim. Just pour the stuff, will you? I promise to swirl and sniff before every sip."

Jim groaned, called her a philistine and filled her glass to the halfway point. Then, after he'd poured considerably more for himself and Frederick, he resettled himself in his corner of the sofa and told them he was leaving the Catholic Church.

"Do you mean you are going to stop being a priest?"

"I have no intention of leaving the priesthood, Olympia, but I am reviewing my options."

"I don't understand." Olympia shifted in her chair and discreetly swallowed a yawn. "I didn't think there were any options. I always thought once a Catholic, always a Catholic."

"But Roman isn't the only kind of Catholic, Olympia. You of all people should know that."

"So what are your options?"

I've looked into both The Eastern Orthodox Rite as well as The Anglican Communion. I feel more inclined toward the Anglican Church, which as you know here in the States is called the Episcopal Church."

"Good heavens, C of E, whoever would have guessed? I'll make an Englishman out of you yet, Father Jim." Frederick raised his wineglass in Jim's direction.

Olympia sat up a little straighter in her chair. This was momentous, and she refused to let herself look sleepy in the face of it.

"Now that you mention it, I have heard of Roman Catholic priests who have become Episcopal priests. What will you have to do?"

"There is a proscribed process. I have to be a regular communicant at a local Episcopal Church, and then I can begin the process. I've started attending the Church of the Advent. It's on Brimmer Street, just a couple of streets away from where I live. Lovely people there. It feels right."

Olympia set down her glass beside Miss Winslow's diary and smiled warmly at her best friend. "I know you've been unhappy for a long time, but it wasn't something I could really help you with."

"Not so unhappy as misplaced. I'm gay, and I'm a Roman Catholic priest, and I'm not a pedophile. In some people's thinking the two are synonymous. I'm tired of living in the shadows, hoping no one outs me."

Frederick looked over at Jim and smiled at his friend. "I've said it before, Jim, it's no way to live."

"That's what I've finally come to understand in my soul. My brain has known it for some time now, but it was a journey and a decision that only I could make for myself."

"So what are you going to do next?" asked Olympia.

Jim held up his long, well-kept hands and shook his head. "Right now I don't know. That's what this year on Beacon Hill is giving me, a place and time to think and a church that will accept me for who and what I am. I can't ask for more."

They were interrupted from further conversation by the ring of the telephone on the table beside Olympia. The cats both twitched their ears and looked first at Olympia, then at Frederick.

"This is Olympia Brown speaking." Then she broke into a broad, fond smile. It was her daughter Laura.

"Hi, other Mother, just checking if it's still okay for Erica and me to come down there for a visit this Sunday?"

Olympia's weariness dissolved in an instant. "Absolutely, I can't wait."

"What time do you get back from church?"

"I'm usually home by one. Would you like to go out to a restaurant?"

"I don't think so. Your granddaughter is becoming quite a handful now that she's crawling. She doesn't want to be strapped into a high chair when there's a whole big world out there for her to explore."

"In that case we'll stay right here, and I'll get a take-out or throw something simple together myself. Do I need to get baby food?"

"Oh, no. She's starting to feed herself now. You should see how far she can smear a dish of mac and cheese."

"Has she tried ice cream yet?"

"I haven't dared."

"With your permission I'll get some, and we can all enjoy the show."

Laura chuckled. "Go for it, Grandma, but thanks for asking first."

"I'll have the camera ready. I can't wait to see you both."

When she hung up the phone Olympia was positively glowing. Then she covered a huge yawn and announced that since she was scheduled to be on the nine-thirty ferry the next morning, she needed to make it an early night.

Later, curled into the warmth and comfort of their bed, she could hear the low murmurs of Frederick and Jim in conversation on the other side of the door. As she began floating down into sleep, she thought she heard the sound of Miss

Winslow's clock, but she lost count of how many times it chimed.

Twenty-Two

August 7, 1862

Jonathan is flushed and feverish and he has a dreadful cough. Many children have fallen ill with similar symptoms and some of them have not survived. I am very concerned. Mr. Fuller came by and offered to fetch the doctor but I declined his offer. Now I wish I had accepted. Sometimes I think I am too strong willed for my own good. Then I ask myself, do I really have a choice? I am alone, and my baby cries out for me.

More anon, LFW

Olympia was well along the road to Woods Hole and the ferry terminal by 7:30 a.m. Much as she loved Frederick and Jim, she was delighted to be totally alone, driving her beloved van, steaming travel mug in hand, listening to something high-pitched and fast by Antonio Vivaldi. Before she left, Frederick swore on a metaphorical stack of Bibles that he would have a functional back door in place by the time she returned that evening, and Olympia was wise enough not to ask for details.

Squinting in the morning sun, she wove her way through the tree-lined back roads of the Upper Cape toward Falmouth. She wondered what her conversation with Yolanda would be like and if the poor woman would still be willing to go forward. Then, realizing that she had no control over that, she diverted her thinking to how she might ensnare Jerrold Markham. The whole operation had taken a much more sinister turn after Jim told them what he'd turned up in his research, especially the information concerning the one woman who had died and the other who'd disappeared. She shivered involuntarily and, in so doing, splashed coffee onto the steering wheel. Pay attention to the road, she scolded herself and pressed down on the gas pedal.

Markham was going to be a difficult man to corner, or maybe he wasn't. He was, after all, a man on a mission, and he did seem to have a habit of showing up at the church when he thought she was alone. Maybe that would be enough. Let him continue to make his advances, then casually let him know she would be there by herself some afternoon or evening, but making sure that Frederick and Jim were within earshot and arm's reach. Then she would just let the drama unfold.

But what about the police? She had agreed to talk with them but decided to worry about that after she'd talked with Yolanda and Julia. That made sense, did it not? She agreed with herself that it did, drained the last of her now cold coffee, wished she hadn't, and turned into the Steamship Authority parking lot in Falmouth.

In Brookfield Jim was on his second cup of coffee, and Frederick upended the teapot for the last few precious ounces of his "English penicillin."

"It's the cure for anything from hemorrhoids to a broken heart," he told Jim as he tipped a splash of milk into the mug and settled down at the kitchen table with his friend. The cats had already been secured in the bathroom, and the two men sat, enjoying their drinks in the fragrant summer air that wafted in through the hole in the back of the house.

"So what's your door plan, Frederick?" asked Jim, obviously pleased with the pun he'd been able to slip in when Frederick wasn't looking.

"I'm still working it out in my head, but I know I'll start with measuring the opening and trying to find a door that comes close to those dimensions. I can always shim in any bits that need straightening or filling in with strips of wood, and those I can cut off the boards I used to secure the tarp last night."

If Jim was feeling doubtful, he was not showing it.

"Umm, where do you think you might find such a door? I'm thinking our dear Olympia will probably want one that would fit in design-wise with the rest of the house."

"I'm glad you asked that," said Frederick. "I'm not sure yet, but if I can't find it, we can always build it."

"I have an idea," said Jim, approaching the matter with gentle caution. "I know you can find everything on the internet these days, so why don't we do a little door search before we start?"

"I never thought about that. But now that you mention it, and remembering all that you learned about Jerrold Markham over the last couple of days, it's probably a good idea. It might save a lot of useless expense and running around, except I wouldn't know where to begin looking."

Jim breathed a silent sigh of relief. "Why don't you pick up the kitchen, and I'll go get my laptop?"

"Jolly good," said Frederick.

Before Jim returned to the kitchen with his computer, he sat down on his bed and typed "Craig's List" into the search engine. He might as well check and see if there were any new messages for Monica.

A flood of memories rushed at Olympia as the top-heavy boat swung through a wide turn, and the ferry terminal building in Vineyard Haven came into view. Some of these were wonderful, and others were downright unsettling. She had never had a gun pointed at her before her stay there, and she'd never met so many wonderful people concentrated in one colorful and quirky place. As the boat nudged the sides of the slip and finally swayed to a stop, she edged her way into the crowd shuffling toward the rear starboard exit. It was with good reason and some anxiety that she wondered exactly how this particular visit might turn out, but she didn't have long to wait. No sooner had she blinked her way into the bright sunshine on the exit ramp than she heard a voice calling her name. It was Julia Scott-Norton, the president of the board and prime mover of the community church she had served the previous summer.

"What an unexpected treat, Olympia. What brings you back? Are you on the trail of yet another nefarious character?"

Oh, if you only knew, thought Olympia, smiling and trying to look noncommittal. "Actually, I've been invited to spend the day with a parishioner in the church I'm serving now. It was an offer I couldn't refuse. I've missed this place far more than I ever thought possible. It's good to be back."

I'm not exactly lying through my teeth, thought Olympia, but damn close. She made a sad face. "Gee, I wish I had thought to call you, and we could at least have had a cup of tea together, but this sort of came up all of a sudden. I promise when I come back again I'll be sure to give you some advance warning."

"Any chance you'd consider another summer pastorate if we promise not to have any criminals for you to catch or match your wits against?"

"I wouldn't say no," replied Olympia, "but next summer is a whole year away. We'll have time to talk it over before then. That's another good reason for a return visit."

"It's none of my business, but what about your dear Frederick? Have you said yes to him yet?"

"No," said Olympia and looked down at, then away from, the piercing eyes of a very lovely, curious and perceptive lady.

She was saved from any further explanation by a freckle-faced, fair-haired woman who came up behind Julia and said, "Reverend Olympia? I'm Yolanda."

Olympia nodded yes and did the introductions, referring to her only as Yoli and deliberately omitting mention of her last name.

Julia smiled at Yolanda with pleasant curiosity apparent in her eyes. "I don't believe we've met before, and I know almost everyone here at least by sight. Have you lived here long?"

Yolanda flicked a nervous glance at Olympia, who chimed in.

"Actually, she's down visiting her cousin Sia who lives in Oak Bluffs. I'd love to stay and chat, but I know Sia's expecting us, so I don't want to keep her waiting."

"Of course," said the ever gracious Julia, "but think about next summer, will you? Maybe this time you can have the peace and quiet we promised you last time."

"We'll definitely have another conversation on the matter," said Olympia in a neutral tone. "I look forward to it."

"Where would you like to go?" asked Yolanda as they walked to where she was parked.

"I'd love to meet your kids," said Olympia, "but that wouldn't allow us much privacy. Why don't we grab some coffee and a couple of muffins at the Black Dog Bakery and find a quiet bench along State Beach? As I remember, they don't really fill up with bathers until noon or later."

"Perfect. What kind of muffin, and how do you like your coffee?"

"Black, please, mild to medium for the coffee and a raisin bran muffin. Those are the best."

Yolanda pulled open the car door. "Why don't you wait in the car, and I'll run over and get our food?"

"Good idea. I'd prefer not to advertise my presence here. It's a small island, and word gets around fast."

"Tell me about it."

When Yolanda returned the two made small talk until they found a mutually acceptable bench. There, Olympia donned her oversized sunglasses and an outlandishly floppy sun hat.

"Hold on, you'll need some of this too." The young mother with so much on her mind thoughtfully held out a tube of sunblock to Olympia. "This stuff is a must on a day like this."

When the two were slathered and settled, Yolanda saved Olympia any discomfort by beginning the conversation herself.

"The newspaper photos don't do you justice, Olympia. You are so much more animated in person."

"Pictures don't jump around, but I sure do," laughed Olympia.

"I might as well start off telling you I talked to my husband last night," said Yolanda.

Olympia went wide-eyed behind her dark glasses. "You did what? I thought you didn't want to say anything to him until you and I had a chance to go over things."

"I know. That was the original plan. But the more I thought about it, the more I realized I would only be furthering this whole sick charade if I left him out of what I hope will be the end of it."

"What did he say?"

"I should probably tell you what I said and then tell you what he said."

Olympia nodded silently. She knew this was very fragile territory.

"I called him when I knew he'd be alone in his office. I asked if he was willing to hear me out, and he said yes but wished it could be in person. I told him why I was not ready to come back yet and that you were coming down today, and then, well, I just told him everything. When I finished we were both crying. He wanted to know when I was coming home."

"What did tell him," asked Olympia?

"I said you'd be here today, and we were going to talk everything out. I told him you'd said that we needed to go to the police and get their cooperation, and there was probably no way we could keep it quiet after that. Then I asked if he was ready for all that might involve."

"What did he say then?"

"He said he was willing to do anything necessary to have us all back together, and he'd go with us when we go to the police."

"Wow!" said Olympia.

"My husband is a very strong man, Olympia, and a very determined one. I don't think I ever really knew how much I loved him until all this happened. I can't believe I was so stupid and naïve, and in spite of it all, he's willing to take me back."

"Don't say that. You were and are not stupid. You are a victim, Yolanda. Jerrold Markham knows exactly how to snare an unsuspecting target, and he'll stop at nothing to get his way."

Wisdom told Olympia not to say anything about the suspicious death and disappearance of the two women Jim had learned about in his internet search

"Did you tell your husband that you wanted to press charges?"

"All he said was, if that's what it would take to stop someone like Markham, he'd support me all the way. But when I asked if he thought it might affect his practice, he said that if some patients felt they needed to change doctors, it was their issue and not his. He said his family was his first priority."

"Wow," said Olympia for a second time.

"So what do I do now?"

Olympia wasn't ready for such a direct question. "I suppose you decide when you want to come back, and when you are ready, we meet with the police. I have every reason to believe this man is too wily and too dangerous to leave anything to chance. We need the heavy artillery on this one."

"Then I'll come back tomorrow or the day after. It won't take me that long to pack up. I didn't bring all that much. The cottage was completely furnished, right down to the corkscrews. All I have to pack is our clothes and a couple of things I picked up at the thrift shop."

Olympia wasn't prepared for that either, although, when she would think back on it all, she would realize she wasn't surprised. Yolanda had proved herself to be a woman of action.

"You hungry?" asked Yolanda.

"Starving. I missed breakfast, and that muffin was a drop in the metaphorical bucket."

Yolanda chuckled. "I suppose now that we've got the big stuff out of the way, we could go back to my cottage. I'd love you to meet my kids and have you get to know them a little bit before I go back home and all hell breaks loose."

Which it absolutely is going to, thought Olympia, but what she said was, "I'd love to." Then she added, "When you do come back, you and the kids need to keep out of sight. If anyone sees you, and word gets to Markham, all hell could break loose before we want it to."

Twenty-Three

"What in God's name am I doing?" Olympia was on the return trip leaning against the rail on the top deck of the ferry when she spoke these words aloud. The whining and grinding of the engine throttling down prior to docking obliterated them to anyone nearby, but the question remained real. What had she gotten herself into, and was it really in God's name that she was doing it, or was it entirely a self-inflicted and self-directed drama where she was playing the lead again? She didn't have time to wait for an answer, because the other passengers were already swarming, lemming-like, toward the exit stairways, and she knew she had to join them.

Later, alone in her car and driving back to Brookfield, she began the longer conversation. She started by asking herself why it was that she seemed to be plagued by troublesome situations she felt called — or in this case, was intentionally hired--to make right? Was it that she was attracted to conflict and danger like a moth to a flame, or was this binding and healing really her ministry? Was this the work she was meant to do? Certainly she felt morally called to stand up against injustice when she witnessed it. It was one of her principles of ethical living, but what else? Did she really get a secret thrill out of the encounter with danger?

Certainly Frederick and Jim were not pleased when she unwittingly put herself in harm's way, but this time she had taken the assignment, knowing there was a problem. The charge of duty had not been to find out why the minister left. It had been to comfort and reassure a shattered congregation and eventually guide them back into a place of stability. However, it would seem that the main reason for the resignation of the former minister and the disappearance of one of the members lay not within the congregation but across the street.

Furthermore, it would appear that this man had not a scruple to his name and had been wreaking havoc in people's lives for quite some time. Unlike some of her other adventures, her eyes were wide open, and she knew what had to be done.

The real question was, how it could be accomplished without causing collateral damage? If Jim's research were to be believed then human lives could be at stake here — and if she wasn't careful, hers could be one of them. It was not a comforting thought, and she knew she had to act fast to make sure it all came together with the right person in charge.

Timing was going to be the key to success along with human endurance. Her inner dialogue was interrupted by a simultaneous pinging and flashing of the dashboard warning light informing her that she needed gas right now. It was a timely diversion. She would think on all of this later after a good meal and a glass of wine and maybe...well, she winked at her own image in the rearview mirror, that would be the perfect nightcap, wouldn't it?

Frederick greeted her with a bow and a flourish of his tea towel. He was standing in the opening of the fully functional and historically appropriate kitchen door. He then announced that Julia Grafton had called, asking that Olympia call her the minute she returned. She muttered something about it never raining except when it pours, but the aphorism was lost in Frederick's enthusiastic welcome home hug, and the words squashed into his shoulder.

"What's that you're chuntering on about?"

"Nothing really, love. What's for supper? I see the telltale tea towel, and I can smell garlic. What have you made?"

"A phone call. You smell pizza, and I was just doing up the last of the breakfast dishes when you pulled in."

"I love you, Frederick."

"Well, what brought that on—not that I'm objecting, you understand?"

"Later, Darling, I need wine and food right now."

"Later what?" Frederick put on his happy, hopeful face.

"Think positively, but let me call Julia before I do anything else. Hungry and tired as I am, I fear this won't wait."

"I left the number by the phone on your desk," he called after her.

Olympia wondered as she headed for the phone in the bedroom whether her use of the word *fear* had been accidental or a subconscious warning. She dialed the number written on the scrap of paper Frederick had taped to the handset and then settled into her chair.

"Julia, this is Olympia Brown returning your call."

"Thank you for getting back to me. I've come to a decision."

Olympia immediately feared the worst, that the poor woman had changed her mind and was no longer willing to bear witness against Markham. Her response was quiet and cautious.

"Can you tell me what you've decided?"

"I'm coming back there, that is, if you'll have me. I know it's a lot to ask, but I'm afraid if I stay and think about it for too long, I'll chicken out."

Olympia took a deep breath. "Tell me what you have in mind. I'll do anything I can."

"I was pretty sure that would be your response. Here's what I'm thinking. I'm not ready to face any members of the congregation yet and maybe not ever, but that's a different issue. The point is I want to come back there to file charges against Markham. If that goes well, maybe then I'll think about making my amends to the congregation."

"That's a pretty momentous decision," said Olympia.

"That's why I asked that you call as soon as you could. If I tell you and buy a plane ticket, I've committed myself, right?"

"You need to know that, much as I hope you don't, you can always change your mind, and I'd never hold it against you.

This has to be soul wrenching for you. I'll help in whatever way I can. I guess you know that by now."

"You're a very good minister, Olympia. We ministers are the worst at letting ourselves be ministered unto."

"Tell me about it," said Olympia, "and you are a very strong woman."

"I might not have said that until this morning, but the more I thought about what that disgusting man is doing, I knew it was more than my ego and pride at stake. If I were going to be totally honest, the word *revenge* is curiously comforting right now."

"Now I know you're human," laughed Olympia. "Where would we be without a little healthy and well-targeted revenge? Now let's talk logistics."

"I don't want to be a bother. I thought I would stay at a B&B near you. I know where Brookfield is, and it's far enough away from Millbridge that I'm not likely to run into anyone I know."

"Are you allergic to cats?" Olympia was doodling swirls and curves all over the scrap of paper with Julia's number on it.

"No, I love cats, but what does that have to do with what we are talking about?"

"Everything and nothing. If cats aren't a problem, I have more rooms in this house that anyone has a right to. Some of them are habitable, and some are still in process. It's an antique New England farmhouse that Frederick and I are slowly restoring. I can offer you anything you'll need. You can have a private room with a bathroom right next door, hot and cold running cats, and a nosy but very personable house-ghost that we are happy to share with you. Her name is Miss Winslow. She's a Mayflower descendent."

"House-ghost?"

"She's almost a member of the family, not mischievous or scary at all. In fact, she's quite protective of us."

"You're joking," said Julia in a tone that said she hoped it wasn't true.

"Come see for yourself. She'll love you."

"You're serious."

"Absolutely. I never thought about asking you to come back here, but if you can, I think we'll have everything we need to unmask that man for the monster he is and get him off the streets for good.

Olympia cocked her head. She could hear an unmistakable sound coming from the sitting room behind where she was sitting.

"Speak of the devil, Julia, did you hear that?"

"I heard something that sounded like a bell or a clock chiming. What was it?"

"That, my dear, was Miss Winslow signaling her approval. She's letting me know she wants you to stay here as well, and you'll adore Frederick. Everyone does. So when can you come?"

"Let's see. Today is Thursday. Is it okay if I come on Monday? That way you can get Sunday out of the way, and I can tie up a couple of loose ends out here. It's summer, so I won't need to pack very much.

"It's New England." Olympia was now doodling a snowman wearing sunglasses.

"Okay, I'll bring a sweater and an umbrella."

"I have umbrellas. Just call me or e-mail me with your flight numbers and times, and one or the other of us will pick you up."

"Okay. Um, I know what you look like, but what does Frederick look like?"

"He's English, and he'll be driving a canary yellow Ford pickup. You can't possible miss him. No one can. How do you know what I look like?"

"I Googled you."

"Sounds obscene."

Julia chuckled. "Actually, you're pretty impressive. I didn't think they taught crime solving in seminary." Julia's voice was sounding stronger and more confident.

"Everybody needs a hobby, Julia. It seems as if I've taken up scaring the pants off myself."

"If I were you, and considering what you are taking on, I might suggest another descriptive phrase."

Now it was Olympia's turn to laugh.

"I'm looking forward to meeting you, Julia; you sound like my kind of woman."

"I was once, and maybe I will be again after we get this whole miserable thing behind us."

"I'm committed to it. Just call and let me know when you'll be here."

"How late do you stay up?"

"I'll give you my cell phone number. Why don't you call me in the morning? I think I'm probably going to bed early tonight."

"Will do."

Olympia was grateful that Julia couldn't see her smug anticipatory grin. Some things are truly best left unsaid.

Later, when the pizza was a sticky memory, the wine glasses still needed washing, and Frederick and Olympia were having an after-dinner cup of tea, she brought him up to date.

He set down his teacup on the table beside him and looked at her over his reading glasses. "You mean both women are willing to go public and press charges?"

"That's what they said. Of course, anything could change between now and then, but I'm going forward on the premise that they will indeed carry through."

"So when do we talk to the police? You said you would, Olympia, and although I have no legal right to do so, I must insist."

"Frederick, even if we were married you still couldn't insist that I do anything. Marriage isn't like that anymore. You could emphatically implore me to do something, and I suppose you could even try to insist, but unless I decided to do whatever, then you'd be, uh, pissing in the wind, for lack of a better turn of phrase."

"So will you marry me?"

"Frederick, will you be serious?"

"Don't shout. I am serious. I just saw an opportunity, and I took advantage of it."

"Okay."

"Okay, you'll go to the police first thing in the morning, or okay, you'll marry me?"

"Both."

"I'm not joking, Olympia. There is too much at stake here for you to be playing sillybuggers."

"I'm not playing sillybuggers as you call it, neither am I joking about marrying you. I said both, Frederick, and I meant both. Yes, I will marry you. Now let's go to bed and celebrate."

"But ..."

"Quick, before I change my mind!"

August 14, 1862

This has been a most frightening week but I thank God I am on the other side of it. Jonathan became very ill, and there were times that I truly feared for his life. In the end, Mr. Fuller did fetch the doctor to attend us and then stayed on to help. After some very long and prayer filled nights my precious little boy has begun to mend and I will be forever in Richard Fuller's debt. In the long hours sitting by my son's bed we talked and talked and talked. It was as though a dam had burst and a river of words gushed out. There was no stopping them, nor did we try and in so doing we have allowed ourselves to become friends. I said earlier in these most private pages that we all make choices and we all have secrets. This cannot and will not change, but now I have a friend who will guard my secrets as tenderly I will guard his.

When Jonathan is fully restored to health, I shall take him and my writing materials off to Cambridge and spend some time with Aunt Louisa. Richard Fuller has graciously agreed to care for the house and even take my cat Sammy to stay with him until I return. I count myself most fortunate to be his friend.

More anon. LFW

Twenty-Four

"So when and where shall it be?" Frederick was assembling his tea while Olympia was making poached eggs on toast for the two of them.

"Frederick, what on earth are you talking about?"

"Last night you said that you'd go to the police before you took this thing any further, and you also agreed to marry me. 'How soon and where' applies to both issues."

Olympia nodded, spatula in hand. "I'm not going to go to the police until I've talked with both Julia and Yolanda. They are the ones who have the most to lose if it goes wrong, so we all have to be on the same page."

"That makes sense. So when do we get married?"

"How about this afternoon?" Olympia lifted the eggs out of the boiling water and dropped them, one by one, on the waiting pieces of toast. "You do know that it's the spoonful of vinegar in the boiling water that makes the eggs hold together, don't you?"

"Olympia, I do not give a rat's arse about vinegar and water and how the combination affects the poaching of an egg. I want to marry you. Will you please get bloody serious?"

He was clearly irritated, and Olympia was instantly contrite.

"I'm sorry, Frederick. I guess I'm just nervous. I do love you, but the thought of getting married really scares me. On the other hand, who else would I ever want to marry? I need to get over this little fear of marriage thing of mine."

Frederick's voice softened. "Practically speaking, you probably shouldn't be planning a wedding and laying siege to a sexual predator in the same paragraph. Let's see this latest adventure of yours to its conclusion before we bring the subject of marriage up again. Believe me, my darling, it is almost enough that you've finally said yes. You've made me a very happy man."

Frederick was positively beatific as he reached for his plate of eggs and toast. Nothing more needed saying, and for one of the few times in her life, Olympia didn't break the spell.

Later, Olympia was on her way to Millbridge, where she could work on her sermon in the privacy of her office. As was her wont, she was reviewing her current battle plan in the total peace and isolation of her beloved van. One thing was missing; she needed coffee. The breakfast and lunch spot (and village grapevine) Frederick had discovered the day she went for her first interview with the church was right along the way. She glanced at the clock on the dashboard. If she got there early enough, they might still have some of their prized apricot-ginger scones to go with it. These were always a sell-out, and locals either placed a special order the day before or waited in line when the doors opened at six in the morning to make sure they got some. After ordering a double cinnamon cappuccino to go, Olympia snagged the last two scones on the tray.

Once she was back on the road, she continued with the mental review of her options. First she would meet with Julia and Yolanda separately, then again with the two women together. After that, if he was willing, she hoped to meet with Yolanda and her husband Nick. Somewhere in the unfolding schedule she needed everyone involved to meet Jim and Frederick because, wittingly or unwittingly, they too had become part of the offensive. Then what? That was the X- factor. She felt as if she had all the ammunition and no gun. What was, or would be, the actual offense with which he could be charged? Olympia shuddered, splashing coffee on her light beige slacks and under it, her leg. Damn! The complexity of it all was daunting.

Maybe it would be a good idea if the police did take over. She blinked and shook her head. Up until that very minute the thought had never occurred to her not to be on the front line and leading the charge. Reality and common sense had finally prevailed, and she accepted that this really was a job for professionals. Olympia was a professional in her chosen field. She was an ordained minister, not a credentialed detective.

"Nah, I just play one on television," she said aloud to the steering wheel as she signaled for a right and then nosed the faded blue van into her Reserved for the Minister space in front of the church. She was surprised to see Franna's car. She didn't usually come in on Fridays.

As she got out of the van she glanced over her shoulder toward the church across the street. Was it nerves? She couldn't see if Jerrold's car was there because he usually parked it in the back, but what she did see was a figure pull back from the church office window at the moment she looked up.

Once inside the church, she offered the second scone to Franna, who squealed her delight and ripped open the bag. "M-m-m, still warm. I'd better go make some coffee. Want some?"

Olympia held up her three-quarters-full paper container and sloshed it around. "No, thanks, Franna, I'm good. This should get me through until at least ten, but I have to be honest and tell you that second scone almost didn't make it here. Bythe way, what are you doing in here on a Friday? "

Franna laughed. "I have some catching up to do. I should only be here for an hour or two."

"Any messages or parish emergencies I need to address while I finish my coffee?"

"One of each," said Franna. "The rose ladies are at it again. They both think they are supposed to be doing the flowers for this Sunday. Rosemary Madder is hyperventilating in the Ladies Parlor, and Letitia just bent my ear for the last half-hour, accusing me of being careless with the schedule. I didn't dare tell her someone had erased her name and written Rosemary Madder in its place. Then there really would be an all-out war. I tried to take the blame and said I must have done it in a distracted moment, but she wouldn't have it."

"Better that than the two of them facing off with loppers and weed killer at dawn." Olympia chuckled at the comical image forming in her mind. "Okay, that's the emergency. What's the message?"

Franna made a face and gestured with her thumb toward the church on the other side of the village green. "He called to see if you were in yet. I told him you weren't and asked if there was a message. He just cut me off and said he'd call back later. He really aggravates me. I think it's even worse now that I told you what I know. It's really hard to be civil to him, especially now that he seems to be coming on to you."

Olympia thought for a moment before responding. She wasn't sure how much she should share with Franna. On the other hand, Franna knew most what was going on—not all, but most.

"Franna, can you come into my office and shut the door? I want to tell you something, but I can't risk anyone hearing me."

"Don't you think you'd better go talk to Rosemary first and sort all that out? I'll go make myself some coffee and zap that scone in the microwave, and you go pour oil on troubled flower petals."

"Good thought. Any leftover cookies out there?"

"Possibly, but they might be stale."

"Sugar is sugar. Stale or fresh, bring them on. I need courage, and it's too early for a glass of wine."

Franna pressed her hands together, bowed her head and whispered, "Yes, Minister."

As she headed out toward the kitchen, Olympia took a deep breath and walked into the church parlor to greet the fulminating flower gardener who lay in wait.

"I suppose you've heard!" Rosemary Madder was on her feet and quivering in outrage when Olympia entered the room. Her gut response was to play innocent, but age and experience caught up with her. This was a very delicate, and at the same time totally absurd, situation, and it demanded all of her pastoral skills. As a minister and a compassionate human being, she knew most people wanted to be recognized and valued for what they did. The trouble was that in this church there were two expert gardeners, each vying for what they believed to be one crown. In that fleeting thought Olympia realized she might have a solution to this thorny issue, but now was not the time to breathe even a hint of it. The woman was on the edge of tears.

"Come and sit down, Rosemary. Shall I make us some tea first? Franna told me there was a mix-up on the flower schedule."

"Mix-up!" shouted the distraught woman. "That awful woman took my name off the calendar and wrote in her own, and it went out in the church newsletter. So even if I do them anyway, everybody will think the flowers are hers. I mean, it's not like I can put a sign in front of them with my name on it. I wait for this Sunday all year, Reverend. My roses are at their very best, and I even have a new one this year called Parson's Blessing. I figured it would be a perfect way to honor your work with us. We need all the blessings we can get right now." She slumped against the velvet back of the Victorian sofa in what amounted to a full body scowl.

Oh, God, what do I say now? thought Olympia. She twisted the ring Frederick had given her, praying the right words would come.

"Rosemary, do you think there might have been a misunderstanding? I don't believe Letitia would deliberately do something like that."

The glower deepened. "You're new here. You don't know what she's like. I've been dealing with that woman for over forty years."

They were interrupted by Franna, who stuck her head in the door to ask if they needed anything.

"No thanks, Franna. Save the cookies, I may need them later."

Rosemary looked annoyed. "I don't want to interrupt your morning, Reverend, I should probably just go." This was followed with a long, sorrowful sigh.

Olympia reached over and patted her hand. "The cookies can wait, Rosemary, I don't really need them anyway. You and your roses are far more important. We need to make this right for both of you."

The woman stiffened. "What do you mean, both of us? She's the one who swapped names. I'm the victim here. She ..."

Olympia held up her hand. "Rosemary, the more I think about it, the more I think we three should sit down and have a conversation. If we do we might find a way to have two expert gardeners attend the same church without sparks flying."

"No disrespect, but you are a dreamer, aren't you? What do you think you can do that we haven't been able to do in all these years?" Rosemary was sitting up straight now with her arms crossed and her chin high.

"Listen," said Olympia.

"Hmph!"

"Are you willing to give it a try?"

"I suppose. You probably mean well."

Olympia ignored the little jibe. "Oh, and by the way, I intended to call you earlier, but my life has become just a little complicated in the last few days." When Rosemary looked concerned, she added, "Mostly family stuff." She just couldn't say whose family it was. She leaned forward and changed the subject. "I've got a wedding coming up in a couple of weeks. It will be a small wedding, and the brides are on a very tight budget. I wonder if you might be willing to make a floral arrangement for the altar for them?"

"Did you just say brides?"

"I did."

"Two women are getting married in this church?"

"They are."

"Well, fancy that."

"Does that bother you?"

Rosemary broke into a broad smile. "Just the opposite. It's about time we let people marry who they want to, and I'm proud to be part of one of the churches that does it."

Will wonders never cease? thought Olympia and rewarded the woman with an enthusiastic thumbs-up.

"So you'll do it?"

"The flowers for the wedding and a three-way conversation with Letitia?"

Olympia nodded.

"You're asking for a lot."

"Rosemary, what's one more hour against forty years of aggravation?"

"Oh, all right."

"I'll give Franna some times that work for me, and she can arrange it with the two of you. But I'm going have a chat with Letitia first."

This was greeted with another harrumph and just the hint of a sideways smile.

"Would you like to come and meet the brides the next time they come in?

"I'd love to," said Rosemary.

The rest of the morning was relatively calm. After Rosemary left, Franna came into the office with fresh coffee and the stale cookies, and with the plate between them they attended to church business. When Olympia told her what had transpired with Rosemary and her plans to try and get them both together in the same room, her administrator was openly dubious.

"But this is a church and miracles happen," said Olympia.

"And pigs fly," said Franna.

Then Olympia got serious and told her what she felt she could share without breaking confidence. She said both Julia and

Yolanda had said they were willing to press charges, and then she asked if Franna was willing. Would she step up if needed?

"I'd love to," said Franna rubbing her hands together. "I never would have, if the two women weren't going to, but frankly there's nothing I'd rather see than him get his comeuppance."

"It may well be more than that."

"What are you talking about?"

Olympia rubbed her chin. "That chapter is still unfolding, but it's enough to say that if everything that we've learned about him turns out to be true, there may be enough evidence to send him to jail for a very long time."

Franna went wide-eyed. "Oh, my God, what do you want me to do until then?"

"Act normal. Treat him as you always have. Everything from now on depends on him not getting the slightest hint there's anything going on."

"Well, that shouldn't be hard. I barely give him the time of day as it is. He knows I have no use for him."

"Well, then, keep calm and carry on," said Olympia.

"I've heard that phrase before."

"It's one of Frederick's lines. These things rub off on you after a while."

"Sounds like something the Queen might say. Say, you going to be here by yourself this afternoon?"

"Yes, but I'll keep the door locked. I've got a bunch of phone calls I have to make. I'd rather do it from here."

By three in the afternoon she had learned that Yolanda would be back tomorrow, and a sheepish Letitia Blume would be willing to come in for tea and a chat the next morning. She was just about to congratulate herself on getting through the day without having to deal with Jerrold Markham when she heard a loud knocking on the outside door. Instinct told her who it probably was. One of these days I'm going to ask that the doorbell get fixed or maybe even ask them to install an intercom, she thought. Meanwhile, I'll just act normal and open the door, slowly and not too far.

She was right.

"Oh, hi, Jerrold, what's up?" Olympia stood in the open doorway with her right shoulder resting against the back side of the door and her hand on the doorknob.

He smiled. "I'm going out for a coffee, can I bring you one?"

"That's really nice of you, but I was just about to head for home."

He put on his best crestfallen little boy look and scuffed his shoe on the pavement. "Well, then, how about lunch sometime next week? We haven't had time to catch up on local clergy stuff. We can call it a business meeting, if you promise not to tell anyone we're enjoying ourselves."

Olympia paused before saying, "Sure, I just need to think for a minute."

He raised a cautious eyebrow. "Is there a problem having lunch with me?"

"No, not at all. I was just mentally checking my calendar, and Wednesday and Thursday are both good. I've got appointments on either side of lunchtime on both days, so we can't be too long."

He bowed low. "Your wish is my command, Reverend Madame. Let's say Wednesday, and why don't we go back to that Greek place?"

"Sounds like a plan, Reverend Markham."

Twenty-Five

When Olympia got home that evening she had a lot to report to Frederick — and he told her, after a resounding homecoming kiss, that he probably had just as much to tell her.

"Wine and dinner first," said Olympia.

"Am I surprised?" asked Frederick. He stepped back into the kitchen, twirled on one toe, picked up one of two stemmed glasses filled with something pale and cool and held it out to her.

"*Pour toi, ma cherie.*"

Olympia accepted the glass and raised it in his direction.

"I love it when you talk dirty, Frederick; what's for dinner?"

"I was going to ask you the very same thing. We can dig around and see what we can create, or I can call for take-out. " said Frederick.

"We did take-out last night. I know we have half a box of pasta, and I think there's a hunk of gorgonzola and a few mushrooms lurking somewhere in the depths of the fridge. If we have any cream hiding in there as well, I can have a killer supper ready for us in twenty minutes."

"Jolly good!"

Frederick didn't have to be asked twice when offered a good meal that he didn't have to prepare. He could cook and sometimes did, but it was work, and often not a thing of beauty. Olympia actively enjoyed creating in the kitchen, and Frederick showed his appreciation by cleaning up afterward.

By seven in the evening they were finished with dinner and enjoying an evening stroll around the neighborhood, relating the particulars of their respective days to one another. She told him about the wars of the roses, and more importantly, she now had three women willing to press charges and would go to the police when she had spoken with them all. He told her Jim had called and said he'd found even more evidence of Markham's trail of deceit. Also, "Monica" had heard from Gerry Marks again and was planning to meet him sometime next week.

Olympia looked puzzled. "How can he meet him without revealing who he is? Did he say anything more specific?"

"No, he said he planned to come down after you've had a chance to sit down with the witnesses. Maybe you should talk to him yourself."

"By the way, I'm having lunch with Markham on Wednesday."

"You're what?' Frederick stopped walking and pulled Olympia around so she was facing him.

Olympia waved him back with her free hand. "Calm down, love. We will be in a public place in the middle of the day. I've gone to lunch with him before. It will be a good way to see which way the wind is blowing, so to speak, and if possible keep him interested without actually leading him on. Don't you see, it's a perfect opportunity? I'll make him think I enjoy his company, and then I can observe how he operates."

"I don't like it, Olympia."

"Okay, I have an idea. He has no idea what you look like. Why don't you, or you and Jim, go to the restaurant and sit at a different table? Would that make you less worried?"

"I'll think about that. Are you sure you know which restaurant it will be?"

"He's the one that suggested it. It's a local Greek place. If you want I'll give you the address and directions, and you can go on your own. Think about it. A little third-party observation wouldn't hurt."

After that the two walked along hand-in-hand without speaking. The bright, warm, late June evenings were a special treat to Frederick. From time to time he would say it was the one thing he missed about living in England, sitting outside in the summertime and reading the paper at 10:30 in the evening. The New England smells of backyard cooking and the sounds of children playing outside after supper drifted in and out of Olympia's consciousness as she turned the unfolding events over in her mind.

"You're thinking," said Frederick as they turned into the driveway.

"What makes you say that?"

"The furrowed brows and blank stare give you away every time."

"Oh."

"So what's the plan?"

"It's still gestating."

"All right, then maybe we could talk about the wedding?"

Olympia stopped on the granite block step outside the kitchen door and looked Frederick straight in the eye. "I said yes, but I didn't say when to the yes."

"True enough, but can we get out our datebooks and at least pick a month … or even a season?" Frederick put his hands on her waist and began to move closer.

"I wonder what Randall and Malcolm will say?"

"Don't forget Laura."

Olympia bit her lip. "Let's go inside and start writing things down. Planning something like this will be a lot nicer than setting a trap for a dangerous animal."

"I dare say it is, Olympia, but we need to proceed with extreme caution. Both endeavors are deadly serious business."

Olympia turned away from him and walked into the kitchen. "I didn't think weddings were especially deadly. Heck, I'm in the business."

Frederick cocked his head and responded. "They are if they go wrong, dear lady. You had one that has scarred you in ways I still don't, and may never, know. The fact that I'm also divorced says that we are both matrimonially challenged in our own ways. I certainly don't want to repeat any history, yours or mine. I may be eager to marry you, my darling, and you may find this hard to believe, but I'm not in a rush."

Olympia reached out to the man she loved and drew him to her.

"Thank you, Frederick."

In his cozy Beacon Hill kitchen, Jim carefully slipped the salmon fillet he'd just poached onto a warmed plate. On one side of it he placed a steaming, buttered baked potato and on the other side a generous serving of green peas. Tradition demanded that salmon be served with green peas, and when it came to certain foods, Jim was a traditionalist. Over the months of living alone in Boston, he'd discovered he had both a flair and a passion for cooking. He'd always enjoyed good food and wine but mostly as a partaker rather than a creator. When he was living in the rectory, teaching and his clerical duties left little time for a hobby. Things were different now, very different.

He placed the colorful plate onto a wooden tray, set a chilled glass of Vouvray next to it and carried his dinner into the living room, where he habitually took his meals. Good food, good wine and the evening news on TV. What more could a man want? Jim wasn't ready to answer that question yet, but he was getting closer to the time when he knew he would have to.

When he finished his dinner he would call Olympia and Frederick and report his latest findings on Markham as well as the developing electronic tragicomedy of Gerry Marks and Monica. The thought of it all was enough to sour his stomach. If Jerrold and Gerry were indeed the same man, and by now Jim was almost certain they were, then Markham not only needed to be stopped, he needed to be permanently removed from society. Forcing his mind elsewhere, if even for a little while, he picked up the remote with his right hand and his wine glass with the left. Outside on the streets of historic, genteel Boston, the sun was still shining, and the sounds of an active city neighborhood punctuated the evening newscast. Jim set down his glass and picked up his knife and fork in pleasant anticipation.

Olympia's daughter was doing an inventory of her apartment in Somerville. She was carrying Erica on her hip, bouncing and swaying the way mothers instinctively do. The baby was waving and clapping her dimpled hands to her mother's version of "Old MacDonald" as Laura two-stepped through the rooms trying to decide what she should take, what she should store, and what she should send to Goodwill. She was alternating between confident anticipation and abject terror at the impending move and change, but like her biological mother, she was not one to back away from a challenge. She did need to talk some things over with that mother and was glad she was going down to Brookfield on Sunday. She wouldn't be able to settle everything that was going on in her mind, and maybe she never could, but a yes or no to the question she planned to ask on Sunday would get one more detail out of the way. Then she'd have a better idea of what to pack and what to ship. Laura stopped and looked out of the window and through the trees at a sky that was beginning to go pink and wondered if the sunsets would be different in California.

Even though it was still light enough to read, Jerrold Markham pulled down the window shades and drew the curtains in his study. He was at home in the church parsonage with no meetings or other pastoral obligations. This was a rare privilege, and he wanted total privacy.

Because he wasn't married he wasn't expected to do much parish entertaining, and for the most part there was no need. He had a steady stream of hot casseroles, homemade bread and cookies, and enough dinner invitations to feed three men. Jerrold liked being fussed and fawned over by the church ladies and pretty much accepted it as his due. He knew never to show the slightest bit of overt favoritism within the congregation and did it so well that even the men in the church made jokes about safety in numbers and Pastor Jerry's girls.

When he did begin to favor one, he knew exactly how to do it so that no one was ever the wiser. And when he grew bored and restless, he knew exactly how to end it. Well, he did most of the time.

He'd been on his best behavior since his involvement with, and the sequential disappearances of, Julia Grafton and Yolanda Nikitas. That had never happened to him before, and it still unsettled him to think about it. Until then he had always been the one to call it quits. Maybe he should stay with the internet connections from now on. They were nameless, faceless, fast and predictable, but they weren't exciting or challenging. There was something about the long courtship right under people's noses that was as much a high for him as was the final conquest. He was soon bored with what passed for the sex part. It was the thrill of the chase and the challenge of forbidden fruit that he couldn't stop craving, nor did he ever intend to.

He needed to be far more careful in the future. Julia and Yolanda, whereabouts unknown, could mean serious retroactive trouble if people started checking up on him. He preferred not to think about how frantically he'd had to cover his tracks on two other occasions. Now he only went after women with too much to lose if they were ever found out.

Jerrold Markham liked to be in control, and he usually was. That's why Olympia, even though she was no beauty, was such a challenge. It was clear that she, too, liked to be in control. He would win in the end. He always did. Jerrold smiled in anticipation, leaned back in his leather chair and opened his laptop.

Twenty-Six

When Olympia arrived at the church the next morning, she took care to lock the door behind her and tape up a sign that read Bell Broken – Please Knock. She expected Letitia Blume at ten and was not about to leave the door unlocked while she waited. Franna was not in on Saturdays, and Olympia came in alone sometimes so she could work on her sermon. Between the cats, Frederick and other sundry things she could find to putter with, she found there were fewer distractions in her office than at home.

She sniffed the musty air in the closed-up room and pushed up the window behind her chair. That's when she noticed the message light on her answering machine was blinking. She hit the play button and listened to Jerrold Markham's oily voice saying he was terribly sorry, but he had a pastoral emergency and needed to cancel their lunch on Wednesday, and could they please make it Thursday? Too bad, she thought. Here I was all geared up for a game of cat and mouse, but to be honest, I'm not sure who is stalking whom. In this particular case, each was the cat and each was the mouse, circling one another for totally different and equally dark reasons.

Olympia realized she was mildly disappointed but shrugged it off and was preparing to get started on her sermon when she spotted a pink memo sheet from Franna. It read, "Rose ladies can meet this afternoon at 3:00. If that works for you, call them and let them know. GOOD LUCK!"

Oy vey was her first reaction, but she realized that if she did meet with the two of them that day and get it sorted out, it would be one less thing to deal with in what was becoming an overfull to-do list. Prudently she decided not to call Rosemary Madder until after she had spoken with Letitia, just in case the whole thing blew up in her face. She checked her watch. She had an hour to devote to coming up with a subject and title for her sermon.

By the end of the morning Olympia counted two minor successes to her credit, a good talk with Letitia Blume and a healthy start on her sermon. There would be a third on the list if the meeting that afternoon, agreed to by both ladies, didn't erupt into a shower of compost and blood-red rose water.

At ten minutes to three Olympia poured lemonade and a splash of ginger ale into a tall pitcher and added some ice cubes. She set this, along with three matching glasses and a plate of cookies, on a sturdy plastic utility tray and carried everything into the Ladies Parlor just as she heard the knock at the door.

Olympia gulped, set everything down, took a deep breath and went to greet her guests. She was not surprised to find both of them standing there. She suspected they had probably hidden behind separate trees so as not to let the other arrive first.

"Come in, ladies. I've made us some lemonade with a little something extra. It's my special recipe."

For a few minutes they fussed over where they should sit, tasted the enhanced lemonade and politely declined the cookies. The conversation between the two ladies sounded like something out of an Oscar Wilde play. They were overly, even archly, polite and solicitous.

"Letitia, dear, would you care for a cookie?"

"Why no, thank you, Rosemary, darling, I'm watching my weight. Can't be too careful, can we?"

"Watching it go up," muttered Rosemary.

"What was that, dear?"

Olympia cleared her throat just in time to avert disaster. "Ladies, shall we sit and have a moment of silence together before we begin?"

As she was driving home Reverend Doctor Olympia Brown found herself erupting into giggles as she thought about the meeting she had just successfully concluded. At first the two women acted more like petulant five-year-olds fighting over a teddy bear than women of a certain age and standing in the community trying to come to an understanding. What Olympia wisely realized was that they were not mean, selfish and egotistical. They were fragile, sensitive and justly proud of the one thing they knew they did well. They both wanted recognition and feared that without their prized roses they would be nobodies. The pity was there were two of them competing for what they believed could be only one award. Olympia hoped she could help them see it differently.

As the afternoon and the lemonade and the cookies dwindled, Olympia helped them understand that this need not be an either-or situation. She asked if there might be a way to consider having a shared regency. She remembered saying that two were often better than one, and if they could find a way to work together in the future, they might even tend each other's gardens if one wanted to go away on a trip or needed a little time away.

Slowly the wheels of kindness turned, and eventually the ladies began talking to each other instead of Olympia. At that point Olympia excused herself, ostensibly to go to the ladies room but in reality to give the two of them time together without a referee. When she returned the emotional temperature in the room had gone from the frozen arctic to a warm sunny day in Millbridge. The two were sitting closer together, chattering on about pruning, fertilizers, climbers and all manner of things floral.

Olympia knew better than to say that everything was coming up roses, but she thought it and stifled a chuckle when she did. She'd done it—no, they'd done it. It was only a beginning, but it was a good beginning. Ministry was not about the flowing robes and expounding platitudes from an elevated pulpit. Ministry was listening and being present to another human being.

She signaled left, turned onto her street and coasted down the little incline to her driveway. She was home and eager to catch Frederick up on the very mixed blessings of her day, but the fact that his pickup was not in its habitual spot told her the man of the hour was not yet there.

Once inside she greeted the cats with a handful of kitty treats and began to rummage around in the kitchen for something she could turn into their supper. It didn't take long to come up with the makings of two potentially superb omelets, some greens that could be coaxed into a salad and some bread ends that with a little butter, garlic, parsley and a short stint in the oven would perfectly round out the meal. The phone rang as she was laying out the ingredients.

She'd had years of practice doing more than one thing at a time. Whether it was holding a child on her hip or talking on the phone, Olympia believed herself to be the original multi-tasker. The word had become so trendy these days, but she and every other mother on God's green earth had been doing it for millennia. Olympia picked up the phone, tucked the handset under her ear and continued her meal preparations without missing a beat.

"Oh, hi, Jim, any new developments on your end of the Markham front, and when are we going to see you?"

"One question at a time, Olympia. Yes, there are new developments, and if it's okay with you, I'd like to come down tomorrow night. I think we need to move on this thing as soon as we can."

"What are you talking about?"

"My e-mail persona Monica made a lunch date with her internet friend, Gerry Marks, for Wednesday of next week, only she's going to stand him up."

"Jim, will you stop talking in code and just tell me what happened?"

Jim chuckled at her predictable impatience and was clearly enjoying stretching it out.

"What I just said. Monica, my invented lady, set up a meeting with Gerry, her ardent electronic mystery suitor, and plans to stand him up. But Father Jim will be going to the very same place in his priest-suit and dog-collar and will take some nice clear photographs through the window of a nearby bookstore of the man who is being stood up."

"You're joking."

"Hardly."

"Ver-r-y interesting. I was supposed to have lunch with Jerrold Markham on Wednesday, and he left me a message on the church phone asking if we could change it to Thursday."

"We may have just struck paydirt, Reverend."

With the handset tucked under her ear, Olympia broke the eggs into a bowl. Then she set out the cheese and the spinach leaves. Everything seemed to be falling into place. She didn't like it when things came together too easily. It tended to make one overconfident, and overconfidence can lead to carelessness.

Olympia had the uncomfortable feeling that this whole thing was taking on a life of its own. Much as she loved and trusted Jim, she was surprised to find herself just the tiniest bit annoyed with his progress and presumption. Was she being a selfish control freak? She didn't like asking herself that question, and she wanted even less to know the correct answer. One of these days Olympia needed to have a face-to-face with herself about such feelings.

"Before I do anything else I need to talk with Yolanda and Julia and see where they are on all of this. The next step really does depend on them. Add to all of this, my daughter is coming down on Sunday, as well, and she's bringing the baby. She says she needs to ask me something, but she's not staying the night."

"I hope I get there in time to see them. See you then."

The omelets proved to be delicious, the bread duly resurrected itself in the oven, and the salad got a pass. When Olympia offered to bake apples for dessert, Frederick suggested that since it was so warm, they might go out for ice cream instead.

Later, sitting side by side in the back garden and spooning up the last of their rapidly melting confections, Olympia caught Frederick up on the Jerrold Markham situation, including Jim's clandestine photography.

Frederick shut his eyes and shook his head. "That man never ceases to surprise me. What in my lady queen's name is he going to come up with next?"

"We'll probably find out when he comes down here. I think I told you that Laura and the baby are coming for the afternoon on Sunday. She has something she wants to talk to me about but wouldn't say what it was over the phone. Jim will be here after that for supper and may or may not spend the night. Julia Grafton is flying in on Monday. I'm hoping I can sit down with her and Yolanda and see if I can get their permission to go to the police. And somewhere in the middle of all of this, we need a few minutes to talk about the wedding."

"I'd say you've got a rather full dance card this weekend, my love. Do you really think you can throw in wedding planning as well? On the other hand, you do everything else at nineteen to the dozen, so why not add this to the mix?"

Olympia set her empty ice cream cup on the grass beside her chair, where it was immediately set upon by Cadeau. "Believe it or not, now that I've come this far I am not about to have a drive-through wedding. I want the real deal with flowers, a new dress and maybe even a bridesmaid."

Frederick looked at her in amused wonder. "Well, as I live and breathe, do I get a buttonhole and groomsman as well?"

"Doesn't your suit have buttonholes already?"

"What do you yanks call flowers that men wear on their lapels at formal occasions?"

"Flowers," said Olympia. "If you want to put on airs, it's a *boutonnière*."

"If you are going to get yourself a new dress, I do believe I'll need a new wedding suit."

Olympia was clearly warming to the subject. "What about this coming October? Something small, right here in the back yard. I should be finished up in Millbridge by September. We'd have time to pretty up the garden by then. What do you think?"

Frederick was positively starry-eyed. "I think yes to all of the above, but I also think we should go in and start practicing."

"Practicing what?"

"What married people do," he said with a knowing leer.

"The dishes?" she said innocently.

August 23, 1862

I have neglected my writing for almost two weeks while Jonathan was ill. Surely I will need to have a title for this fledgling work, but to date, nothing comes to mind. Perhaps I shall ask Aunt Louisa in my next letter to her. The early vegetables are starting to come in. I must go across the street and share my simple harvest with Richard Fuller. He does so much for us and asks for nothing in return. It is the very least I can do.

More anon, LFW

Twenty-Seven

Olympia scooped up her sermon, her clerical robe and her hymnal, then added an umbrella to the pile on the back seat before setting off to church. The weather forecast for the afternoon was for thundershowers, possibly severe with potentially damaging winds. Olympia hoped it would all hold off so she and Laura might be able to be outside, but this was New England, and there was simply no telling. Frederick was right when he said, "The weather simply is, and there is nothing we can do about it other than be prepared for all eventualities." Dear Frederick, she thought. He really is a keeper.

After church Olympia detoured by her favorite Italian bakery and picked up an assortment of pastries to have after dinner that evening. Next she stopped at an ice cream shop and bought a quart each of French vanilla and ginger peach. This was courage-comfort food, she told herself by way of rationalization. Her mother always said, "Nothing exceeds like excess," and in such self-indulgent matters, Olympia always took her mother's word.

As she was driving home the sky overhead was darkening into an angry, greenish-grey, and the wind was picking up dramatically. When she pulled into the drive she was grateful to see that Laura and the baby had already arrived. The first few minutes of the visit were consumed with hugs and kisses and exclamations of delight, the quick change of a very smelly diaper and the first clap of thunder.

"I guess we're not going out," said Olympia.

"Not a problem," said Laura.

"Would you like something cool to drink? I make a yummy mix of ginger ale and lemonade. If I run fast, I think I can grab some sprigs of fresh mint before all hell breaks loose outside."

"Go for it, Grandmom." Laura settled baby Erica on the floor with a few plastic containers and lids she'd brought with her. The two cats peered out from under the sofa. Babies were not something they were used to, and curious as they were, it would take a while for them to emerge. Olympia dashed back in, accompanied by a flash of lightning. A deafening crash of thunder caused the cats to vanish completely and Erica to start howling. While Laura comforted her daughter, Olympia switched on some lights. The sky outside was now almost black, and a ferocious wind was tearing at the trees and the shutters while raindrops the size of golf balls slammed against the windows.

Frederick came out of their bedroom and joined them in the sitting room. There was nothing any of them could do but wait it out. By now Erica had been quieted, but her dark blue eyes were wide and her expression wary as she clung to her mother with both hands.

"You both got here just in time," said Frederick. "I had no idea it was going to be this bad."

"Maybe you'd better go get the flashlights, my love. I'll go dig around for some candles and some matches. By the look of this, we may just need them."

Outside the storm was building to a terrifying volume and intensity. The power went off when a simultaneous crack of thunder and streak of lightening screeched through the air and hit something close by. This was followed by the crash and thud of something massive falling on or beside the house. Olympia ran to the kitchen window to see that their magnificent oak had been split in half, and most of it was now blocking the end of the driveway. Miraculously, it had somehow missed the house and their cars. "Thank you, Jesus," she whispered into the din and ran back to light a candle and huddle with the others in the sitting room. Erica's chin began to quiver, and she started wailing into her mother's shoulder.

Laura yelled over the noise, "Is there a cellar under the house, and do you think we should go down there?"

"We have a basement," said Frederick.

"Well, if we hear something that sounds like a train coming toward the house, we'd all better get down there fast. I don't mind telling you, I'm scared." Laura tightened her grip on the baby.

"Me, too," said a grim-faced Olympia.

And then, almost as quickly as it had set upon them, the storm began to ease up. In less than ten minutes they could see a double rainbow through the gaping space left by the broken oak tree.

"What do we do now?" asked Laura.

"You stay here and take care of the baby, and Frederick and I will go out and survey the damage and see if anybody in the neighborhood needs help."

"Make sure you look out for downed wires and dangling branches," said Laura.

"I will, sweetie," said her mother, teary with affection and the awareness that her daughter was genuinely concerned for her safety.

As they went out the door Frederick asked what they might be able to make for supper since they had no power.

"We've got a hibachi and some charcoal, so I suppose we can come up with something, and if we can't, we can always have ice cream for supper and Italian pastries for dessert."

"Works for me," called Laura from the sitting room, "but what are the rest of you going to have?"

That produced a laugh all around as Frederick and Olympia went on their way. The rest of the afternoon was a flurry of activity devoted to storm damage and cleanup. One of Olympia's neighbors had a chain saw and offered to help them clear enough of the branches to be able to make the street passable and use their driveway. Within the hour a power crew was on site, and all that could be heard was the sound of multiple chainsaws, chippers and neighbors shouting to one another over the din. As people do in an emergency, everyone was helping one another. Olympia and Frederick, with the help of their neighbors, hauled and piled logs at the end of the drive and then cleared away the remaining twigs and leaves as best they could. By five that evening the road was passable, the driveway was usable. Olympia and Frederick staggered in and sprawled in the sitting room, dirty, sweaty, smelly and exhausted.

"Why don't you two get cleaned up, and I'll go look for something to put together for supper? It's not like I've never scrounged up a meal out of nothing before."

"I'm not sure I can put one foot in front of the other, never mind climb the stairs," groaned Olympia.

"Oh, come on, love, you can do it." Frederick held out his hand to help her out of the chair.

"You first, Frederick, I need a few more minutes to pant and sweat."

When he'd gone, Olympia turned to her daughter with a wry smile. "So what did you want to talk about, Laura? Something about the new job? When do you start?"

"That is what I wanted to talk to you about. I'm supposed to start September fifteenth. I will need a car there, and I can't afford a new one yet. Mine is pretty dependable, and I'm sure that it can make it. If I was travelling by myself I wouldn't think twice about it, but if I broke down, I don't want to be standing beside the highway with a baby on my hip and my thumb out."

"What are you asking me, honey?"

Laura bit her lip and hesitated. "I'm asking if you'd be willing to drive out there with me?"

"Of course."

"What about the church?"

"I'll be finished up by then, and I'd absolutely love to go with you." Olympia paused, "Umm, what about your mother? Shouldn't you ask her? Maybe she'd want to go with you."

"To be honest, I asked you first because it's you I want to come with me. This might be the only chance we ever have to spend that much time together. If you weren't able to, then I would have asked her."

"Well, the answer is still yes."

The energy that fifteen minutes ago Olympia had sworn she didn't have returned with an ebullient rush. Suddenly she wanted that shower more than anything else in the world — and food. As she started toward the stairs Jim came in through the kitchen door, calling hello to all and sundry and asking if he was in Kansas.

"What the hell are you talking about, Jim?" asked a bewildered Olympia.

"It looks like a tornado hit out here, and I'm Dorothy looking for a green-faced wizard and a yellow brick road."

"It wasn't a tornado, but it damn sure acted like one. I think they call them micro-bursts or something like that. Anyway, it tore up half the trees on this street and didn't even break a branch on the next street over. Other than a good part of the oak that went down and having no power, we're fine, thank God."

"So what are we going to do for supper?" he asked, setting down the paper sack containing the wine.

"Take-out," said Olympia. "There's a menu for Café Eleganza tacked on the wall beside the telephone in the kitchen. Italian. The food's great."

"But I brought French wine," said Jim, feigning great theatrical distress.

"I think we can manage." Olympia turned to her daughter. "Laura, would you get people something to drink? I'll be back in twenty minutes, and Jim ..." Olympia stood behind Laura so she couldn't see her holding a finger to her lips. "We can talk about Monica and Gerry later. That's church stuff, and I've done enough of that for one day, thank you."

Jim nodded a wordless flicker of understanding in her direction and turned back toward the kitchen to get the take-out menu and some glasses.

That evening after Laura had left them, Jim shared the rest of what he had learned about the shadowy past of Jerrold Markham. It was a very troubling picture.

When he was finished Frederick said, "Changing the subject, may we assume you are spending the night, Jim?"

"You may. I've had a tad too much wine to drive, and besides, I want to go and talk to the police. I'm the one who's done the research."

"Do I remember you saying there was something else you wanted to talk about tonight?"

"You do, and I'm not being unduly secretive when I say let's get this mess settled first. My news will wait. I'm not going anywhere, nor do I think you are."

"Only to California in September, but I'll be gone just a week or two at the most."

"Don't forget you're going down the aisle in October," chimed in a beatific Frederick.

"What?" said Jim.

"Kinda looks that way," Olympia confirmed.

"Why, Reverend Doctor Olympia Brown, I never thought I'd see it, but I do believe you're blushing."

September 1, 1862

The heat and humidity have finally broken and there is a definite chill in the evening. With Richard's help, I spent the day hunting and gathering and packing for my stay with Aunt Louisa in Cambridge. Poor Jonathan is quite confused and out of sorts, and Sammy the cat went into hiding at the sight of the first travelling case. I think that time away will be good for me, and with Louisa to help with Jonathan I shall be able to make some progress with my writing. Richard has offered to care for

Sammy and to take us to the train tomorrow morning in his carriage. I am fortunate indeed to have such a trusted friend. He promised to write, and I promised to reply.

More anon, LFW

Twenty-Eight

Before she left for work on Monday morning, Olympia called Detective Steve Vages at the Millbridge Police Department and asked if she could meet with him later that morning.

"Is this about Mrs. Nikitas?" he asked in a low voice.

"Yes, it is, but I don't want to say more until I get there."

After that her plan was to go off to the church as she customarily did on a Monday morning, check in with Franna and take care of whatever else needed her attention. She needed everything to look normal. She was pretty sure Jerrold Markham was checking on her comings and goings from behind the curtains on his office window, and that's just what she wanted him to be doing.

Jerrold Markham was experiencing the titillating thrill of distinct possibility. The chase was definitely on. Olympia had agreed to have lunch with him, then didn't seem to be bothered when he had to put it off for a day and actually insisted they reschedule. And there was Monica to look forward to, as well. No doubt whatsoever that she was interested, but Monica was an arrangement of pleasurable convenience, not an adventure. Jerrold preferred a challenge.

He looked across the street to see if the good Reverend had arrived and was pleased to see that disgrace of a van she insisted on driving pull up in front of the church. Maybe he'd drop over there this afternoon after that obnoxious busybody administrator left for the day. Perhaps he'd go out and buy a yellow rose for Olympia. Roses always worked.

Olympia breezed into the office, greeted Franna, checked her messages and made a few calls. She then announced she was going out for an hour or so and asked if Franna would like her to bring back a sandwich or something for lunch.

Franna shook her head. "That's so nice of you to offer, but I have to leave a little early today, so I won't be here when you get back. Don't worry, though. I'll make up the time."

Olympia made a face. "I do not worry about your hours, nor will I ever. You do the job and then some. We probably owe you time."

Franna flushed with pleasure and turned back to the computer on her desk.

Olympia approached the main desk in the reception area of the station house and stood, waiting to speak. "I have an eleven o'clock appointment with Detective Steve Vages. My name is Reverend Olympia Brown."

The uniformed officer scribbled something on a pad of paper and pushed the button on the intercom. "There's a lady minister out here to see you, Steve. You want me to send her in?" After listening for a moment, he said, "Second door on the left, Ma'am, he's waiting for you."

Olympia thanked him and followed instructions. Vages was already on his feet when she came through the door and directed her to the least scruffy chair in the room.

When they were both seated Olympia got right to the business at hand, but not before Vages asked permission to record the session. With that precaution in place, Olympia began to speak.

"Yolanda Nikitas and the children are home, and Rev. Julia Grafton, the former minister of the church I'm currently serving, is coming here tomorrow. Both women are willing to make a statement and press charges of sexual assault, intimidation and blackmail against Jerrold Markham."

The man looked astonished. "How in the world did you manage to arrange all of that? That's supposed to be our job."

"Believe me, Dectective, I didn't plan it this way. Almost from the time I took the job at All Souls, I've been hearing subtle and not-so-subtle rumblings about something being very wrong in the neighborhood. Then Yolanda actually called me from where she was hiding and told me what happened and why she had to run away. She became involved with Markham, and when it turned sour and she told him she planned to speak out, he threatened harm to her and the children. She was terrified. I took a chance and called Julia Grafton and got pretty much the same story. He starts with very subtle, very persistent advances, then the sad story about how lonely the job is. Finally he gets around to saying he's a man, he has desires, blah-blah-blah, until he gets what he wants. When these two women figured out they each were one of many and separately confronted him, he became abusive and threatening."

Steve shook his head in disgust. "You'd never know it to hear him talk. He really comes on like a conservative pillar of the community. Always advocating family values, pro-life and, of course, almost fanatically anti-gay."

"He did start moralizing about a same sex wedding I'm doing next month, but I wouldn't let him finish the sentence. It hasn't stopped him though."

"What are you saying, Reverend?"

"I have every reason to believe he's marked me as his next conquest, and I'm letting it unfold so that I can be one more live witness to the way he works. So far, his approach has been almost verbatim to what the two women described to me. So help me God, it's like the man has a script."

Vages looked slightly bemused. "You're pretty devious for a woman of the cloth, Reverend."

"Without going into my colorful past, let's just say this isn't the first time I've had a bit part in bringing a stinker to justice."

"I'll have to have more information before I can get a detail onto this. I need to talk to the two women and hear their stories myself. Then I'll take it to the prosecutor and see if we have enough hard information to build a case. You may think you have proof of his wrongdoing, and Dr. Nikitas certainly has reason to want to see this man taken down, but a straying wife or even an errant minister isn't front page news these days."

"You're right. Two people having an affair might be unethical, but it's not illegal. Yolanda's disappearance was front page news when everybody thought she'd been abducted. The fact is, there's more. A priest friend of mine has an inside connection with the Boston Police Department. With their help he's been able to do an extensive internet search into Markham's past and is prepared to give it all to you. It's pretty ugly."

Vages shook his head and whistled.

For the rest of their time together Olympia explained who Father Jim was and what his role had been thus far. In the end they agreed that Jim would come over to the station that afternoon and provide Steve with all the evidence and documentation he had thus far. Then he could decide when the two women would come and make their formal statements.

"You've thought of just about everything, haven't you, Reverend?"

"No, Steve, I've told you what I've heard firsthand from two victims who were afraid to come forward. I've added to that what I am experiencing. Now I'm coming to you, as the expert and an officer of the law, and asking you to put this rat out of our misery and permanently out of action."

"Well said, Reverend. I've got a wife, a mother and two daughters. Men like Markham make my skin crawl. I'll do everything I can."

When Olympia got back to the church office, she called Jim and asked him to call Officer Vages and set up a time to show him everything he'd turned up through his Boston connection. She was just finishing up the salad she'd picked up for lunch and wondering if there were any leftovers from coffee hour when she heard the church door opening and footsteps approaching the office. Twenty seconds later Jerrold Markham was standing in the doorway. He was holding a single yellow rose.

Olympia was unpleasantly startled. She'd forgotten to lock the door behind her. This was going to be tricky. She literally had to keep him at arm's length while at the same time not endangering their going to lunch later in the week. She decided to try a light approach.

"Not another rose!" She clapped the back of her hand to her forehead.

He looked crestfallen. "You don't like roses? I saw this one in the florist's window, and it's so perfect and beautiful I just had to get it for someone who would appreciate it. I couldn't think of anyone else. I guess I was wrong." He stood there, holding the rose and pouting.

Olympia laughed, perhaps just a little too heartily. "Wrong, wrong, wrong, my friend. Pull up a chair. I love roses, and I'm very touched that you thought of me. You just don't know the back-story." Once he was seated she told him at great length and in minute detail the saga of the rose ladies. He listened dutifully, but it was clear he was not really interested.

When she finished and was about to launch into another story, he interrupted her, saying he really wanted to give her the rose as a thank you, because he was so grateful to have a kindred spirit he could trust just across the street. Then, toying with the ribbons on the rose, he began to tell her how lonely he was, how hard it was to find a woman he could trust, and how he hoped they would be friends for a long time to come.

Olympia assured him that good friends and trusted colleagues were rare treasures, and she was pleased and honored that he thought of her in this way. Then she looked at her watch and gasped.

"Oh, good grief, I was supposed to be home by now. I've got dinner guests, and I need to prepare. I guess I lost track of time."

Jerrold stood his ground and held out the rose. "You will accept it, won't you?"

When she reached for it Markham took her hand in his and held it. "You are such a good person. Can I have a hug before you leave? It would mean so much to me."

Olympia slipped her hand out of his and stepped back. "Let me think about that, Reverend Markham. I promise I'll give you an answer on Thursday."

When Jim returned to Olympia's house that evening, he was still wearing his black shirt and clerical collar. Olympia had suggested he wear it when he went to the police station to add credibility to what he had to say. He told her and Frederick that Vages said that once he had the sworn statements of Yolanda and Julia, there would be more than sufficient evidence to put out a warrant for the arrest of Markham; but now that he knew there was more, he was determined to get it all before taking action. He said if they moved too quickly, Jerrold Markham, alias-alias-alias, could bolt before they had enough evidence to keep him in custody.

It was clear that the man had a long history of starting churches and then walking away, leaving a lot of unanswered questions, broken hearts and empty bank accounts. The records showed that if anyone did try and press charges, there never seemed to be sufficient evidence to bring the man to trial. Then Markham, or whatever his real name is, would lie low for a little while, then relocate and open up another church. Until now nobody had ever put the pieces together and tracked him down.

"Kudos to you, Olympia."

"Actually, Jim, to both of us. That man is a viper."

"And he's just as poisonous," said Jim.

"What now?" asked Frederick.

"Vages is going to try and contact some of those other churches and see if anyone is willing to come forward now that we have the makings of a real case here."

"Then what?"

"Not so much then as when. They need a little more time to gather evidence before they move in on him. Markham is very smart. He's been in operation this long because he knows how not to get caught. We all know most sexual crimes go unreported due to shame, intimidation or the fear of humiliation and disgrace. That's one of the reasons he's never been brought to justice," Jim finished up.

"So how much time are we talking about here?" asked Olympia.

"Vages couldn't say — a couple of days, possibly a week. The really troubling thing, not that sexual assault isn't bad enough, is the whole issue of women connected to this who are gone. One is a questionable suicide, and the other simply vanished without a trace. That second case is still open. In the case of the suicide the husband of the woman who died insisted she died by her own hand, even though the victim's brother and sister begged him to investigate it further. Unless he was willing to ask for further investigation, there was nothing further the police could do."

"So it would seem that if some of these allegations can be proved, Pastor Markham could permanently be taken out of action," Olympia concluded.

"That's the goal. That's why it's so very important that we continue as if we suspect nothing and keep it going until Vages is ready to move."

"We, meaning me," said Olympia. "Right now, I'm the only one who's having any direct contact with him."

"Don't forget Monica," said Jim.

"I suppose she can keep him interested and buy us some time, as well."

"As long as she can remain electronic, we can. That may begin to prove more difficult, but I'll do what I can," Jim promised.

"So my job is to act natural, stay out in the open and keep him interested until otherwise directed."

"Right on all counts, Olympia."

Twenty-Nine

On Tuesday Jim headed back to Boston, saying he had some legal business to attend to as well as to prepare for his Wednesday encounter with Gerry Marks. Olympia stayed at home in Brookfield while Frederick went off to collect Julia Grafton from Logan airport. When they returned, Olympia settled Julia into her room, and Frederick set bread and sandwich makings on the kitchen counter and started a fresh pot of coffee. As Julia and Olympia came back downstairs, Miss Winslow's clock chimed impatiently from its spot on the mantel.

"Don't worry, Miss Winslow, I'll introduce you," said Olympia. In response to Julia's puzzled look she added, "I do believe I mentioned our house-ghost, did I not?"

After lunch Frederick discreetly went out to work in the garden so the two women could be alone. Julia was an attractive and engaging woman. Olympia guessed she was probably in her late forties and therefore a few years younger than herself. She had shoulder-length brown hair, chemically enhanced with a shower of golden streaks. The effect was very pleasing and complemented her oval face and warm coloring. She was wearing light cotton slacks and a matching blouse, good for looking nice and staying cool while travelling.

Because she had given herself the day off, Olympia was wearing a pair of old jeans that she'd sheared off at the knees, sandals and an oversized tee-shirt with the words Ladies Sewing Circle and Terrorist Society blazoned across the chest. The absurdity of the message served to break the ice without being obvious. Olympia knew not to rush or pressure the woman and instead let her direct the conversation.

They talked about the weather, laughed and gossiped about the rose ladies and eventually got around to the man across the street. By mid-afternoon Julia had repeated the story of her involvement with Markham and affirmed that she was still willing go to the police. There was one problem, and it was a big one. Julia was concerned for her former church. She wanted to meet with a few key members of the board and tell them what had happened.

This last condition turned out to be a curve ball Olympia hadn't expected, but when she thought about it, she knew it would be the only ethical way that Julia could go forward.

It all depends on the timing, she thought. Doesn't everything?

By way of transition Olympia offered to give Julia a historical tour of the house and introduce her to Miss Winslow. Then she suggested that Julia might want to go upstairs and have a little rest or perhaps go out and explore the neighborhood. Olympia needed to speak with Dr. and Mrs. Nikitas in private. Julia opted for the walk, saying she was tired and would undoubtedly want to nap later, but she was too full of nervous energy and needed to walk some of it off.

Olympia poured herself a tall glass of cold water and carried it to her desk in the bedroom, sat down and dialed Yolanda's cell phone number. She was feeling the strain of the awful responsibility of it all, but at this juncture there was no way out but through. Yolanda answered the phone and agreed to come over with Nick in an hour. Before she hung up, Olympia asked Yolanda how she was feeling.

"Bruised, raw, exhausted and never more grateful for what I have and almost lost."

"How's Nick doing?"

"Much the same, but we're going to make it. I don't mind telling you I'll be glad when I can go out. It is so weird, hiding out in my own house. But never mind, it'll be over soon. We'll see you in an hour … and thank you for everything."

"Do you know how to get here?"

"My aunt used to live in Brookfield. Just give me the street and number, and I'll be able to find it."

"Yolanda, I have to tell you that Julia Grafton is here. She's agreed to press charges, as well. If you aren't ready to see her yet, I don't mind coming over there."

"Thank you for asking, but I'm more than ready to meet her. We've both been injured by the same despicable man. We'll make a stronger case together than separately. Besides, she was my minister. I trust her."

At the end of the meeting with Nick and Yolanda, Olympia felt as if she had no bones left in her body. Nick had been adamant that they go to the police as soon as possible and get everyone on board. Olympia agreed, and then with Nick and Yolanda's permission, she asked Julia to come in from the back yard to join them. It was a little awkward at first, but curiously enough Nick was the one who put everyone at ease. Once he met Julia his outrage at Markham's vile deceptions instantly expanded to include both wronged women. Olympia hoped he would be able to contain himself and not go off on his own. This was a highly charged situation, and Nick was an emotional man. She knew the combination could be explosive.

Before inviting Frederick to come in, she explained who he was and what his connection to all of this would be in the days to come.

When all that could be said so far had been said, and everyone was holding a glass of wine or a cup of tea, Frederick proposed a toast. He held up his tea mug, cleared his throat and said, "To brave women and to the men who love them enough to see this through."

As the five of them raised their glasses the ring of the doorbell coincided with a double chime from the clock on the mantel.

Olympia set down her glass and started toward the door. "It's the pizza man. Frederick, will you get some paper plates and napkins? I think we'll just eat right here in the sitting room."

Later, when Nick and Yolanda had gone home and Julia was upstairs in her room, Frederick and Olympia went into the kitchen. Frederick was clearing things up, the cats were picking the cheese bits off the pizza boxes, and Olympia was sitting at the table with her chin on her hands, staring into space.

"A penny for your thoughts, my love."

"I'm too tired to think, Frederick. I'm brain-dead. Olympia felt herself on the verge of tears.

"Go to bed, darling. It will all look better in the morning."

She bit her lip and shook her head. "I'm not so sure about that, but then I'm not very sure about anything right now. You're right. I need to go to bed."

On Wednesday afternoon, Gerry Marks was drumming his fingers on a white plastic table in the back left corner of the food court at the South Shore Plaza. He was wearing sunglasses, a Canadian Tilley hat and a light cotton sweater casually tossed over his shoulders and looped in the front. There was a single yellow rose tied with a ribbon on the table in front of him.

To the casual observer he was the picture of a healthy, well-groomed outdoor adventurer of indeterminate age. Closer inspection would reveal the deepening lines around his mouth, and skin that was beginning to sag under his jaw. The sweater was carefully arranged to distract the eye from any aging imperfection. He had a well-used backpack, one with lots of buckles and zippers and just the right amount of wear on the corners, positioned on the floor beside him. It was clear that he was waiting for someone. He kept checking his watch and then looking toward the nearest entrance. After better than a half hour of this, he reached into his back pocket, pulled out a phone and tapped out a text message. More waiting and staring at the phone in his hand, and then the sound of a text alert.

"Wicked srry, husbd home early. Wil e-mail t-nite."

A deflated Gerry Marks texted back, "Ok, still wnt 2 mt u real soon! U wont b sorry."

After that he put the phone back in his pocket, hiked his backpack over his shoulder and looked around one last time. He wondered if she might possibly be somewhere nearby, checking him out. He'd done that himself. No luck. There was nothing other than what he expected to find at lunchtime in a shopping mall. He saw mothers pushing tired babies in strollers, older couples sharing a fast food lunch and stuffing the extra salt and sugar packets in their pockets, and a priest coming out of one of the bookstores, talking on his cell phone. What was a priest doing here in the middle of the day? On the other hand, why not?

Gerry stood, picked up the rose, snapped it in half and tossed it into the nearest trash basket.

With his cell phone pressed tightly against his ear and his arm partially blocking his face, Jim passed close to where Marks was standing. As he did, he angled the phone out slightly and snapped one more picture. After that he went directly to his car and drove straight to Brookfield, where he would download and print the pictures that would confirm what he and Olympia already suspected.

Thirty

On Thursday morning Jim Sawicki and Frederick drove Yolanda and Nick Nikitas, along with Julia Grafton, to the Millbridge police station where Detective Steve Vages would take their statements. Because it was important that the women not be seen, Steve suggested they slip in through a rear entrance where he would meet them with the necessary paperwork. He explained that once the interviews and the paperwork were completed, he could proceed with getting a warrant for Markham's arrest.

When they'd returned from the police station and dropped off the two women, Jim and Frederick drove to Olympia's church. If asked, they would say they were planning to get married and wanted to check out the building. Since no one knew them by sight, it was a perfectly reasonable explanation of why they were there. Olympia chuckled at the thought of it. Despite the gravity of the situation, it was funny as hell; and when it all was done and dusted, as Frederick was wont to say, it would be a story they would tell for years to come.

Meanwhile, just act normal. Olympia kept repeating these words to herself like a mantra all the way to the church.

Everything was falling into place, and it was now Olympia's job to keep Markham interested until he, too, was in place. She was seriously conflicted. She hated lying and subterfuge, but she also hated what Markham and those like him did to people who trusted them, the women he would cruelly exploit, knowing they would be too shamed or afraid to speak out. It was the ultimate abuse of power. She also knew she was playing a very dangerous game.

She pulled into her reserved spot in front of the church, set the hand brake and headed for the side door. Franna wasn't in on Thursdays, so Olympia was making coffee for one instead of two when she heard the phone ringing. She made a dash for it and wished she hadn't. It was Jerrold Markham, confirming their lunch and asking if they could make it a little later. Her heart sank, and she took a deep breath. Just act normal, she told herself for the thousandth time.

"Not really, Jerrold. I, uh, have a couple coming in this morning. They want to look at the church for their wedding. I promised to meet with them later this afternoon, so I have to be back by three-thirty. If we are going to have that extra time we talked about, we have to stick with plan A and leave here by half past twelve."

"That's okay. I was just hoping we could maybe make an afternoon of it." He sounded disappointed.

"Ask me another time, Jerrold."

"I'll hold you to it, Olympia, and don't forget that hug you promised me."

She forced a chuckle that sound more like she was choking. "I promised to give you an answer, and an answer is what you will get. I'll see you later."

At quarter after twelve Markham called back to ask if she was ready to go.

"I will be in fifteen minutes like we planned. Why do you ask?"

"It's just that I notice there's a car I don't recognize parked behind yours. I wondered if you were busy."

"It's the couple I told you that wanted to look at the church for their wedding."

"But I saw two men get out of it."

"That's right, Jerrold, it is two men, and I will be doing their wedding. If I didn't know better, I'd say you were spying on me."

"You know what I think about gays and gay marriage. I just happened to be looking out the window when they drove up."

Now is not the time to get into an argument, thought Olympia. "You don't have to think about it, I'm the one who will be doing the ceremony. If we are going to be friendly colleagues, I'm afraid there will some things we'll just have to agree to disagree about."

"You're right, Olympia. Let's not disagree. I'm really looking forward to our lunch. I'll pick you up in ten minutes."

Olympia had not considered the possibility of him driving. That was not in the plan. "I thought I'd drive. You've never been in my aging hippie-mobile. It's an adventure."

"I want to drive, Olympia. Call it a man thing, but I'm just not used to having women drive when I'm in the car."

Call it a control thing, she amended privately, and the thought made her uneasy. Just act normal.

"Okay for this time, but I drive the next time."

"We'll see."

When she hung up the phone, she went and found Jim and Frederick in the sanctuary. She hastily told them of the change in plans and asked that they follow Jerrold's black and silver BMW at a discreet distance.

"I'm not feeling good about this, Olympia," said Frederick.

Olympia brightened. "Hey, I've got a better idea. Why don't you leave right now and go directly to the Taverna and wait for us there? I printed out the directions for myself. Here, you can have them. He knows how to get there." She held out a sheet of paper. "I'll ask him to stop somewhere and stall for time so you can get there and find a table before we arrive."

Frederick was looking worried.

"Frederick, its broad daylight, we all know where I'm going, and you've got Jim with you. It's as if I've got two bodyguards. I'll be fine."

Frederick still looked worried.

Olympia went back to her office to collect her purse and a light sweater. Even though it was summer, air conditioned buildings could be freezing, and she remembered being chilly the last time they'd been there. She waited inside the church until Jim and Frederick drove off, then stepped outside and locked the door.

Markham's spotless BMW was waiting at the curb. She slipped in, greeted Jerrold, adjusted the seatbelt and settled into the ergonomic comfort of the elegant vehicle. Along with the rugged scent of leather and the rest of the expensive car's interior, she could detect a splash of aftershave overlaid with lingering tones of peppermint mouthwash.

Act normal.

After a few minutes on the road, Olympia looked puzzled and asked, "Isn't the Taverna in the opposite direction?"

"Right in one," said Jerrold. "I'm taking you someplace special."

"Where?"

"If I told you, then it wouldn't be a surprise, would it?"

Act normal.

"But I was looking forward to going back to the Greek place. The food is terrific, and I'm starving."

It didn't work. Jerrold smiled in her direction. "You'll get plenty to eat, you greedy girl, and still get back by half past three. I promise."

Olympia was at a total loss as to what to do next. Jim and Frederick would likely panic and tell Steve Vages to call out the militia, but they didn't know what Jerrold's car looked like or where they were going.

Damn damn damn!

On the other hand, if he got her back to the church when he said he would, there really wasn't time for anything to happen. Okay, she told herself, back to plan A, only without Jim and Frederick within shouting distance. It wasn't the worst thing. They were going to a restaurant. There would be people there.

"You look thoughtful, something on your mind?"

"Huh? Oh, nothing, just wondering if I'll be able to find something vegetarian at this place."

"Do you think I'd forget that, Olympia? I called ahead and made sure of it. Now sit back and relax, and let me surprise you. I've been looking forward to this."

Damn damn damn, and act normal.

When Olympia hadn't arrived at the Taverna within twenty minutes, Jim and Frederick each tried to conceal his growing concern from the other. After thirty minutes they called Steve Vages, who told them to get over to the station ASAP.

Olympia tapped Markham on the arm. "Do you mind pulling into a gas station? I need to use the ladies room."

"Hold on, we're almost there. This place will have a much nicer one, I promise you."

Within five minutes Jerrold signaled for a left, pulled into the parking lot of The Barker Tavern and handed the keys to the parking valet. It was a genuine stage coach tavern more than two hundred years old that reminded Olympia of her own antique home. Unlike her work-in-progress, this structure had been beautifully restored and graciously appointed. Markham had indeed pulled out all the stops.

They were quietly escorted to a table with a reserved sign and a single yellow rose perfectly positioned on the white linen table cloth. Olympia looked at the flower and winced. In the dim interior she could see other diners seated at tables arranged in such a way that people could converse without being overheard. Underneath the sweater draped over her arm, she adjusted her watch so she could see it without Markham noticing.

It's a little after one now and he promised to have me back by three-thirty, she thought. That's two and a half hours. Act normal.

Olympia sat in the chair that was held out for her and looked around. "I've never been here before, although I've certainly heard of it. The food is supposed to be outstanding."

"The ladies room is in the back corner beyond the bar, if you still need it," said Markham.

"I hadn't forgotten. I was just too busy being impressed. Thanks, I'll be right back."

"Shall I order you something to drink?"

"Just coffee, thanks. I have to meet my grooms when I get back."

Olympia caught his look of distaste as she stood and walked away from the table. Once inside the ladies room, she pulled out her cell phone and rapidly dialed Jim's number. "Where are you?" he shouted into her ear.

"I'm fine. I'm at the Barker Tavern in Blackwater, which is about fifteen miles east of Millbridge. There are loads of people here, and he's way too intent on impressing me to try anything. He's promised to get me back to the church by three-thirty. Are you still at the Taverna?"

"No, Olympia, we're at the Millbridge Police station. Just keep him there. We'll get there as soon as we can."

"Don't you dare," hissed Olympia. She was afraid to yell for fear of being overheard. "Everything is going beautifully. He has no idea I'm onto him, and he's playing it for all it's worth. So far he's following the same script he used for Yolanda and Julia. I recognize it. We've got time—days, weeks even. This is only act one, scene two."

"I don't like the idea of you being alone with him."

"I'm not. We are surrounded by other diners. If you're that concerned, come wait in the parking lot and follow us back to the church. I'm really not worried, and for God's sake don't bring the police. The last thing we need right now is to have them make a move before we have a solid case."

She could hear Jim relaxing. "You've got a point, but I'll check with Vages. Either way, Frederick and I will get over there and follow you home. We should be there within the hour."

Thirty-One

When Olympia returned to the table there was a steaming cup of coffee waiting for her. She held the cup almost to her lips, inhaled the rich steamy aroma and favored Markham with a beatific smile. She loved the smell of freshly brewed coffee. He leaned closer and returned the smile.

"I never did acquire a taste for coffee. Not even decaf. Maybe it's the caffeine. Take your time and enjoy it. There's no rush."

Olympia tasted the coffee. It was stronger than what she was used to, but it was delicious. A waiter appeared at her elbow with the menus, and a second waiter placed a basket of hot rolls and a plate of fresh butter on the table between them. More delicious smells. Olympia opened the menu and took another sip of her coffee.

"So what made you decide to become a minister?" Markham was smiling at her.

"It's a long story, but not for today. Another time perhaps."

"Then maybe we should look at the menu."

Olympia sipped and nodded. She was feeling warm and happy and ready for that wonderful food Jerrold had promised her. Oh, yes, menu ... look at the menu. Why are the words blurry? Olympia was having trouble reading the words before her. Glasses, must be my glasses ... must clean ... my ... glasses.

"Olympia, are you feeling all right?"

Jerrold's voice slipped through an unfamiliar mist.

"Feeling a little, um ... soft."

Jerrold hastily summoned a waiter.

"I'm terribly sorry. My wife seems to be feeling faint. We need to leave. Can you please notify the parking valet and help me get her out to the car?"

Jerrold and the waiter stood on either side of Olympia and gently pulled her to her feet.

"Purse?" She said dreamily.

In one motion Jerrold slipped the waiter a twenty dollar bill and picked up Olympia's handbag, and together they started toward the door.

"Don't try and talk, dear. You just need some fresh air. Walking will help. We'll open the windows once we're in the car. Steady now."

Jerrold thanked the valet, handed him a five and waved him off. Then, after buckling a completely unresisting Olympia into her seat, he lifted her left hand to his lips and traced a wet circle on her upturned palm with his tongue.

"Where we going?" She licked her lips. Her speech was slurred.

"I'm afraid you are going to be late for your meeting with those disgusting queers, my dear sweet pudgy Reverend. I'm going to take you to a nice little motel, take off your clothes and screw your brains out. Won't that be nice? Tell me that's just what you want."

Olympia's head lolled to the side. Her tongue felt thick and uncooperative.

"I said, tell me that's what you want."

"Thas jus whad I wan."

"Now say thank you."

"Thanyou."

"That's a good girl," said Jerrold Markham.

Vages was hesitant to let Frederick and Jim go on their own, but when they repeated what Olympia had said and promised to call in if they felt she was in any kind of danger, he reluctantly agreed. Then he printed out the driving directions to the restaurant and told them to take every reasonable precaution. With Frederick calling out the directions, Jim wasted no time and made it to the tavern in just over thirty-five minutes without incurring a speeding ticket. There was no black and Silver BMW in the parking lot. Jim looped around the back just in case but came up empty.

This was not looking good.

Jim pulled crosswise into a space, and the two men flew out of the Toyota and ran into the restaurant. The elegant maître d' who had so recently assisted Markham and Olympia greeted them and asked if they had a reservation.

Jim shook his head and held up his hand. "No, thanks. We're looking for someone. Did a man and a woman come in here within the last hour? The man is tall and rugged looking. The woman is medium height with short salt-and-pepper hair and big glasses."

The maître d' nodded. "They were here, but they've just left. The poor man's wife was taken ill. I helped him take her to the car."

Frederick gasped and caught the man by the arm. "Did you see which way they went?"

"I try not to interfere with people's private lives. She was probably overcome with the heat or," he dropped his voice, "you know, women's problems."

"I think not," said Frederick, "but thank you very much."

Jim was already outside in the parking lot, calling Steve Vages.

"We just missed them, Steve. The waiter told us they'd been there, but they left because Olympia was taken ill. They had to help her get to the car. I don't like the sound of that."

Vages responded. "Look, Jim. We've got some pretty sophisticated tracking and surveillance devices these days. We know she's got her cell phone with her. As long as it's turned on, we can locate her. What's the number?"

"Jim recited the number and asked, "But what if it isn't turned on?"

"We're putting out an APB to every town in a two-hundred-mile radius with the description of the car and the license plate, black and silver late model BMW, license plate BMW-X13."

"When did you get all that?"

"About an hour after you left the station on Tuesday. You and your reverend friend tied up a whole lot of loose ends that led me right where I needed to go. We were waiting for this last piece of evidence. Now I can get a warrant out for his arrest. We just have to find him. From what you say he hasn't had time to get very far."

"So what should we do? I can't just sit here. I'll go nuts." Jim was pacing back and forth in the tavern parking lot.

"Go back in and ask the manager where the nearest motels are. You start there. We're on our way. If you should spot the car, call us at once, and stay put. Do not, under any conditions, try and confront him by yourselves."

"What about Olympia?"

"This is really tricky. I think she'll be all right if we don't spook him. Leave it to the professionals, Jim. I mean it. Otherwise she could be in even more danger than she is right now."

"I didn't want to hear that."

"I didn't want to say it," said Steve.

"What should I tell Frederick?"

"Tell him we're going to find her."

After registering as Mr. and Mrs. John Milton and asking for a room in the back, away from the main road, Markham drove around the grey stucco Family Value Motel and parked in the shade. Olympia followed him into the freshly disinfected room and sat like a china doll on the edge of the double bed. Her eyes were unfocused as she picked at the pink chenille tufts on the faded coverlet. Markham locked the door, slipped the safety chain into the slot, turned the cheap noisy air conditioner up to high and walked slowly toward her.

"Well, then, my clever little Reverend, what shall we do first?"

Detective Steve Vages wasted no time.

"Searching for a serial rapist in a black and silver BMW, license plate BMW-X13. He has a potential victim in the car with him. The two left the Barker Tavern in Blackwater within the hour. The man is dangerous and may or may not be armed. Use every caution, but find them and bring him in unharmed, if possible.

Jim and Frederick raced off in the direction indicated to them by the man in the restaurant. Blackwater, with its ponds and rivers, was a summer tourist attraction and had a number of restaurants, hotels, B&Bs and motels to accommodate them.

"Do we stop at every one of them, or do we decide which ones Markham might use?"

"I think we can rule out the B&Bs. Too family oriented, owners on site, usually in-home operations."

Jim was trying to drive safely, look in all directions and keep Frederick and himself from imagining the worst. Giving in to their fear would help no one.

"I suggest we start with the motels. They're the most anonymous, and they take cash," said Jim.

Frederick pointed ahead. "On the right, the Family Value Motel. Think we should start there?"

Jim shook his head. "Too seedy. Markham drives a BMW. Do you really think he'd hole up in a fleabag operation like that? I think we should start with something a little more upscale."

Special Officer Karen Connors held up her hand. "I'm getting a weak signal off the cell phone. They're still in Blackwater."

"Get on it, and pray the battery doesn't die," said Vages.

After putting his palm-sized video camera in place and clicking it on, Jerrold Markham pulled the plastic arm chair over to the bed and sat facing Olympia. His breath was quickening. "Now then, my lovely little captive, let's get those shoes off. I like working from the bottom up."

Olympia lay back on the bed and offered no resistance as Jerrold methodically removed one shoe and then the other. Then he began massaging and kissing her feet. He had a window of about three hours if he'd got the dosages right. That part was always a little tricky, because he didn't like them to come around too soon. Still, they never really remembered what had happened until he showed them the video. That's the part that kept them quiet and allowed him to enjoy it again and again, long after the chase was over.

Jim and Frederick had checked out five of the eight motels in Blackwater. They tried using Gerry Marks and all of the other aliases Jim could remember from the internet search, but they were striking out, and precious minutes were passing.

Jim pulled into a driveway and reversed direction. "That last one was the end of the line here. There are two more places on the main road. If they're not there, then we go back to that first one, but I can't believe he'd spend even two minutes in a place like that."

"Maybe they're not in a motel. Maybe he has a house rental or something we haven't thought of." Frederick's voice was tight and high pitched with fear.

Jim gripped the steering wheel and drove on. "Hold on, my friend, the police have state-of-the-art tracking equipment. Everybody's on it."

"We've lost the signal, Steve."

"She's somewhere in or near Blackstone. Keep checking the GPS, and keep driving. Signals can fade and then come back. Don't give up on it."

Olympia Brown was totally relaxed and feeling perfectly wonderful. The man who had started by kissing her feet was now starting to unbutton her blouse. She tried to help him, but her fingers weren't working very well. No matter, he was getting there.

"There's the car." Steve cut the motor and coasted to a silent stop a few spaces away from Markham's BMW.

"How do you know which room they're in?" said Special Officer Karen Connors.

"I don't. He parked away from the building, so I have no idea. Go check at the desk. Get heavy if you have to."

"Then what?"

"How are we going to go in?"

"I'll know when you get back."

She returned in less than a minute.

"Mr. and Mrs. John Milton are in room 114. What's the plan?"

Vages held up his hand. "Hang onto the gun. We don't know where inside the room they are. The walls are thin. If we fire at random, we could hit one or both of them. I'm going to shock and scare the bejeezus out of them. I'll break in the door with the car and then hit the brakes. You get out and wait till I'm through, and then you come in after me with the heat.

Jim had just pulled up outside the office of the Family Value Motel when they heard the crash. "Bloody hell," said Frederick.

Leaving the car where it was, Jim and Frederick followed the uniformed desk clerk around to the back of the building. They all watched as Detective Inspector Steve Vages jumped out of the crumpled car and with his assistant ran screaming, "Police, don't move!" through the dusty, ragged hole.

"What the hell's going on?" screamed the desk clerk. She had a plastic name tag pinned on her shirt pocket printed with the name Midori.

Jim caught her by the arm. "They're making an arrest, keep back. They might shoot."

"Holy shit," said Midori Herlihy.

"That's one way of putting it," said Jim. "You stay here."

As Jim and Frederick ran toward the broken door, they could hear the sirens of back-up vehicles approaching the scene. By the time they got there Markham was already in handcuffs and glowering as he listened to Steve Vages reciting the Miranda warning. Officer Connors was buttoning up Olympia's blouse and trying to keep her from struggling to get up and walk.

"Olympia!" yelled Frederick and Jim.

"She's okay," said Steve. "She's been drugged, but it should wear off pretty soon. She won't remember squat. We got here in time."

Thirty-Two

It was almost a month since Markham had been taken into custody, and there were only a couple of weeks left in Olympia's church contract. Despite the late summer heat Frederick was drinking his customary cup of tea, and she had an oversized mug of black coffee on the table in front of her.

"Any more news on the Markham mess?" asked Frederick.

"Actually there is. Steve Vages caught me in the office this morning before I left. It seems that several of the congregations that were misused and abused by Mr. Markham claim they have victims who are now willing to come forward. If even half of what is suspected and alleged can be proved, then he'll be out of action for good. And now that he's named a murder suspect, they're holding him without bail." Olympia shivered and shook her head. "I guess I got lucky."

Frederick reached for her hand. "I'm not prone to violence, Olympia, you know that, but given half a chance I'd have gladly beaten that man to smithereens."

"You landed one damn good one. From what I hear, you smashed his perfectly proportioned nose all over his perfectly tanned face."

"I'm surprised Vages didn't try and stop me."

"Steve assures me that he never saw a thing. He thinks Markham must have been so startled by the car coming through the wall that he jumped up and fell against the dresser."

"Is that right?" said Frederick with a sly grin.

Olympia pulled the most recent list out of her pocket and set it on the table between them. "So on the schedule we have, I drive to California with Laura in early September, my son Malcolm's wedding is later in September, and you and I pick a date for our own wedding in early October."

"Yes to all of the above," said Frederick. He took a sip of his tea and added, "I wonder what the big news is that Jim has for us."

"Probably something about his priesthood. I know he's talking with the Episcopalians."

"From what I understand they're a lot more inclusive over here then they are in England."

"I've always gotten along well with the ones I know." Olympia stuck her finger in her coffee and wiped it on a napkin. It needed a shot in the microwave.

"Anything more from Julia Grafton? You said the church asked if she would consider returning to their pulpit."

"That one was a bit more delicate. Her response was one of deep gratitude, but in the end she said no. She said she felt that after all that had happened, she needed to move on. If she stayed there, the shadows would always be present to her and to them."

"I can understand that," said Frederick."

"I needed to help them get to a place of understanding, but eventually they got there. What they finally said was that when she decided to look for a new church, they would give her a five-star recommendation."

Frederick smiled over his tea cup. "That's wonderful. What about Yolanda and Nick? Have they come back into the fold yet?"

"They're in counseling. They came back with the kids last Sunday. They sat together and even came back for the coffee hour. The rest of the congregation was wonderful. Didn't make a fuss, but I saw lots of little hugs and gestures of welcome. It was really touching. This is a wonderful church. I'm going to miss it come September."

"Speaking of churches, what about those poor people in Markham's congregation? They must be in a state."

"They were wounded and humiliated, and after the initial shock wore off, they were outraged. But you know what? The interfaith clergy group stepped right in to care for them. We offered counseling, and we're taking turns with the Sunday services. What a group. I meant it when I said I'm going to miss that place."

"That's wonderful—and getting back to the future, do you have your travel dates set with Laura?"

Olympia nodded. "We're leaving right after the first weekend in September. Without rushing, it'll take us about ten days. I'll fly back as soon as I'm sure she's settled. I'll be back in plenty of time for Malcolm's wedding. I am doing the ceremony, but other than that, all we have to do is host the rehearsal dinner for them."

Frederick looked alarmed. "How do we do that? What's expected?"

"Not a damn thing, my love. I got a head count from the kids and made reservations for twenty at Café Eleganza. They have a private function room, and the food is great. You can propose a toast."

"I can do that. So what about October?"

"Let's wait until Jim gets here to talk about that."

Detective Inspector Steve Vages put down the phone and pressed the intercom. "Hey, Karen, can you step in here for a few minutes? I just got a call from State Police in Georgia. They've located the body of the missing woman in one of the Markham cases. She'd been dismembered and buried in pieces behind a house where he lived."

Special Officer Karen Connors came into the room and took the nearest chair. "When we're through with him they'll likely want to put him on trial down there, as well."

Vages nodded in agreement. "No doubt about it. That guy was some operator. I can't believe no one came forward until now."

"I can, Steve. I work with rape and assault victims. That's my job. These women are shamed and terrified. That's what the perps usually count on and why they get away with so much for so long. You know, they found child porn on his computer, as well as the videos of all the women he victimized. What a sicko."

"Well, this sorry SOB is out of operation. With the evidence we've got, he's not going to see the light of day for years to come, if ever. What a creep."

"Worse than a creep, Steve, but if it's any comfort, the treatment he's going to get once he's in jail is not going to be pretty. You know what they do to abusers."

Vages nodded and smiled. "That does make me feel better, and Georgia still has a death penalty. One can always hope."

"Better not tell that to the good Reverend," said Karen.

"The law is the law, but you're right. She'll find out soon enough. We don't have to say anything."

"She's a piece of work," said Karen.

"You got that right."

Jim arrived in Brookfield shortly after four in the afternoon. When Olympia offered him a glass of her enhanced lemonade, he declined, saying that he was in a celebratory mood and inviting them to dinner.

"I know of a great Thai place," said Olympia.

Jim wrinkled his nose and shook his head. "Far too pedestrian, my dear. There's a place I've been dying to try. It's called Elderberry Wine. Five stars, the whole works, and loads of vegetarian selections. It's about a half-hour from here. I made reservations for six-thirty."

"So what are we going to do until then?" asked Frederick.

"I wouldn't say no to a cup of your English penicillin, dear boy."

When Frederick came back with Jim's tea, Olympia asked him if he was going to keep them on tenterhooks until they got to the restaurant, or was he going tell them his good news?

Jim held up his tea cup in a mock toast. "I just learned that I've been accepted as a candidate for priesthood in the Episcopal Church. I'll be able to be who I am and do what I'm called to do and still be Father Jim."

"Oh, Jim," said Olympia.

Jim could only smile and sniff and nod through his tears.

"Then you can marry us," said Frederick.

"And be the best man too," added Olympia.

Jim smiled and sniffed and nodded for a second time and then took a sip of his tea.

Later that evening, when Jim had gone to bed upstairs and Frederick and Olympia were clearing up, Frederick stopped her in the kitchen, saying he had something to ask her."

"I already said yes," said Olympia.

"I only ask women to marry me once. This is something completely different."

Olympia waited.

"With your permission, I'd like to buy your daughter a new car."

"What!"

"When my mother died I came into a little money. I had no particular use for it at the time, so I just put it away for a day when I might need it. I can't think of a better use for it. She can get something sturdy and practical and good looking for a young woman on the way up. What do you think?"

"I think you are the goodest man in creation."

"Goodest is not a word, Olympia."

She held out her arms and invited him in. "Shut up, Frederick. If I weren't so grateful for who and what you are, I'd probably smack you upside the head."

Later on, they'd tell Jim they could have sworn they heard Miss Winslow laughing in the next room.

September 7, 1862
Cambridge, Massachusetts

The days are warm, the nights are cool, and the leaves are just beginning to turn from green to gold. I am here in Cambridge with Aunt Louisa and writing for hours at a time. I find it curious that the more I write, the more I feel the pain of the last two years slowly breaking apart and slipping away. And, loud hurrahs, I have a title for my novel! I shall call it Bright Days, Dark Nights.

Over these tumultuous weeks and months I have learned that I can only write what I know, and what I know, I can only write from my heart. For this I am deeply grateful.

More anon, LFW

Author's Postscript

Contrary to popular belief, I don't think all power corrupts, but when individuals in power use their position to intimidate and exploit other human beings, they can leave their victims anywhere from wounded to permanently scarred … to dead.

Sexual misconduct by members of the clergy has been the stuff of international headlines for the past decade, but sexual abuse has been going on since one human being assumed, or was granted, dominance over another. What *is* new is that more and more people are no longer remaining silent but are coming forward with their pain, humiliation and outrage to seek justice.

A Predatory Mission is about a sexual predator who is finally stopped because his victims dared to speak out. They find the courage to do so because they sense a sympathetic and determined advocate in Olympia Brown. The message in the story is not only, "Beware." It is also, "Speak out!" Silence allows abusers to continue their destruction of human hearts and lives.

If you are being or have been abused, find a trusted person and speak your truth. Predators can be stopped, and their victims can be assisted, but only if they seek help.

Sex Abuse Help Resources

US Telephone Numbers:
If you are in immediate danger or need emergency assistance, call 911 first.

800.656.HOPE

Horizon's Domestic Violence Hotline:
800.621.HOPE (4673)

Safe Horizon's Crime Victims Hotline:
866.689.HELP (4357)

Safe Horizon's Rape, Sexual Assault & Incest Hotline:
212.227.3000

TDD phone number for all hotlines:
866.604.5350

US Websites

www.rainn.org/get-help/national-sexual-assault-hotline

www.safehorizon.org

UK Websites

www.rapecrisis.org.uk
www.napac.org.uk
www.thesurvivorstrust.org

Meet Author Judith Campbell

Rev. Dr. Judith Campbell is an ordained Unitarian Universalist minister and the author of several books and articles. She has published children's stories and poetry, as well as numerous essays on the arts, religion and spirituality.

She holds a PhD in The Arts and Religious Studies and a Master of Arts in Fine Arts, and she offers writing workshops and religious retreats nationally and internationally.

When she isn't traveling and teaching, she spends her time in Plymouth, Massachusetts, and on the island of Martha's Vineyard with her husband and best friend, Chris Stokes, a "Professional Englishman," together with their annoyingly intelligent cats, Katie and Simon.

To learn more about The Sinister Minister or to invite her to lead a writing workshop, preach at your church or speak at your library or book group, please visit her website at www.judithcampbell-holymysteries.com. "Rev Judy" loves to talk to her readers.

Preview of the sixth Olympia Brown Mystery
coming from Mainly Murder Press in 2014

A Proper English Mission
by Judith Campbell

The Moorlands
A Non-Conformist and Free Christian retreat
and conference center
With commanding views of the West Yorkshire Moors,
central heating and all modern conveniences.
Offering gracious accommodations, traditional English fare,
and discreet professional assistance for your business, social
or religious event.
For information and to make reservations
contact Managing Director Celia Radisson
18643136603

~

Celia Radisson had been managing director at The Moorlands for just six months. She had been the board's first choice out of the final three candidates because of her outstanding qualifications, references and much-needed energy and vision. They hired her so she could breathe new life into the elegant but stodgy old establishment and, with their guidance, bring it into the twenty-first century.

There were, however, those within the organization who held a very different view. They felt someone from the inside should have been promoted to that position. Someone with more seniority, who knew everyone and understood how things were done there should have been given that job. Now, as the tensions were reaching the breaking point between vision and tradition, between growth and comfort, between the elevated and pushed aside, it was time to take action. The key element in all of this was to make sure whatever happened that ultimately succeeded in getting rid of Celia in no way implicated any one of them. Time and tradition were on their side, and once they knew what they had to do, there was no need to rush.

On the other hand, there were those who said, like Macbeth, "If it were done when 'tis done, then 'twere well it were done quickly."

One

Frederick looked up from his book as his newly espoused wife entered the room.

"Who was that on the phone, my love?"

"You aren't going to believe this," said the Reverend Doctor Olympia Brown.

"I'm not going to believe what?"

"How do you fancy a trip to England?"

He put down the book.

"That was Michael Radisson, my minister-friend from the UK. He's asked me to co-lead a creative worship retreat for some of the Unitarian ministers over there.

Frederick leaned back in the chair and crossed his arms. "Hang on a minute. Out of the blue a friend you haven't seen for a years just up and calls you and asks you to come over there and lead a retreat. Now why don't you tell me the rest of the story, because I know there is one."

"Funny you should ask."

"I'm waiting," said Frederick.

"Well, there seems to be something nasty going on at a certain retreat house where his wife is the Managing Director."

"Such as?"

"That's what he'd like me to find out. He thinks someone there, possibly one or more staff members, are making an uncomfortably determined effort to be rid of her."

Frederick was looking less convinced and more skeptical by the minute. "That sort of thing happens all the time in business. It's mean spirited, but it's not new. How is this particular campaign being made manifest, and why is it so bad that he thinks you should make an appearance?"

"The Manager-Director is Michael Radisson's wife Celia. She says that of late all sorts of things have mysteriously and inconveniently gone wrong, toilets backing up, power going out, reservations getting lost and staff calling in sick more and more frequently. Last month the freezer quit on the weekend before a big society wedding, and all the food was spoiled. She's convinced there is a deliberate and organized effort to make her look incompetent. She says it feels like the plagues of Egypt with each successive 'unfortunate incident' getting more pointed and damaging. We all know what the last plague was, although I think I might be carrying the metaphor a bit too far."

"Crikey," said Frederick, "and just what does he think you'd be able to do in such nefarious circumstances?"

"He thinks if a total outsider, someone with no knowledge of the history of the place or the interpersonal dynamics of the people involved, were to come and do a little ..."

"Skulking around?" finished Frederick.

"Well, something of the sort. He thinks I might see things others don't and ask the kinds of questions proper English people would never think to ask."

"Oh, you'd do that, all right. However, I'm not sure if England's green and pleasant land is ready for the likes of you, my dear."

"Whatever do you mean?"

"I mean that you do fit some of the stereotypes we English hold deep in our hearts about you Yanks."

"Such as?"

"No offense, Reverend Lady, but you do always say what you think, you often go where you shouldn't go, and you don't ever take no for an answer—and that's only chapter one."

"There's something wrong with that?"

"Certainly not in your way of seeing things, but it might dismay the landed gentry for you to hit them full bore without proper warning. You are a rather a force of nature, you know."

"All of that notwithstanding, what do you think?"

"Think about what?"

Olympia made a face. "This is getting circular. I started all of this by asking if you wanted to go to England for a couple of weeks."

At first Frederick looked resigned, and then he brightened. "I say, we never had a proper English honeymoon. If we go, I could take you to meet the family."

"Frederick, we've only been married for six weeks."

He gasped and clapped the back of his hand to his brow. "Is that all? It seems like forever."

"Frederick!"

He winked at her. "Call your friend Michael back and find out more of what he's thinking. If he can make arrangements for us over there, I can probably get a couple of weeks off from the bookstore. You don't have a church commitment in the immediate future, so as long as we can arrange cat care, there's nothing to hold us back. Someone's got to look after you, and I do speak the language."

"Very funny."

Coming in 2014 from Mainly Murder Press
www.MainlyMurderPress.com

Lightning Source UK Ltd.
Milton Keynes UK
UKOW041831200613

212602UK00001B/25/P